THE
BARONET'S
SONG

BETHANY HOUSE PUBLISHERS
Minneapolis, Minnesota 55438

The Novels of George MacDonald Edited for Today's Reader

Edited Title	Original Title

The two-volume story of Malcolm:

The Fisherman's Lady	*Malcolm*
The Marquis' Secret	*The Marquis of Lossie*

Companion stories of Gibbie and his friend Donal:

The Baronet's Song	*Sir Gibbie*
The Shepherd's Castle	*Donal Grant*

Companion stories of Hugh Sutherland and Robert Falconer:

The Tutor's First Love	*David Elginbrod*
The Musician's Quest	*Robert Falconer*
The Maiden's Bequest	*Alec Forbes of Howglen*

Companion stories of Thomas Wingfold:

The Curate's Awakening	*Thomas Wingfold*
The Lady's Confession	*Paul Faber*
The Baron's Apprenticeship	*There and Back*

Stories that stand alone:

A Daughter's Devotion	*Mary Marston*
The Gentlewoman's Choice	*Weighed and Wanting*
The Highlander's Last Song	*What's Mine's Mine*
The Laird's Inheritance	*Warlock O'Glenwarlock*
The Landlady's Master	*The Elect Lady*
The Minister's Restoration	*Salted with Fire*
The Peasant Girl's Dream	*Heather and Snow*
The Poet's Homecoming	*Home Again*

MacDonald Classics Edited for Young Readers

Wee Sir Gibbie of the Highlands
Alec Forbes and His Friend Annie
At the Back of the North Wind
The Adventures of Ranald Bannerman

———

George MacDonald: Scotland's Beloved Storyteller by Michael Phillips
Discovering the Character of God by George MacDonald
Knowing the Heart of God by George MacDonald
A Time to Grow by George MacDonald
A Time to Harvest by George MacDonald

Introduction

In 1879 one of the best-loved of all George Mac-
Donald's Scottish novels was published, the captivating
chronicle of the winsome little orphan, Sir Gibbie. An immediate success, the novel was serialized in several maga-
zines, and within a year and a half was published in at least
six different editions by various publishers in Great Britain
and America.

As celebrated as MacDonald's novels were in his own
time, their impact continues long after his death. In 1916 C. S.
Lewis casually picked up a copy of *Phantastes* and found the
entire course of his life altered. He said, "A few hours later I
knew I had crossed a great frontier." Thirty years later he
reflected on the worlds MacDonald had opened for him and
said, "... when the process was complete ... I found that I
was still with MacDonald and that he had accompanied me
all the way."

Many others through the years have similarly found
MacDonald's writings to have affected them. G. K. Chesterton,
for instance, referred to him as "a Scot of genius who could
write fairy tales that made all experience a fairy tale."

In the Preface to her 1962 edition of *Sir Gibbie,* Elizabeth
Yates comments on the book: "... from the moment it caught
me up I was conscious of a breadth and depth and height of
feeling such as I had not known for a long time. It moved me
the way books did when as a child. ... I could not put the book

down until it was finished, and yet I could not bear to come to its end. Once at its last page, I felt I would have to do what I had often done as a child—turn back to the first page and begin reading all over again. I longed to tell everyone I knew to read it.... It would not do to tell them anything about it. This was not only a book, it was an experience." She closed by saying, "Now and then a book is read as a friend ... and after it life is not the same ... for it has become richer, more meaningful, more challenging. *Sir Gibbie* did this to me. *Sir Gibbie* holds within its covers to do something to all who read it."

C. S. Lewis says, "Most myths were made in prehistoric times ... but every now and then there occurs in the modern world a genius ... who can make such a story. MacDonald is the greatest genius of this kind I know."

He then says that MacDonald's writing gift "produces works which give us ... as much delight and as much wisdom and strength as the works of the greatest poets. It is in some ways more akin to music than to poetry. It goes beyond the expression of things we have already felt. It arouses in us sensations we have never had before; ... it gets under our skin, hits us at a level deeper than our thoughts or even our passions."

Both C. S. Lewis and W. H. Auden characterize MacDonald's creative power as "mythopoeic imagination." Yet while lauding him as a mythmaker, Lewis hails him as a poet and weaver of fantasies, saying, "It was in this mythopoeic art that MacDonald excelled; ... the meaning, the suggestion, the radiance is incarnate in the whole story." Perhaps Richard Reis captured it best when he said that MacDonald "achieves a universality ... which transcends time."

What is this peculiar quality inherent in the story of the waif with shaggy golden hair? Why has Gibbie endured in memory though the book in its original form has been out of print since early in this century? What is it that captivates readers of all ages?

Is *Sir Gibbie* myth? Is it poetry? Is it fantasy? Is it music? Or does Gibbie's magic spring from MacDonald's having simultaneously captured the essence of all four? The story tugs at us, the myth calls forth eternity in our spirits, the poetry moves us, the fantasy delights our imaginations, while all along the music makes our hearts sing.

To once again quote Lewis, "What he does best is fantasy—fantasy that hovers between the allegorical and the mythopoeic. And this, in my opinion, he does better than any man."

Several factors emerge as fundamental for an understanding of George MacDonald's writing. First, he firmly held that the deepest insights about life were not to be found in distant obscurities but in everyday relationships and ordinary contacts with the world. Therefore, his books are filled with commonplace lives. We see an agrarian world of thatched cottages with their peat fires, porridge and milk, oats and potatoes, cattle and sheep, green meadows, desolate moors, thudding wooden machinery, and wild mountains. MacDonald never forgot his humble childhood. This was the Scotland he loved, and his truths, like his people, were simple yet subtle.

In his 1914 Introduction to a new edition of *Sir Gibbie,* MacDonald's son Greville comments, "It would be hard to find any book in the English tongue that . . . more plainly displays the hidden grandeur . . . in common life than *Sir Gibbie* . . . the most direct and most beautiful of all George Mac-Donald's novels."

In thus conveying the soul of Scotland—its land and its people—with his descriptions of farming, shepherding and fishing, MacDonald pioneered an entire movement of realistic Scottish fiction. Many others followed him in what came to be known as the "kaleyard school" of writing.

Second, the image of childhood appears throughout his books. He loved to make up stories for his own children and read to them. On one occasion a close family friend, Lewis Carroll, asked George to read a story he had written to his own children. They loved it, and the author enlarged and published it as *Alice in Wonderland.*

MacDonald once said, "I do not write for children, but

for the childlike, whether of five, or fifty, or seventy-five."

All these elements converge in the simple yet profound story of *Sir Gibbie*—the myth, the poetry, the fantasy, the love of Scotland, and the wonder of childhood.

Almost exactly a hundred years after *Sir Gibbie*'s first publication, I "met" George MacDonald, and *Sir Gibbie* was one of the first of his books I read. Though he wrote more than fifty books in his career, no more than a scant handful were in print in the early 1970s. However, my wife and I found what we could and soon fell in love with his moving tales.

It gradually became one of my consuming passions to share the out-of-print fiction of George MacDonald with the reading public. Unfortunately, the bulk of his novels were unavailable, they were usually written in a Scotch dialect unintelligible to today's reader, and they often ran well over 500 pages.

Therefore, I undertook the editing of MacDonald's originals, reducing them to a more manageable size and substituting contemporary English for the Gaelic dialect. *The Fisherman's Lady* and *The Marquis' Secret* were the first two published; this new edition of *Sir Gibbie* and its sequel follow them in the series from Bethany House.

I have rewritten every page, condensing, tightening, editing, and translating. The original *Sir Gibbie* of over 400 pages has been trimmed by about half, and I have translated into current usage such difficult-to-understand passages as:

> Gien the j'ists be strang, an' well set intil the wa's, what for sudna ye tak the horse up the stair intil yer bedrooms? It'll be a' to the guid o' the wa's, for the weicht o' the beasts 'll be upo' them to haud them doon, an' the haill hoose again' the watter ... I'm thinkin' we'll lowse them a' else; for the byre wa's 'ill gang afore the hoose.

As young Gibbie journeys from the city, up the river Daur, to his refuge of Glashgar, so we travel with him into the world of George MacDonald, back to childhood, up the mountain, and on toward the heritage that awaits us. If, as has been suggested, the term myth is to be applied to events which have meaning beyond their literal significance, then Gibbie's pilgrimage surely qualifies. For Gibbie is symbolic of all who are engaged in life's grand adventure onward and upward into the high realms of relationship, wisdom, and love.

Michael Phillips
Eureka, California
July 1982

Contents

Glossary

bairn—child
bossy—a seat of straw
bannock—oatmeal cake
brae—hillside
brogues—shoes
broonie—brownie, elf
burn—brook
byre—stable or barn
cantrip—trick
close—enclosed
couples—a pair of rafters that meet at the top and are tied
cowherd—one who tends cows
crofter—tenant farmer
girnel—a meal barrel
gowan—daisies
gowk—simpleton
hirsute—hairy, shaggy
laird—lord, proprietor of the land
loch—lake
manse—minister's house
Pan's pipes—a kind of wooden recorder
rick—small piles or stack of corn or grain in the field
tarn—bog, marsh
water-brose—grain cereal with liquid poured on top

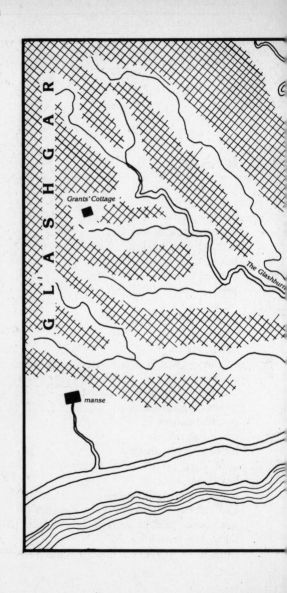

The Region of Gormgarnet

Gamekeeper's Cottage

GLASHRUACH

The Lorrie

m e a d o w

barn

house

MAINS

RIVER DAUR

1   The City's Urchin

"Come out o' the gutter, ye urchin!" cried Mrs. Croale in a harsh, half-masculine voice, standing on the curbstone of a short, narrow, dirty lane. About thirty yards from her, a child, apparently about six but in reality about eight, was down on his knees raking with both hands in the grey dirt of the street.

At the woman's cry he lifted his head, ceased his search, raised himself without getting up and looked at her. They were notable eyes out of which he looked—a deep blue and having long lashes, but more notable for their bewitching expression of confidence. Whatever was at the heart of the expression, it was something that enticed question and might want investigation. The face as well as the eyes was lovely— not very clean but chiefly remarkable from a general effect of something I can only call luminosity. The hair, which stuck out from his head in every direction, would have been of the red-gold kind had it not been sunburned into a sort of human hay. An odd creature altogether the child appeared, as from his bare knees on the curbstone he shook the gutter-drops from his dirty little hands and gazed at the woman of rebuke. It was but for a moment. The next, he was down raking in the gutter again.

The woman took a step forward; but the sound of a sharp, imperative little bell made her turn at once and reenter

17

the shop from which she had just issued. Meantime the boy's attention seemed entirely absorbed in the gutter. Whatever passed him by, he never lifted his head but went creeping slowly on his knees along the curb still searching in the flow of the sluggish, nearly motionless current of black muck.

It was a gloomy morning toward the close of autumn. The days began and ended with a fog, but often between, a golden sunshine glorified the streets of the grey city. At this moment a ray of sunlight from between two tall houses suddenly fell upon the pavement and gutter, revealing to the boy the glistening object of his search. He made a dart upon all fours and pounced like a creature of prey upon something in the mud. He sprang to his feet and bounded with it into the sun, running and all the while rubbing it upon what he had for trousers, for which there was nothing below the knees but a few streamers. His feet as well as his knees and legs were bare and red and rough. He held up his find into the radiance of the sunlight, regarding it admiringly. It was a little earring of amethyst-colored glass. The boy was in ecstasy over his find. He rubbed the glass on his sleeve, sucked it to clear from it the last of the gutter, then held the earring once more in the sun, where, for a few blissful moments, he contemplated it in speechless wonder. He then caused it to disappear somewhere about his garments—I will not venture to say in a pocket— and ran off, his little bare feet sounding thud, thud, thud on the pavement.

Through street after street he sped, the whole built of granite—a hard, severe city; not beautiful, yet in the better parts handsome as well as massive and strong. To the boy the great city was but a house of many rooms—all for his use, his sport, his life. He did not know much of what lay within the houses; but that only added the joy of mystery.

It was in one of a third-rate sort that the urchin at length ceased his trot and drew up at the divided door of a baker's shop, opening in the middle by a latch of bright brass. But the child did not lift the latch—only raised himself on tiptoe by the help of its handle to look through the upper half of the door into the tantalizing shop. The smell that came through it could seem to the child as that of the tree of life in the Paradise of which he had never heard: scones and rolls, biscuits hard and soft, and those brown discs of delicate pie-crust known as buns. But most enticing of all to the eyes of the little wanderer of the street were the penny loaves, hot smoking from the oven. The main point which made them more attractive than all the rest to him was that sometimes he did have a penny, and a penny loaf was the largest thing that could be had for a penny in the shop. So, lawless as he looked, the desires of the child were moderate, and his imagination within the bounds of reason.

Behind the counter sat the baker's wife, a stout, fresh-colored woman, simple and honest. She was knitting and dozing over her work, and never saw the forehead and eyes which gazed at her over the horizon of the door. There was no greed in those eyes—only much interest. He did not want to get in, had to wait, and while waiting enjoyed the scene before him. He knew that Mysie, the baker's daughter, was at school and would be home within half an hour. He had seen her with tear-filled eyes as she went, and learned from her the cause, and had in consequence unwittingly roused Mrs. Croale's anger. But though he was waiting for Mysie, such was the absorbing power of the spectacle before him that he never heard her approaching footsteps.

"Let me in," said Mysie with a touch of indignation at being impeded on the very threshold of her own father's shop.

The boy started and turned, but instead of moving out of the way, began searching in some mysterious receptacle hid in the recesses of his rags. A look of anxiety once appeared but the same moment vanished, and he held out in his hand the little crop of amethystine splendor. Mysie's face changed, and she clutched it eagerly.

"That's real good of you, wee Gibbie!" she cried. "Where did you find it?"

He pointed to the gutter, and drew back from the door.

"I thank you," she said heartily and, pressing down the thumbstall of the latch, went in.

"Who's that you're talking with, Mysie?" asked her mother.

"It's only wee Gibbie, Mother," answered the girl.

"What do you have to say to him?" resumed the mother; "he's hardly fit company for the likes of you who has a father and mother. You must have little to say to such a runabout laddie."

"Gibbie has a father, though they say he never had no mother," answered the child.

"A fine father!" rejoined the mother with a small scornful laugh. "Such a father, lassie, that would make truth of saying he had none! What said you to him?"

"I thanked him, 'cause I lost my earring going to school this morning and he found it for me. He was waiting for me by the door. They say he's always finding things."

"He's a good-hearted creature!" returned the mother, "—for one, that is, that's been so ill brought up."

She rose, took from the shelf a penny loaf, and went to the door.

"Here, Gibbie!" she cried as she opened it; "here's a fine piece for ye."

But no Gibbie was there. Up and down the street not a child was to be seen. The baker's wife drew back, shut the door, and resumed her knitting.

Though the sun remained hot for an hour or two in the middle of the day, in the shadows dwelt the cold breath of coming winter. To Gibbie, however, barelegged, barefooted, almost barebodied as he was, sun or shadow made small difference except as one of the musical intervals of the life that make the melody of existence. Hardy through hardship, he knew nothing better than a constant good-humored sparring with nature and circumstances for the privilege of being, enjoyed what came to him thoroughly, never mourned over what he had not and, like the animals, was at peace. When Gibbie was not looking in at a shopwindow or turning on one heel to take in all at a sweep, he was oftenest seen trotting. Seldom he walked. A gentle trot was one of his natural modes of being. And through this day he had been on the trot all the sunshine through, nevertheless, when the sun was going down there was wee Gibbie upon the trot in the chilling and darkening streets.

He had not had much to eat. He had been near having a penny loaf. Half a cookie which a stormy child had thrown away to ease his temper, a small yellow turnip the green-grocer's wife had given him, and a handful of the seaweed called "dulse" from a fishwife with a creel on her back was all he had eaten. It had been one of his meager days. But it is wonderful upon how little those rare natures capable of making the most of things will live and thrive. There is a great deal more to be gotten out of things than is generally gotten out of them, whether the thing be a chapter of the Bible or a yellow turnip. Truly Gibbie got no fat out of his food, but what he did receive was far better. What he carried was all muscle—small but hard and healthy, and knotting up like whipcord. There are all degrees of health in poverty as well as in riches, and Gibbie's health was splendid. His senses also were marvelously acute; his eyes sharp, quick, roving.

While Gibbie thus lived in the streets like a town sparrow, the human father of him would all the day be sitting in a certain dark court, as hard at work as an aching head and bloodless system would afford. The said court was off the narrowest part of a long, poverty-stricken street called the Widdiehill. In the court, against a wing of an old house, around which yet clung a musty fame of departed grandeur, rose an outside stair leading to the first floor. Under this stairway was a rickety wooden shed; in the shed sat the father of Gibbie, cobbling boots and shoes as long as, at this time of the year, the light lasted. Up that stair, and two more flights inside the house, he went to his lodging, for he slept in the garret. But when or how he got to bed, George Galbraith never knew, for by then, invariably, he was drunk. In the morning, however, he always found himself in it—generally with an aching head and always with a mingled disgust at and desire for drink. During the day, alas! the disgust departed while the desire remained, strengthening with the approach of evening. All day he worked with might and main, such might and main as he had—worked as if for his life, and all to procure the means of death.

Wee Gibbie was his only child, but about him or his well-being he gave himself almost as little trouble as Gibbie caused him. Not that he was hardhearted; if he had seen the child in want, he would, at the drunkest, have shared his whiskey with him; if he had fancied him cold, he would have put his last garment upon him. But to his whiskey-dimmed eyes the child scarcely seemed to want anything, and the thought never entered his mind that, while Gibbie always looked smiling and contented, his father did so little to make him so. He did not do well for himself, and he shamefully neglected his child. But he did well by his neighbors; he gave the best of work and made the lowest of charges. He was a man of such inborn honesty that the usurping demon of a vile thirst had not even yet, at the age of forty, been able to cast it out.

His friends addressed Galbraith as "Sir George," and he accepted the title with a certain unassumed dignity. For if it was not universally known in the city, it was known to the best lawyers in it that he was a baronet by direct derivation from the hand of King James the Sixth. The bearer of the title, however, had seen better days. George's father was a man of some standing who had given his son more than a fair education, not without some distinction. While his father was yet alive, George married the daughter of a small laird in a neighboring county. He took her home to the ancient family house in the city—the same in which he now occupied a garret and under whose outer stair he now cobbled shoes. During his father's life they lived there in peace and tolerable comfort, though in a poor enough way. His wife died, however, soon after Gibbie was born; and then George began to lose himself altogether. The next year his father died, and creditors appeared who claimed everything. Mortgaged land and houses were sold, and George was left without a penny or any means of livelihood. For heavy work he was altogether unfit; and had it not been for a bottle companion—a merry, hard-drinking shoemaker—he would have died of starvation or sunk into beggary.

The shoeman taught him his trade, and George was glad enough to work at it, both to deaden the stings of conscience and memory and to procure the means of deadening them still further.

How Gibbie had gotten thus far alive was a puzzle not a creature could have solved. It must have been by charity and ministration of more than one humble woman, but no one now claimed any particular interest in him—except Mrs. Croale, and hers was not very tender. It was a sad sight to some eyes to see him roving the streets, but an infinitely sadder sight was his father; he looked the pale picture of misery. When the poor fellow sat with his drinking companions in Mistress Croale's parlor, seldom a flash broke from the reverie in which he seemed sunk. Yet those drinking companions would have missed George Galbraith, silent as he was; for he was courteous, always ready to share what he had, and never looked beyond the present tumbler—altogether a genial, kindly, honest nature.

2   Mistress Croale's

The day went on and went out, its short autumnal brightness quenched in a chilly fog. All along the Widdiehill, the gas was alight in the low-browed dingy shops. In his shed under the stair it had been dark for some time—too dark for work, that is, and George Galbraith had lighted a candle. He never felt at liberty to quit so long as a man was recognizable in the street by daylight. But now at last, with a sigh of relief, he rose. His hand trembled with expectation as he laid from it the awl, took from between his knees the great boot on which he had been stitching a patch, lifted the yoke of his leather apron over his head and threw it aside. After one hasty glance around, he caught up a hat, which looked as if it had been brushed with grease, pulled it on his head with both hands, stepped out quickly, closed the door behind him, turned the key, left it in the lock, and made straight for Mistress Croale's. Above the door of her establishment was a small board, nearly square, upon which was painted in lead color on black the words, "Licensed to sell beer, spirits and tobacco to be drunk on the premises." There was no other sign. It was to this, his earthly paradise, that George now hastened.

George was a tall man of good figure, loosened and bowed. His face was well-favored, but not a little wronged by the beard and the dirt of the week, through which it looked haggard and white. He looked neither to the right nor left but walked on with dull gaze, noting nothing.

"He's his own worst enemy," remarked the kindly grocer's wife as he passed her door.

"Ay," responded her customer who kept a secondhand shop nearby, "ay, I daresay. But, eh! To see that poor neglected bairn o' his runnin' about the town—with little jacket left but the collar and rags for trousers! Eh, woman! It makes a mother's heart sore to see it. It would make *his* mother turn over in her grave!"

George was the first arrival at Mistress Croale's that night. He opened the door of the shop like a thief, and glided softly into the dim parlor where the candles were not yet lit. Mistress Croale was seated on a horsehair sofa in the twilight, a busy fire crackling in the grate.

"Come on in," she said hospitably as she rose.

The woman had a genuine regard for Galbraith, but in her secret mind she deplored that George should drink so inordinately and so utterly neglect his child as to let him spend his life in the streets. She comforted herself, however, with the reflection that seeing he would drink, he drank with no bad companions.

The usual company was soon assembled, the candles lit, and the toddy measured out. The conversation was for some time very dull. But the fire burned cheerfully and the kettle made many journeys between it and the table; things gradually grew more lively. Stories were told, often without any point but still with effect; reminiscences were offered and accepted with laughter; and adventures were related in which truth was no necessary element to reception. In the case of one of the company, for instance, not one of those present believed a word he said; yet as he happened to be endowed with a small stock of genuine humor, his stories were regarded with much the same favor as if they had been authentic.

But the revival scarcely reached Sir George. He said little or nothing, but between his slow gulps of toddy sat looking vacantly into his glass. It is true he smiled absently now and then when the others laughed, but that was only for manners. Doubtless he was seeing somewhere the saddest of all visions—the things that might have been. Was the chief joy his drink gave him the power once more to feel himself a gentleman? What faded ghosts of ancestral dignity the evil potion called up in the mind of Sir George—who himself hung ready to fall, the last, or all but the last, mildewed fruit of the tree of Galbraith!

In the descending frosty dark of the autumn evening, Gibbie too found himself outside Mrs. Croale's establishment. Under the window of the parlor he would stand listening for a moment, then, darting off a few yards suddenly and swiftly like a frightened bird, fall at once into his own steady trot—up the lane and down, till he reached the window again, where he would stand and listen. Whether he made this departure and return twenty or a hundred times in a night, neither he nor any other could have told. Never moth haunted lamp so persistently. Ever as he ran, up this pavement and down that, on the soft-sounding soles of his bare feet, the smile on the boy's face grew more and more sleepy; but still he smiled and still he trotted, still paused at the window and started afresh.

He was not so much to be pitied as you may think. Never in his life had he yet pitied himself. The thought of hardship or wrong had not occurred to him. It would have been difficult, if not impossible, to get the idea into his head that existence bore to him any other shape than it ought. Things were to him as they had always been. How could he question what had been from the beginning?

It was now late. The streets were empty. Neither carriage nor cart, wheelbarrow nor truck, went anymore bumping and clattering over their stones. They were well lighted with gas, but most of the bordering houses were dark. Now and then a single footfarer passed with loud, hollow-sounding boots along the pavement. A cold wind—a small, forsaken, solitary wind, moist with a thin fog—seemed, as well as wee Gibbie, to be roaming the night, for it met him at various corners and from all directions. But it had nothing to do and nowhere to go and was therefore not like Gibbie, the business of whose life was even now upon him, the mightiest hope of whose conscious being was now awake.

All he expected or ever desired to discover by listening at the window was simply whether there were yet signs of the company's breaking up; and his conclusions on that point were never mistaken. Seldom had he there heard the voice of his father. This night, however, as the time drew near when they must go and Gibbie stood once more on tiptoe with his head just on the level of the windowsill, he heard his father utter two words: "Up Daurside." They came to him through the window, in the voice he loved, plain and distinct. The words conveyed nothing to him at all, but the mere hearing of them made them memorable. For the time, however, he forgot them, for he perceived that the company was on the point of separating. From that moment he did not take his eyes off the door until he heard the first sounds of its opening. As it was hard on a midnight so cold that his feet threatened to grow indistinguishable from the slabs of pavement, he was driven, in order not to lose his toes to frostbite or to lose sight of the door, to practice the already cultivated art of running first backward, then forward, with scarcely superior speed. But it was not long before the much-expected sound of Mistress Croale's voice heralded the hour when patience would blossom into possession. Gibbie bounded up and stood still as a statue at the very door until he heard Mistress Croale's hand upon the lock; whereupon he bolted, trembling with eagerness, into the entry of a court a few houses nearer to the Widdiehill.

One after another the pitiable company issued from its paradise, and each stumbled away, too far gone for leave-taking. Most of them passed Gibbie where he stood, but he took no heed; his father was always the last—and the least capable. But often as he left her door, never did it close behind Galbraith until with her own eyes Mistress Croale had seen Gibbie dart like an imp out of the court—to take him in charge and all the weary way home hover, not very like a guardian angel in appearance but not the less one in truth, around the unstable equilibrium of his father's tall and swaying form.

And thereupon commenced a series of marvelous gymnastics on the part of wee Gibbie. Imagine a small boy with a gigantic top six times his own size, which he keeps erect on its peg not by whipping it round but by running round it himself, unfailingly applying at the very spot and at the very moment the precise measure of impact necessary to counterbalance its perpetual tendency to fall in one direction or the other. Home the big one staggered, reeled, gyrated and tumbled; round and round him went the little one, now behind, now before, now on this side, now on that, his feet never more than touching the ground but dancing about like those of a tiny prizefighter. His hands and arms acted like flying buttresses all about a universally leaning tower, propping it here, propping it there, with wonderful judgment and skill. Not once in the last year and a half, during which time wee Gibbie had been the nightly guide of Sir George's homeward steps, had the self-disabled mass fallen prostrate in the gutter, there to snore out the night.

The first real struggle of the evening commenced when they reached the foot of the outside stair over the baronet's workshop. All up the outside and the two inside stairs, his waking and sleeping were as the alternate tic-tac of a pendulum; but Gibbie stuck to his business like a man, and his resolution and perseverance were at length, as always, crowned with victory.

The house in which lords and ladies had often reposed was now filled with very humble folk who were all asleep when Gibbie and his father entered; but the noise the two made in ascending caused no great disturbance of their rest. If any of them were roused for a moment, it was but to recognize at once the cause of the tumult with the remark, "It's only wee Gibbie luggin' home Sir George," and to turn on the other side and fall asleep again.

Arriving at last at the garret door which stood wide open, Gibbie had little need of light in the nearly pitch darkness of the place, for there was positively nothing to stumble over between the door and the ancient four-post bed, which was all of his father's house that remained to Sir George. With heavy shuffling feet the drunkard lumbered laboriously bedward, and the bare posts and crazy frame groaned and creaked as he fell upon the oat chaff that lay waiting him in place of the vanished luxury of feathers. Wee Gibbie flew at the man's legs and did not rest until, one after the other, he had gotten them onto the bed. If they were not very comfortably deposited, he knew that, in his first turn, their owner would get them right.

And then came the culmination of Gibbie's day! In triumph he spread over his sleeping father his dead mother's old plaid of Gordon tartan—all the bedding they had. Without a moment's delay—no shoes even to take off—he crept under it himself and nestled close upon the bosom of his unconscious parent. A victory more! Another day ended with success. His father was safe, and all his own! The canopy of the darkness and the plaid lay over them as if they were the only two in the universe! His father, unable to leave him, was his for whole dark hours to come. It was Gibbie's paradise now! His heaven was his father's bosom, to which he clung as no infant yet ever clung to his mother's. He never thought to pity himself that the embrace was all on his side, that no answering pressure came back from the prostrate form. He never said to himself, "My father is a drunkard, but I must make the best of it; he is all I have." He clung to his one possession—only clung. This was his father—all in all to him.

The conscious bliss of the child was of short duration, for in a few minutes he was fast asleep. But for the gain of those moments, the day had been well spent.

3   Sir George

Such were the events of every night, and such they had been since Gibbie first assumed this office of guardian—a time so long in proportion to his life that it seemed to him as one of the laws of existence that fathers got drunk and Gibbies took care of them. But Saturday night was always one of special bliss for the joy to come. All Sunday his father would be his. On that happiest day of all the week, he never set his foot out of doors except to run to Mistress Croale's to fetch the dinner which she supplied from her own table and for which Sir George paid in advance on Saturday.

The streets were not attractive to the child on Sundays; there were no shops open. As to going to church, such an idea had never entered his head. He had not once for a moment imagined that anybody would like him to go to church, or that church was at all a place to which Gibbies with fathers to look after should have any desire to go. As to what church-going meant, he had not the vaguest idea; it had not even waked the glimmer of a question in his mind. All he knew was that other people went to church on Sundays. It was another of the laws of existence, the reason of which he knew no more than why his father went every night to get drunk.

There was a strange remnant of righteousness in Sir George which showed itself in his determination never to taste drink before it was dark in winter or in summer before

29

the regular hour for ceasing work had arrived; and to this rule he kept, but with far greater difficulties, on the Sunday as well. Mistress Croale would not sell a drop of drink, not even on the sly, on the Sabbath day. George was thus driven to provide his own Sunday-night whiskey and drink it at home.

When darkness had fallen, too much ashamed to begin his drink before the child—he hated to uncork the bottle before him—Sir George sent Gibbie to Mistress Croale. She was always kind to the child and could not help feeling that no small part of what ought to be spent on him came to her; and on Sundays, therefore, partly for his sake, partly for her own, she always gave him a small glass of milk and as much dry bread as he could eat. When he returned greatly refreshed he found his father, as he knew he would, already started on the business of the evening. He had drawn the chest, the only seat in the room, to the side of the bed against which he leaned his back. A penny candle was burning in a stone blacking bottle on the chimney piece, and on the floor beside the chest stood the bottle of whiskey, a jug of water, a stoneware mug and a wine glass.

There was no fire and no kettle. Gibbie was far from shocked; it was all in the order of things, and he went up to his father with radiant countenance. Sir George put forth his hands and took him between his knees.

"Gibbie," he said solemnly, "never drink a drop of whiskey; never drink anything but water, clear water, my man."

As he said the words he stretched out his own hand to the mug, lifted it to his lips, and swallowed with a great gulp.

"Don't do it, I tell you, Gibbie," he repeated.

Gibbie shook his head with positive repudiation.

Here followed another gulp from the mug.

"Gibbie," resumed Sir George, after a brief pause, "do you know what folk'll call you when I'm dead?"

Gibbie again shook his head—with expression this time of mere ignorance.

"They'll call you 'Sir Gibbie Galbraith,' my man," said his father, "and rightly, for it'll be no nickname, though some may laugh at you 'cause your father was a cobbler and you never had shoes on your feet. Poor fellow! But don't heed what they say, Gibbie. Remember that you're Sir Gibbie and have the honor of the family to hold up. And remember, my man, that you cannot do and drink. For it's this cursed drink that's been the ruin of all the Galbraiths as far back as I can think. My grandfather was a big, bonny man, Gibbie, but he drank up almost everything there was till there was hardly an acre left upon all Daurside to come to my father, nothing but one small house. He was a good man, my father, but his father taught him to drink while he was still young and gave him no schooling. If a kind neighbor, that knew what it was to drink, had not taught me my trade, the Lord knows what would have become of you and me, Gibbie, my man. Go to your bed now and leave me to my own thoughts, not that they're always the best of company, laddie."

Gibbie obeyed, and getting under the Gordon tartan, lay and looked out, like a weasel from its hole, at his father's back. For half an hour or so Sir George went on drinking. All at once he started to his feet and turned toward the bed, his white face distorted with agony. He paused, stretched down his hand to the floor, lifted the mug and drank a huge mouthful; then with a cough set it down and fell forward upon the bed groaning, and his voice died gradually away. Gibbie watched it all, and the awe of the unknown made his soul very still. But with his father on the bed he soon fell asleep.

Gibbie slept some time. When he woke it was pitch dark and he was not lying on his father's bosom. He felt about with his hands till he found his father's head. Then he got up and tried to rouse him and, failing, tried to get his legs onto the bed. But in that too he was sadly unsuccessful. What with the darkness and the weight of him, the result of the boy's endeavor was that Sir George half slipped, half rolled onto the floor. Assured then of his own helplessness, wee Gibbie dragged the miserable bolster from the bed and got it under his father's head; then covered him with the plaid and, creeping under it, laid himself upon his father's bosom where he soon slept again.

He woke very cold. The room was no longer dark, for the moon was shining through the skylight. He turned to have a look at his father. The pale light shone full upon his face and it was that, Gibbie thought, which made it look so strange. He moved closer to him and stared aghast! He had never seen him look like that before, even when most drunk! He threw himself upon him in fear—he could not even have told of what. He would not wake. He was gone to see what God could do for him there, for whom nothing could be done here.

Gibbie did not know anything about death, and went on trying to wake him. At last he observed that although his mouth was wide open, the breath did not come from it. Thereupon Gibbie's heart began to fail him. But when he lifted an eyelid and saw what was under it, the house rang with the despairing shriek of the little orphan.

4   Alone in the Streets

Gibbie's agony passed and life became again life, and he ran about the streets as before. Some may think that wee Sir Gibbie—as many now called him, some knowing the truth and others in kindly mockery—would get on all the better for the loss of such a father; but it was not so. In his father he had lost his Paradise and was now a creature expelled. The streets and the people and the shops, the horses and the dogs, even the penny loaves, though he was hungry, had lost half their precious delight when his father was no longer in the accessible background, the heart of the blissful city. As to food and clothing, he did neither much better nor any worse than before; people were kind as usual, and kindness was to

Gibbie the very milk of Mother Nature. Whose the hand that proffered it or what form it took, he cared no more than a stray kitten cares whether the milk set down to it be in a blue saucer or a white. But he always made the right return. The first thing a kindness deserves is acceptance, the next is transmission; Gibbie gave both without thinking much about either. For he never had taken, indeed never learned to take, a thought about what he should eat or what he should drink or wherewithal he should be clothed.

He roamed the streets, as all his life before, the whole of the day and part of the night; he took what was given him and picked up what he found. There were some who would gladly have brought him within the bounds of an ordered life; he soon drove them to despair, however, for the streets had been his nursery and nothing could keep him out of them. However Gibbie's habits might shock the ladies of the parish minister Mr. Sclater's congregation, who sought to civilize him, the boy was no more about mischief in the streets at midnight than they were in their beds. They collected enough on his behalf to board him for a year with an old woman who kept a school, and they did get him to sleep one night in her house. But in the morning she would not let him run out. Instead, she brought him into the schoolroom, her kitchen, and began to teach him to write. Gibbie failed to see the good of it. He must have space, change, adventure, air, or life was not worth the name to him. Above all, he must see friendly faces, and that of the old dame was not such. He immediately departed from her house, and it was the last she ever saw of him. Thus, after one night's brief interval of respectability, he was again a rover of the city, a flitting insect that lighted here and there and spread wings of departure the moment a fresh desire awoke.

It would be difficult to say where he slept. In summer, anywhere; in winter, where he could find warmth. Like animals better clad than he, yet like him able to endure cold, he reveled in mere heat when he could come by it. Sometimes he stood at the back of a baker's oven, for he knew all the haunts of heat about the city; sometimes he buried himself in the oat

33

husks lying ready to feed the kiln of a meal-mill; sometimes he lay by the furnace of the steam engine of the waterworks. One man employed there, when his time was at night, always made a bed for Gibbie; he had lost his only child, and this one of nobody's was a comfort to him.

The merits the police recognized in him were mainly two—neither of small consequence in their eyes—the first, that of utter harmlessness; the second, a passion and power for rendering help, taking notable shape chiefly in two ways: The first was the peculiar faculty now rather generally known—his great gift, some said; his great luck, others called it—for finding things lost. It was no wonder the town crier had sought his acquaintance and when secured had cultivated it—neither a difficult task; for the boy, ever since he could remember, had been in the habit, as often as he saw the crier or heard his tuck of drum in the distance, of joining him and following until he had acquainted himself with all particulars concerning everything proclaimed as missing. The moment he had mastered the facts as announced, he would dart away to search and not unfrequently to return with the thing sought. The crier spoke kindly to him, as well he might, and now and then gave him a penny.

The second of the positive merits by which Gibbie found acceptance in the eyes of the police was a yet more peculiar one, growing out of his love for his father and his experience in the exercise of that love. It was, however, unintelligible to them, except on the theory commonly adopted with regard to Gibbie—namely, that he "wasna a' there." It was indeed the main cause of his being, like themselves, so much in the street at night. If the finding of things was a gift, this other peculiarity was a passion: it was to play the guardian angel to drunk folk. If such a distressed human craft hove in sight, he would instantly bear down upon and hover about him until resolved as to his real condition. If he was in such a distress as to require assistance, Gibbie never left him till he saw him safe within his own door. The police asserted that wee Sir Gibbie not only knew every drunkard in the city and where he lived, but where he generally got drunk as well.

He was least known to those to whom he rendered most assistance. Rarely had he thanks for it, never halfpence, but not unfrequently blows and abuse. For the first he cared nothing; the latter, owing to his great agility, seldom visited him with any directness. About the time the company at Mistress Croale's would be breaking up, he would on most nights be lying in wait a short distance down the Widdiehill, ready to minister to that one of his father's old comrades who might prove most in need of his assistance; and if he showed him no gratitude, Gibbie had not been trained in a school where he was taught to expect or even to wish for any.

5 Adrift

When Mistress Croale moved her establishment near the docks in the second winter after his father's death, Gibbie followed and continued to haunt it. What more than anything else attracted him to her new house was the jolly manners and openhearted kindness of most of the sailors who frequented it, with almost all of whom he was a favorite. Scarcely a night passed when he was not present at one or more of the quarrels of which the place was a hotbed. He was not shocked by the things he saw, even when he liked them least. He regarded the doings of them much as he had looked upon his father's drunkenness—as a pitiful necessity that overtook men, one from which there was no escape and which caused a great need for Gibbies. Evil language and coarse behavior alike passed over him without leaving the smallest stain upon heart or conscience, desire or will. No one could doubt it who considered the clarity of his face and eyes, in which the occasional expression of keenness and promptitude scarcely even ruffled the prevailing look of unclouded babyhood.

It is hardly necessary to remark that what kept Gibbie pure and honest was the rarely-developed, ever-active love of his kind. The human face was the one attraction to him in the universe. Gibbie knew no music except the voice of man and woman; at least no other had as yet affected him.

One night in the spring he saw at Mistress Croale's for the first time an African sailor whom the rest called Sambo. Gibbie was at once taken with his big, dark, radiant eyes and his white teeth continually uncovering themselves in good-humored smiles. To Gibbie, Sambo speedily became absolutely loving and tender, and Gibbie made him full return of devotion.

One night Sambo was looking on at a game of cards in which all the rest in the room were engaged. Happening to laugh at some turn it took, one of them who was losing was offended and abused him. Others objected to his having fun without risking money and required him to join in the game. This for some reason or other he declined, and when the whole party at length insisted, Sambo positively refused. Thereupon quickly came all the many steps of the ascent—from displeasure to indignation, wrath, revenge; and then ensued a row.

Gibbie had been sitting all the time on his friend's knee, in whom, as insult followed insult, the blood kept slowly rising. At length a savage from Greenock threw a tumbler at him. Sambo, quick as a lizard, covered his face with his arm. The tumbler, falling from it, struck Gibbie on the head—not severely but hard enough to make him utter a little cry. At that sound the latent fierceness came wide awake in Sambo. Gently as a nursing mother he set Gibbie down in a corner behind him, then with one rush sent every Jack of the company sprawling on the floor, with the table and bottles and glasses atop of them. At the vision of their plight, his good humor instantly returned; he burst into a great hearty laugh and proceeded at once to lift the table from off them. That effected, he caught up Gibbie in his arms and carried him with him to bed.

In the middle of the night Gibbie half woke and, finding himself alone, sought his father's bosom; then, in the confusion between sleeping and waking, imagined his father's death come again. Presently he remembered it was in Sambo's arms he fell asleep, but where he was now he could not tell; certainly he was not in bed. Groping, he pushed a door and a glimmer of light came in. He was in a closet of the room in which Sambo slept—and something was to do about his bed. He rose softly and peeped out. There stood several men, and a struggle was going on—nearly noiseless. Gibbie was half-dazed and could not understand; but he had little anxiety about Sambo in whose prowess he had a triumphant confidence. Suddenly came the sound of a great gush, and the group parted from the bed and vanished. Gibbie darted toward it. The words, "O Lord Jesus!" came to his ears, and he heard no more; they were poor Sambo's last in this world. The light of a street lamp fell upon the bed; the blood was welling in great thick throbs out of his black throat.

For some moments Gibbie stood in ghastly terror. No sound except a low gurgle came to his ears, and the horror of the stillness overpowered him. He never could recall what came next. When he knew himself again he was in the street running like the wind, he knew not whither. It was not that he dreaded any hurt to himself; horror, not fear, was behind him.

His next recollection of himself was in the first of the morning on the lofty chain bridge over the river Daur. Before him lay he knew not what—only escape from what was behind. His faith in men lay in ruins. The city, his home, was frightful to him. Quarrels and curses and blows he had been used to, and amidst them life could be lived. If he did not consciously weave them into his theories, he consciously wrapped them up in his confidence and was at peace. But the last thought had revealed something unknown before. It was as if the darkness had been cloven and through the cleft he saw into hell. A thing had been done that could not be undone, and he thought it must be what people called murder. And Sambo was such a good man! He was almost as good a man as Gibbie's father, and now he would not breathe anymore! Was he gone where Gibbie's father was gone? Was it the good men that stopped breathing and grew cold? But it was those wicked men that had deaded Sambo! And with that his first vague perception of evil and wrong in the world began to dawn.

Brooding thus he fell into a dreamy state in which, brokenly from here and there, pictures of his former life grew out upon his memory. Plainer than all the rest came the last time he stood under Mistress Croale's window waiting to help his father home. The same instant back to the ear of his mind came his father's two words, as he had heard them through the window—"Up Daurside."

"Up Daurside!" Here he was upon Daurside—a little way up too; he would go farther up. He rose and went on, while the great river kept flowing the other way toward the city that had so long been his home.

Meantime, the murder came to the knowledge of the police, Mistress Croale herself giving the information, and all in the house were arrested. In the course of their examination, it came out that wee Sir Gibbie had gone to bed with the murdered man and was now nowhere to be found. Either they had murdered him too or carried him off. The news spread and the whole city was in commotion about his fate. The city was searched from end to end, from side to side, and from cellar to garret. Not a trace of him was to be found—but indeed Gibbie had always been easier to find than to trace, for he had no belongings of any sort to betray him. No one dreamed of his having fled, and search was confined to the city. The murderers were at length discovered, tried and executed. They protested their innocence with regard to the child and therein nothing appeared against them beyond the fact that he was missing. The result so far as concerned Gibbie was that the talk of the city was turned upon his history; and from the confused mass of hearsay that reached him, Mr. Sclater set himself to discover and verify the facts. For this purpose he burrowed about in the neighborhoods Gibbie had chiefly frequented, and was so far successful as to satisfy himself that Gibbie, if he was alive, was Sir Gilbert Galbraith, Baronet. But his own lawyer was able to assure him that not an inch of property remained anywhere attached to the title. There were indeed relations of the boy's mother who were of some small consequence in a neighboring county, also one in business in Glasgow or its neighborhood, reported wealthy; but these had entirely disowned her because of her marriage. All Mr. Sclater discovered besides was in a lumber room next to the garret in which Sir George died, where he found a box of papers—a glance at whose contents showed that they must at least prove a great deal of which he was already certain from other sources. A few of them had to do with the house in which they were found, still known as the Auld Hoose o' Galbraith; but most of them referred to property in land, and many were of ancient date. If the property were in the hands of descendants of the original stock, the papers would be of value in their eyes; and, in any case, it would be well to see to their safety. Mr. Sclater therefore had the chest removed to the garret of the church where it stood thereafter, little regarded, but able to answer for more than itself.

6 Up Daurside

Gibbie was now without a home. He had had a whole city for his dwelling, and for the first time in his life the fatherless, motherless, brotherless, sisterless stray of the streets felt himself alone.

It was a cold, fresh morning, cloudy and changeful toward the end of April. It had rained and would rain again; it might snow. Heavy, undefined clouds hung about the east. Even to him, city-creature that he was, it was plain something was going to happen there. And happen it did presently, with a splendor that for a moment blinded Gibbie. For just at the horizon there was a long crack and the topmost arc of the rising sun shot suddenly a thousand arrows of radiance into the brain of the boy.

To no traveler could one land be so different from another as to Gibbie the country was from the town. He had seen bushes and trees before, but only over garden walls or in one or two of the churchyards. The sun seemed but to have looked up to mock him and go down again, for he had crossed the crack and was behind a thick mass of cloud; a cold, damp wind, spotted with sparkles of rain, blew fitfully from the east. Below him the gloomy river, here deep, smooth, moody, sullen, went flowing heedless to the city. Yet never once did Gibbie think of returning. He rose and wandered up the wide road along the riverbank, farther and farther from it—his only guide the words of his father, "Up Daurside"; his sole comfort the feeling of having once more to do with his beloved father so long departed. Along cultivated fields on the one side and a steep descent to the river on the other, covered here and there with trees, but mostly with rough grass and bushes and stones, he followed the king's highway. There were buttercups and plenty of daisies within his sight—primroses, too, on the slope beneath; but he did not know flowers, and his was not now the mood for discovering what they were.

The exercise revived him and he began to be hungry. But how could there be anything to eat in the desert, inhospitable succession of trees and fields and hedges, through which the road wound endlessly along like a dead street, having neither houses nor paving stone? Hunger, however, was far less enfeebling to Gibbie than to one accustomed to regular meals, and he was in no anxiety about either when or what he should eat.

The morning advanced, and by and by he began to meet a fellow creature now and then upon the road; but at sight of anyone a feeling rose in him such as he had never had toward human beings before. They seemed somehow of a different kind from those in the town, and they did not look friendly as they passed. He did not know that he presented to them a very different countenance from that which his fellow citizens had always seen him wear. He was so uncomfortable at length from the way the people he met scrutinized him that when he saw anyone coming, he would instantly turn aside and take the cover of thicket, or hedge, or stone wall, until the bearer of eyes had passed.

Up Daurside was the one vague notion he had of his calling, his destiny; and with his short, quick step, his progress was considerable. He passed house after house, farm after farm; but he went nearer none of them than the road led him. Besides, the houses were very unlike those in the city, and not at all attractive to him.

He came at length to a field sloping to the road, covered with leaves like some he had often seen in the market. They drew him; and as there was but a low and imperfect hedge between, he got over and found it was a crop of small yellow turnips. He gathered as many as he could carry and ate them as he went along. In the city he would never have dreamed of touching anything that was not given him, except it lay plainly a lost thing. But here, where everything was so different and he saw none of the signs of ownership to which he was accustomed, the idea of property did not occur to him. He came soon after to a little stream that ran into the great river. For a few moments he eyed it very doubtfully, thinking it must, like the kennels along the sides of the street, be far too dirty to drink from; but the way it sparkled and sang soon satisfied him, and he drank and was refreshed.

All day the cold spring weather continued, with more of the past winter in it than of the coming summer. The sun would shine out for a few moments with a grey, weary, old light, then retreat as if he had tried but really could not. Once came a slight snow, which melted the moment it touched the earth. The wind kept blowing cheerlessly by fits, and the world seemed growing tired of the same thing over again so often. At length the air began to grow dusk. But, happily, before it was quite dark, and while yet he could distinguish between objects, he came to the gate of a farmyard; it waked in him the hope of finding some place where he could sleep warmer than in the road, and he clambered over it. Nearest of the buildings to the gate stood an open shed. But just as he entered it, he spied at the farther outside corner a wooden structure, and through the arched door of it, he saw the floor covered with nice-looking straw. He suspected it to be a dog's kennel; and presently the chain lying beside it with a collar at the end satisfied him it was. The dog was absent and its dwelling looked altogether enticing! He crept in, got under as much of the straw as he could heap over him, and fell fast asleep.

In a few minutes, as it seemed to him, he was roused by the voice of a boy in conversation with a dog. He seemed, by the sound of the chain, to be fastening the collar on the dog's neck, and presently left. The dog, which had been on the rampage the whole afternoon, immediately turned to creep in and rest till suppertime, presenting to Gibbie the intelligent countenance of a large Newfoundland. Now Gibbie had been honored with the acquaintance of many dogs, and the friendship of most of them. Even among dogs, however, there are ungracious individuals, and Gibbie had once or twice been bitten. Hence, with the sight of the true occupant of the dwelling, it dawned upon him that the dog must be startled to find a stranger in its house and might, regarding him as an intruder rather than a guest, worry him before he had time to explain himself. He darted forward therefore to get out but had scarcely reached the door when the dog put in his nose, ready to follow with all it had. Gibbie, thereupon, began a loud barking, as much as to say, "Here I am; please do nothing without reflection." The dog started back in extreme astonishment, his ears erect and a keen look of question. What strange animal, speaking like, and yet so unlike, an orthodox dog, could have gotten into his chamber? Gibbie, amused at the dog's fright and assured by his looks that he was both a good-natured and reasonable animal, burst into a fit of merry laughter. The dog took it as a challenge to play, darted into the kennel, and began poking his nose into his visitor. Gibbie fell to patting and kissing and hugging him, glad of any companion, and they were friends at once. Both were tired, however, for both had been active that day, and few minutes of mingled wrestling and endearment, to which perhaps the narrowness of their playground gave a speedier conclusion, contented both, after which they lay side by side in peace, Gibbie with his hand on the dog's back, and the dog every now and then turning his head over his shoulder to lick Gibbie's face.

Again he was waked, this time by approaching steps, and the same moment the dog darted from under him with much rattle out of the kennel, in front of which he stood and whined expectantly. A woman was setting down something before the dog—into which he instantly plunged his nose and began gobbling. The sound stirred up all the latent hunger in Gibbie, and he leaped out, eager to have a share. A large wooden bowl was on the ground, and the half of its contents of porridge and milk was already gone. It was plain if Gibbie was to have any, he must lose no time. Had he a long nose and mouth all in one like the animal, he would have plunged them in beside the dog's. But the flatness of his mouth causing the necessity, in the case of such an attempt, of bringing the whole of his face into contact with the food, there was not room in the dish for the two to feed together. So he was driven to the sole other possible expedient, that of making a spoon of his hand. The dog neither growled nor pushed away the spoon but instantly began to gobble twice as fast as before, and presently was licking the bottom of the dish. Gibbie's hand, therefore, made but few journeys to his mouth, but what it carried him was good food—better than any he had had that day. When all was gone he crept again into the kennel; the dog followed, and soon they were both fast asleep in a tangle of arms and legs.

Gibbie woke at sunrise and went out. His host came after him and stood wagging his tail and looking wistfully up in his face. Gibbie understood him and, as the sole return he could make for his hospitality, undid his collar. Instantly the dog rushed off, cleared the gate at a bound and, scouring madly across a field, vanished from his sight; whereupon Gibbie too set out to continue his journey up Daurside.

This day was warmer; spring had come a step nearer;

the dog had been a comforter to him, and the horror had begun to assuage. He began to grow aware of the things about him and to open his eyes to them. Once he saw a primrose in a little dell and left the road to look at it. Still on his right was the great river flowing down toward the home he had left—now through low meadows, now through upshouldered fields of wheat and oats, now through rocky heights covered with the graceful silver-barked birch, the mountain ash and the fir.

That second day he fared better than the first. But I must not attempt the detail of this part of his journey. It is enough that he got through it. He met with some adventures and suffered a good deal from hunger and cold. Had he not been hardy as well as fearless, he would have died. But now from this quarter, now from that, he got all that was needful for one of God's birds. Once he found in a hedge the nest of an errant and secretive hen and, recognizing the eggs as food authorized by the shopwindows and market of the city, soon qualified himself to have an opinion of their worth. Another time he came upon a girl milking a cow in a shed, and his astonishment at the marvels of the process was such that he forgot even the hunger that was rendering him faint. He had often seen cows in the city but had never suspected what they were capable of. When she caught sight of him, staring with open mouth, she was taken with such a fit of laughter that the cow, which was ill-tempered, kicked out and overturned the pail. Now, because of its troublesomeness, this cow was not milked beside the rest, and the shed where she stood was used for farm implements only. The floor of it was the earth, beaten hard and worn into hollows. When the milk settled in one of these, Gibbie saw that it was lost to the girl and found to him. Undeterred by the astounding nature of the spring from which he had just seen it flow, he threw himself down and drank like a calf. Her laughter ended, the girl was troubled; she would be scolded for her clumsiness in allowing Hawkie to kick over the pail, but the eagerness of the boy after the milk troubled her more. She told him to wait and, running to the house, returned with two large pieces of oat-cake which she gave him.

Thus, one way or another, food came to Gibbie. Drink was to be had in almost any hollow. Sleep was scattered everywhere over the world. For warmth, only motion and a seasoned skin were necessary. The latter Gibbie had; the former, already a habit learned in the streets, had now become almost a passion. By this time Gibbie had gotten well up toward the roots of the hills of Gormgarnet, and the river had dwindled greatly in size. He was no longer afraid of it, but would lie for hours listening to its murmurs over the pebbly bed, and sometimes even sleep in the hollows of its banks or below the willows that overhung it. Every here and there a brown rivulet from some peat bog on a hill, brown and clear, flowed into it. Farm after farm he passed, with an occasional little village of low-thatched houses. By this time he had become greatly reconciled to the loneliness of nature, and no more was afraid in her solitary presence.

At the same time his heart had begun to ache and long after the communion of his kind. For not once since he set out (and that seemed months where it was only weeks) had he had an opportunity of doing anything for anybody—except, indeed, unfastening the dog's collar; and not to be able to help was to Gibbie like being dead.

7 The Barn

May had now set in, but up here among the hills she was May by courtesy only. The green crops were growing darker. The lambs were frolicking, and in sheltered places the flowers were turning the earth into a firmament. And now a mere daisy was enough to delight the heart of Gibbie. His joy in humanity so suddenly and violently checked, he had begun to see the human look in the face of the commonest flowers. The wind, of which he had scarce thought as he met it roaming the streets like himself, was now a friend of his solitude, bringing him sweet odors, alive with the souls of bees, and cooling with bliss the heat of the long walk.

One evening just as it became dark, he found himself at a rough gate through which he saw a field. There was a lovely tall hedge on each side of the gate, and he was now a sufficiently experienced traveler to conclude that he was not far from some human abode. He climbed the gate and found himself in a field of clover. It was a splendid big bed, and even had the night not been warm, he would not have hesitated to sleep in it. So down he lay in the clover and was at once unconscious.

When he woke, the moon was high in the heavens. A short distance from his couch he saw a long, low house in which there was a door, horizontally divided into two parts. Gibbie rose and walked to it and would fain have got in, to try whether the place was good for sleep, but he found both halves fast. In the lower half, however, he spied a hole, which, though not so large, reminded him of the entrance to the kennel of his dog host; but alas! it had a door too, shut from the inside. There might be some way of opening it. He felt about, and soon discovered that it was a sliding valve, which he could push to either side. It was, in fact, the cat's door, specially constructed for her convenience of entrance and exit. The hole was a small one but tempting to the wee baronet; he might perhaps be able to squeeze himself through. He tried and succeeded, though with some difficulty. The moon was there before him, shining through a pane or two of glass over the door; and by her light on the hard, brown clay floor he was able to see about. It was a very old-fashioned barn. About a third of it was floored with wood—dark with age, almost as brown as the clay—for threshing upon with flails. At that labor two men had been busy during the most of the preceding day, and that was why, in the same end of the barn, there rose a great heap of oat straw, showing in the light of the moon like a mound of pale gold. What he saw in the other corner was still more like gold and was indeed greater than gold, for it was *life*—the heap, namely, of corn threshed from the straw. Gibbie recognized this as what he had seen given to horses. But now the temptation to sleep was overpowering and took from him all desire to examine further. He shot into the middle of the loose heap of straw, vanishing like a mole. In the heart of the golden warmth, he lay so dry and comfortable that, notwithstanding his hunger, he was presently in a faster sleep than before.

When at length Gibbie became once more aware of existence, it was through a stormy invasion of the still realm of sleep. The blows of two flails fell persistent and quick, first on the thick head of the sheaf of oats untied and cast down before them, then grew louder and more deafening as the oats flew and the chaff fluttered and the straw flattened and broke and thinned and spread—until at last they thundered in great hard blows on the wooden floor. He wormed himself softly around in the straw to look out and see.

It was well that the man with the pitchfork did not spy Gibbie's eyes peeping out from the midst of the straw; he might have taken him for some wild creature and driven the prongs into him. As it was, Gibbie did not altogether like the look of him and lay still as a stone. Then another sheaf was unbound and cast on the floor, and the blows of the flails began again. It went on thus for an hour and a half, and Gibbie dropped asleep several times. The men at length swept up the corn and tossed up the straw for the last time and went out. Gibbie crept out and began to look about him for something he could eat. The oats looked the most likely and he took a mouthful for a trial. He ground at them severely but, hungry as he was, he failed to find oats good for food. Their hard husks and dryness foiled him utterly. Looking round him he saw an open loft and, climbing on the heap in which he had slept, managed to reach it. At the farther end was a heap of hay, which he took for another kind of straw. Then he spied something he knew; a row of cheeses lay ripening on a shelf suspended from the rafters. Gibbie knew them well from the shopwindows—knew they were cheeses and good to eat, though whence and how they came he did not know, his impression being that they grew in the fields like the turnips. He pounced upon a cheese and lifted it between his two hands; it smelled good, but felt very hard. That was no matter; what else were teeth made strong and sharp for? He tried them on one of the round edges, and, nibbling actively, soon got through to the softer body of the cheese.

At length he crept softly toward the other end of the loft to see what was to be seen there. He found that the heap of hay was not in that loft at all but filled a small chamber in the stable, and when Gibbie clambered upon it, what should he see below him on the other side but a beautiful white horse. Beyond, he could see the backs of more horses, but they were very different—big and clumsy, and not white. They were all eating and this was their food on which he lay! He wished he too could eat it—and tried, but found it even less satisfactory than the oats.

A door opened beyond and a man came in and led two of the horses out, leaving the door open. Gibbie clambered down from the top of the hay into the stall beside the white horse and ran out. He was almost in the fields, had not even a fence to cross, and went straight for a neighboring hollow, where, taught by experience, he hoped to find water from a stream flowing into the great river.

8   Glashgar

Once away from the barn, Gibbie had no thought of returning. *Up Daurside* was the sole propulsive force whose existence he recognized. But when he lifted his head from drinking at the stream and, greatly refreshed, looked up its channel, a longing seized him to know whence came the water of life which had thus restored him to bliss—how a burn first appears upon the earth. He would follow it up and see. So away he went, yielding at once to the first desire that came. He had not trotted far along the bank, however, before he saw that its course was a much longer one than he had imagined, for it turned from the mountain and led up among the roots of other hills; while here in front of him, direct from the mountain as it seemed, came down a smaller stream and tumbled noisily into this. The larger burn would lead him too far from the Daur; he would follow the smaller one. He found a wide, shallow place, crossed the larger, and went up the side of the smaller.

The stream he was now ascending ran along a claw of the mountain, which was covered with almost a forest of pine. He trotted along the bank of the burn, farther and farther up, until he could trot no more but had to clamber over great stones or sink to the knees in bog. Sometimes he walked in the water; sometimes he had to scramble up its steep sides. Its banks were mainly of rock and heather, but now and then a small patch of cultivation intervened. Gibbie had no thought that he was gradually leaving the abodes of men behind; he knew no reason why in ascending things should change. For all he knew, there might be farm after farm, up and up forever, to the gates of heaven.

After so long wandering, Gibbie had hardly enough dress left to carry the name. Shoes, of course, he had none. Of the shape of trousers there remained nothing, except the division before and behind in the short petticoat to which they were reduced; and those rudimentary divisions were lost in the multitude of rents of equal apparent significance. He had never, so far as he knew, had a shirt upon his body; and his sole other garment was a jacket, so much too large for him that to retain the use of his hands, he had folded back the sleeves quite to his elbows. His head had plentiful protection in his own natural crop. All ways his thatch of light hair pointed, as if surcharged with electric fluid, crowning him with a wildness which was in amusing contrast with the placidity of his countenance—a sort of live peace abiding in that weather-beaten little face under its wild crown of human herbage. His eyes—partly, perhaps, because there was so little flesh upon his bones—were very large, and in repose had much of a soft animal expression. His hands and feet were small and childishly dainty, his whole body well-shaped and well put together—of which the style of his dress rather quashed the evidence.

Such was Gibbie to the eye, as he rose from Daurside to the last cultivated ground on the borders of the burn and eventually came upon the highest dwelling on the mountain. It was the abode of a cottar, and was a dependency of the farm he had just left. The cottar was an old man of seventy; his wife was nearly sixty. They had reared stalwart sons and shapely daughters, now at service here and there in the valley below.

It was a very humble dwelling, built of turf upon a foundation of stones, and roofed with turf and straw—warm, and nearly impervious to the searching airs of the mountainside. One little window of a foot and half square looked out on the universe. At one end stood a stack of peat, half as big as the cottage itself. All around it were huge rocks. A few of the commonest flowers grew about the door, but there was no garden. The doorstep was natural stone, and a huge projecting rock behind formed the back and a portion of one of the end walls. This latter rock had been the attraction to the site because of a hollow in it, which now served as a dairy. For up there with them lived the last cow of the valley—the cow that breathed the loftiest air on all Daurside, a good cow, gifted in feeding well upon little.

Gibbie knocked at the old, weather-beaten, well-patched door.

"Come on in, whoever ye be."

Gibbie pulled the string that came through a hole in the door; so lifting the latch, he entered.

A woman sat on a stool, her face turned over her shoulder to see who came. It was a grey face, with good, simple features and clear eyes. The plentiful hair that grew low on her forehead was half grey, mostly covered by a white cap with frills. A clean apron of blue print over a blue petticoat completed her dress. A book lay on her lap. Always when she had finished her morning's work and made her house tidy, she sat down to have her "comfort," as she called it. The moment she saw Gibbie she rose. She was rather a little woman and carried herself straight and light.

"Eh, ye poor outcast!" she said in the pitying voice of a mother. "How did ye get up here? And what do you want here? I have nothing."

Receiving no answer but one of the child's bewitching smiles, she stood for a moment regarding him, not in mere silence but with a look of dumbness. She was a mother and, more, one of God's mothers.

Now the very moment before Gibbie entered, she had been reading the words of the Lord: "Inasmuch as ye have done it unto one of the least of these, ye have done it unto me," and with her heart full of them, she had lifted her eyes and seen Gibbie. For one moment, with the quick flashing response of the childlike imagination of the Celt, she fancied she saw the Lord himself. Often had Janet pondered, as she sat alone on the great mountain while Robert was with the sheep or as she lay awake by his side at night with the wind howling about the cottage, whether the Lord might not sometimes take a lonely walk to look after such solitary sheep of His flock as they to let them know He had not lost sight of them. There stood the child, and whether he was the Lord or not, he was evidently hungry.

In the meantime, Gibbie stood motionless in the middle of the floor, smiling his innocent smile, asking for nothing, hinting at nothing, but resting his wild-calm eyes, with a sense of safety and mother-presence, upon the thoughtful face of the gazing woman. Her awe deepened. Involuntarily she bowed her head and, stepping to him, took him by the hand and led him to the stool she had left. There she made him sit while she brought forward her table, white with scrubbing. Then taking from a hole in the wall a platter of oatcakes, she set it upon the table. She next carried a wooden bowl through a whitewashed door to her dairy in the rock, and bringing it back filled, half with cream, half with milk, set that also on

51

the table. Then she placed a chair before it and said, "Sit down and eat. If you were the Lord himself, my bonny man— and for all I know you may be—I could give you nothing better. It's all I have to offer."

Presently she came back with a look of success, carrying two eggs, which, having raked out a quantity, she buried in the hot ashes of the peats and left in front of the hearth to roast while Gibbie ate the thick oatcake, sweet and substantial, and drank such milk as the wildest imagination of a town boy could never suggest. It was indeed angels' food. Janet took a seat on a low, three-legged stool and picked up her knitting that he might feel neither that he was watched as he ate nor that she was waiting for him to finish. Every other moment she gave a glance at the stranger she had taken in; but never a word he spoke, and the sense of mystery grew upon her.

Suddenly came a great bounce and scramble; the latch jumped up, the door flew open and, after a moment's pause, in came a sheep dog—a splendid thoroughbred collie, carrying in his mouth a tiny, long-legged lamb which he dropped half dead in the woman's lap. Then, having done his duty by the lamb, he sat on his tail and stared with his two brave, trusting eyes at the little beggar that sat in the master's chair eating of the fat of the land. Oscar was a gentleman; he had never gone to school, therefore neither fancied nor had been taught that rags make an essential distinction and ought to be barked at. Gibbie was a stranger, and as a stranger Oscar gave him welcome—now and then stooping to lick the little brown feet that had wandered so far.

Like all wild creatures, Gibbie ate quickly and had finished everything set before him before the woman had finished feeding the lamb. Without a notion of the rudeness of it, his heart full of gentle gratitude, he rose and left the cottage. When Janet turned from her shepherding, there sat Oscar looking up at the empty chair.

"What's become of the laddie?" she said to the dog, who answered with a low whine, half-regretful, half-interrogative. Janet hastened to the door, but already Gibbie's nimble

feet, refreshed to the tip of every toe with the food he had just
swallowed, had borne him far up the hill behind the cottage,
so that she could not get a glimpse of him. Thoughtfully she
returned and thoughtfully removed the remnants of the meal.

When at last she had finished, put the things away
and swept up the hearth, she sat down once more to read. The
lamb lay at her feet with his little head projecting from the
folds of her new flannel petticoat; and every time her eye fell
from the book upon the lamb, she felt as if somehow the lamb
was the boy that had eaten of her bread and drunk of her
milk.

Not for years and years had Janet been to church. She
had long been unable to walk so far; and having no book but
the best, and no help to understand it but the highest, her
faith was simple, strong, real, all-pervading. Day by day she
pored over the great gospel until she had grown to be one of
the noble ladies of the kingdom of heaven—one of those who
inherit the earth and are ripening to see God. For the Master,
and His mind in hers, was her teacher. She had little or no
theology save what He taught her. To Janet, Jesus Christ was
no object of so-called theological speculation, but a living
Man who somehow or other heard her when she called to
Him, and sent her the help she needed.

9   The Kitchen

Up and up the hill went Gibbie. The mountain grew
steeper and more bare as he went, and he became absorbed
in his climbing. All at once he discovered that he had lost the
stream, where or when he could not tell. All below and around
him was red granite rock.

Not once while he ascended had the idea come to him
that by and by he should be able to climb no farther. For

aught he knew there were oatcakes and milk and sheep and collie dogs ever higher and higher still. The sun was about two hours toward the west when Gibbie, his little legs almost as active as ever, surmounted the final slope. Running up like a child that would scale heaven, he stood on the bare round, the head of the mountain, and saw with an invading shock of amazement, and at first of disappointment, that there was no going higher; in every direction the slope was downward. He had never been on the top of anything before. He had always been in the hollows of things. Now the whole world lay beneath him. It was cold; in some of the shadows lay snow, but Gibbie felt no cold. In a glow with the climb, which at the last had been hard, his lungs filled with the heavenly air and his soul with the feeling he was above everything that was uplifted on the very crown of the earth, he stood in his rags, a fluttering scarecrow, the conqueror of height, the discoverer of immensity, the monarch of space. Nobody knew of such marvel but him! Gibbie had never even heard the word poetry, but nonetheless was he the very stuff out of which poems grow; and now all the latent poetry in him was set swaying and heaving.

He sat down on the topmost point. And slowly in the silence and the loneliness, from the unknown fountains of the eternal consciousness, the heart of the child filled. The mighty city that had been to him the universe was lost in the far indistinguishable distance; and he who had lost it had climbed upon the throne of the world. The air was still when a breath awoke—it but touched his cheek like the down of a feather—and the stillness was there again. The stillness grew great and slowly descended upon him. It deepened and deepened. It was as if a great single thought was the substance of the silence and was all over and around him, closer to him than his clothes, than his body, than his hands. In after years when Gibbie had the idea of God, when he had learned to think about Him, to desire His presence, to believe that a will of love enveloped His will, as often as the thought of God came to him, it came in the shape of the silence on the top of Glashgar.

As he sat, with his eyes on the peak he had just chosen from the rest as the loftiest of all within his sight, he saw a cloud begin to grow. The next moment a flash of blue lightning darted across the sky. The clouds swept together, and then again burst forth the lightning. He saw no flash, but an intense cloud illumination, accompanied by the deafening crack, and followed by the appalling roar and roll of the thunder. He clung to the rock with hands and feet. It was an awful delight that filled his spirit. Mount Sinai was not to him a terror. To him there was no wrath in the thunder any more than in the greeting of the dog that found him in his kennel. Gibbie sat calm, full of awe, while the storm roared and beat and flashed and ran about him. It was the very fountain of tempest. The tumult at last seized Gibbie like an intoxication; he jumped to his feet and danced and flung his arms about as if he himself were the storm. But the uproar did not last long. Almost as suddenly as it had come it was gone. The sun shone out clearly but was a long way down the west, and twilight, in her grey cloak, would soon be tracking him from the east.

Gibbie, wet and cold, began to think of the cottage where he had been so kindly received, of the friendly face of its mistress and her care of the lamb. It was not that he wanted to eat. He did not even imagine more eating, for never in his life had he eaten twice of the same charity in the same day. What he wanted was to find some dry hole in the mountain and sleep as near the cottage as he could. So he rose and set out. But he lost his way. At length he found, as he thought, the burn along whose bank he had ascended in the morning and followed it toward the valley, looking out for the friendly cottage. But the first indication of abode he saw was the wall of the grounds of the house through whose gate he had looked in the morning. He was, then, a long way from the cottage and not far from the farm; and the best thing he could do was to find again the place he had slept so well the night before. This was not very difficult even in the dusky night.

He skirted the wall, came to his first guide, found and crossed the valley stream and descended it until he thought he recognized the slope of clover down which he had run in the morning. He ran up the brae, and there were the solemn cones of the cornricks between him and the sky! A minute more and he had crept through the cathole. Happily, the heap of straw was not yet removed. Gibbie again shot into it like a mole and burrowed to the very center, there coiled himself up, and imagined himself lying in the heart of the rock on which he sat during the storm listening to the thunder winds over his head.

In spite of the cocks in the yard that made it their business to rouse sleepers to their work, he might have slept longer the next morning, for there was no threshing to wake him, had it not been for another kind of cock inside him which bore the same relation to food that the others bore to light. He peeped first, then crept out. All was still except the voices of those same prophet cocks, a moo now and then, and the occasional stamp of a great hoof in the stable. Gibbie clambered up into the loft and, turning the cheeses about until he came upon the one he had gnawed before, again attacked it and enlarged considerably the hole he had already made in it.

He heard a woman nearby and thereupon Gibbie ventured to reconnoiter a little farther. Popping in his head again, he saw that the dairy was open to the roof but the door was in a partition which did not run so high. The place from which the woman entered was ceiled, and the ceiling rested on the partition between it and the dairy; so that from a shelf level with the hole he could easily enough get on the top of the ceiling. Urged by the instinct of the homeless to understand their surroundings, this he presently effected by creeping like a cat along the top shelf.

The ceiling was that of the kitchen and was merely of boards which, being old and shrunken, had here and there a considerable crack between them. Gibbie, peeping through one after another of these cracks, soon saw several things he did not understand. Of such was a barrel churn, which he took for a barrel organ and welcomed as a sign of civilization. The woman was sweeping the room toward the hearth where the peat fire was already burning, a great pot hanging over it and covered with a wooden lid. When the water in it was hot, she poured it into a large wooden dish in which she began to wash other dishes, thus giving the observant Gibbie his first notion of housekeeping. Then she arranged the dishes on shelves and rack, except a few which she placed on the table, put more water on the fire, and disappeared in the dairy.

Thence presently she returned carrying a great jar which, having lifted a lid in the top of the churn, she emptied into it, to Gibbie's astonishment; he was not, therefore, any further astonished that no music issued when she began to turn the handle vigorously. As to what else might be expected Gibbie had not even a mistaken idea. But the butter came quickly that morning, and then he did have another astonishment, for he saw a great mass of something half-solid tumble out where he had seen liquid poured in—not that alone, for the liquid came out again too! But when at length he saw the mass, after being well washed and molded into certain shapes, he recognized it as butter, such as he had seen in shops, and had now and then tasted on the piece given him by some more-than-usually generous housekeeper. Surely he had wandered into a region of plenty! Only now when he saw the woman busy and careful, the idea of things in the country being a sort of common property began to fade from his mind and the perception to wake that they were as the things in the shops, which must not be touched without first paying money for them over a counter.

The butter-making brought to a successful close, the woman proceeded to make porridge for the men's breakfast, and with hungry eyes Gibbie watched that process next. The water in the great pot boiling like a warm volcano, she took handful after handful of meal from a great wooden dish and threw it into the pot, stirring as she threw, until the mess was presently so thick that she could no more move the spurtle in it. Scarcely had she emptied it into another great wooden bowl when Gibbie heard the heavy tramp of the men crossing the yard to consume it.

For the last few minutes, Gibbie's nostrils had been regaled with the delicious odor of the boiling meal; and now his eyes had their turn. Prostrate on the ceiling he lay and watched the splendid spoonfuls tumble out of sight into the throats of four men; all took their spoonfuls from the same dish, but each dipped his spoonful into his private cup of milk before he carried it to his mouth. A little apart sat a boy, whom the woman seemed to favor, having provided him with a plate full of porridge by himself; but the fact was, four were as many as could bicker comfortably or with any chance of fair play.

When the meal was over and he saw the little that was left with all the drops of milk from the cups tumbled into a common receptacle, to be kept, he thought, for the next meal, poor Gibbie felt very empty and forsaken. Sad at heart, he crawled away with nothing before him except a drink of water at the burn.

10 Donal Grant

It was now time he should resume his journey up Daurside, and he set out to follow the burn that he might regain the river. It led him into a fine meadow where a number of cattle were feeding. The meadow was not fenced—indeed, little more than marked off on one side from a field of growing corn by a low wall of earth, which was covered with moss and grass and flowers. The cattle were herded by a boy whom Gibbie recognized as the one he had seen as he lay spying through the crack in the ceiling. The boy was reading a book, from which every now and then he lifted his eyes to glance around and see whether any of the cows were wandering beyond their pasture of rye grass and clover. Having, then, all before him, therefore no occasion to look behind, he did not see Gibbie approaching. But as soon as he seemed thoroughly occupied, a certain black cow, with short, sharp horns and a wicked look, gradually edged nearer and nearer to the corn, and it turned suddenly and ran for it, jumping the dyke and plunging into a mad revelry of greed. The cow tore and devoured with all the haste of one that knew she was stealing.

Now Gibbie had been observant enough during his travels to learn that this was against the law and custom of the country—that it was not permitted for a cow to go into a field where there were no others; and like a shot he was after the black marauder. The same instant the herdboy, too, lifting his eyes from his book, saw her and, springing to his feet, caught up his great stick and ran also. He had more than one reason to run, for he understood only too well the dangerous temper of the cow, and saw that Gibbie was a mere child and unarmed, an object most provocative of attack to Hornie—so named, indeed, because of her readiness to use the weapons with which nature had provided her. She was in fact a malicious cow, and but that she was a splendid milker would have been long ago fattened up and sent to the butcher.

The boy as he ran full speed to the rescue kept shouting to warn Gibbie from his purpose, but Gibbie was too intent to understand the sounds he uttered and supposed them addressed to the cow. With the fearless service that belonged to his very being, he ran straight to Hornie and, having nothing to strike her with, flung himself against her with a great shove toward the dyke. Hornie, absorbed in her delicious robbery, neither heard nor saw before she felt him and, startled by the sudden attack, turned and in contemptuous indignation lowered her head. She was just making a rush at Gibbie when a stone struck her on a horn; the next moment the herdboy ran up and, with a storm of fiercest blows delivered with full might of his arm, drove her in absolute rout back into the meadow. Drawing himself up in the unconscious majesty of success, Donal Grant looked down upon Gibbie with the eyes of admiration.

"Haith, creature!" he exclaimed. "You're more of a man

than you look! What made you run into the devil's very horns that way?"

Gibbie stood smiling.

"If it hadn't been for my stick, we'd both been knocked over the moon by this time. What's your name, man?"

Still Gibbie only smiled.

"Where do you come from? Where's your folk? Where do you live?—Haven't you a tongue in your head, you rascal?"

Gibbie burst out laughing, and his eyes sparkled and shone; he was delighted with the herdboy, and it was so long since he had heard human speech addressed to himself!

"The creature's an idiot!" concluded Donal to himself. "Poor thing!" he added aloud, and laid his hand on Gibbie's head.

It was but the second touch of kindness Gibbie had received since he was the dog's guest. His emotion was one of unmingled delight and embodied itself in a perfect smile.

"Come, creature, I'll give you something to eat; you'll no doubt understand that!" said Donal. He turned to leave the corn for the grass, where Hornie was eating with the rest like the most innocent of animals. Gibbie obeyed and followed as Donal led the way.

"I hope none of them's swallowed my lunch!" he said, as they walked. Then, looking around, "I'm not so sure where I was sitting."

Suddenly Gibbie darted off, flitting hither and thither like a butterfly. A minute more and Donal saw him pounce upon his bundle, which he brought to him in triumph.

"Fegs! You're not the gowk I took you for," remarked Donal.

Whether Gibbie took the aside for a compliment, or merely was gratified that Donal was pleased, the result was a merry laugh.

The bundle had in it a piece of hard cheese, such as Gibbie had already made acquaintance with, and a few quarters of cakes. One of these Donal broke in two, gave Gibbie the half, replaced the other, and sat down again to the book he had been reading. Gibbie seated himself a few yards off, where in silence he ate his piece and gravely regarded Donal. His human soul had of late been starved even more than his body, and it was paradise again to be in such company. Never since his father's death had he looked on a face that drew him as Donal's. For age Donal was getting toward fifteen, and was strongly built and well-grown. A general look of honesty and an attractive expression of reposeful friendliness pervaded his whole appearance. Though conscientious in regard to his work, he was yet in danger of forgetting his duty for minutes together in his book. The chief evil that resulted from it was such an occasional inroad on the corn as had that morning taken place. He knew his master would threaten him with dismissal if he came upon him reading in the field, but he knew also his master was well aware that he did read, and that it was possible to read and yet herd well.

It was easy enough in this same meadow; on one side ran the Lorrie, on another was a stone wall, and on the third, a ditch. Only the cornfield lay virtually unprotected, and there he himself had to be the boundary. And now he sat leaning against the dyke, as if he so held a position of special defense; but he knew well enough that the dullest calf could outflank him and invade, for a few moments at the least, the forbidden pleasure ground. He had gained an ally, however, whose faculty and faithfulness he yet little knew. For Gibbie had begun to comprehend the situation. He could not understand why or how anyone should be absorbed in a book, for all he knew of books was from his one morning of dame-schooling; but he could understand that, if one's attention were so occupied, it must be a great vex to be interrupted continually. Therefore, as Donal watched his book, Gibbie for Donal's sake watched the herd and, as he did so, gently possessed himself of Donal's club. Nor had many minutes passed before Donal, raising his head to look, saw the cursed cow again in the green corn, and Gibbie manfully encountering her with the club, hitting her hard upon head and horns and deftly avoiding every rush she made at him.

"Give her it upon the nose!" Donal shouted in terror

as he ran full speed to his aid, abusing Hornie in terms of fiercest vituperation.

But he need not have been so apprehensive. Gibbie heard and obeyed, and the next moment Hornie had turned tail and was fleeing back to the safety of the lawful meadow.

"Hech, creature! You must come from fighting folks!" said Donal, regarding him with fresh admiration.

Gibbie laughed; but he had been sorely put to it and big drops were coursing fast down his sweet face. Donal took the club from him and, rushing at Hornie, belabored her well, and drove her quite to the other side of the field. He then returned and resumed his book, while Gibbie again sat down nearby and watched both Donal and his charge. Surely Gibbie had at last found his vocation on Daurside, with both man and beast for his special care!

By and by Donal raised his head once more, but this time it was to regard Gibbie. It had gradually sunk into him that the appearance and character of the boy were peculiar. He had regarded him as a little tramp whose people were not far off, and who would soon get tired of herding and rejoin his companions; but while he read, a strange feeling of the presence of the boy had been growing upon him. He seemed to feel his eyes without seeing them; and when Gibbie rose to look how the cattle were distributed, he became vaguely uneasy lest the boy should be going away. For already he had begun to feel him a humble kind of guardian angel. He had already that day enjoyed a longer spell of his book than any day since he had been herdboy at the Mains of Glashruach.

For a minute or two he sat and gazed at him. My reader must think how vastly, in all his poverty, Donal was Gibbie's superior in the social scale. He earned his own food and shelter and nearly four pounds a year besides, lived as well as he could wish, dressed warmly, was able for his work, and imagined it no hardship. Then he had a father and mother whom he went to see every Saturday and of whom he was as proud as son could be—a father who was the priest of the family, and fed sheep; a mother who was the prophetess, and kept house ever an open refuge for her children.

Poor Gibbie earned nothing—never had earned more than a penny at a time in his life, and had never dreamed of having a claim to such penny. Nobody seemed to care for him, give him anything, do anything for him. Yet there he sat before Donal's eyes, full of service, of smiles, of contentment.

Donal took up his book, but laid it down again and gazed at Gibbie. Several times he tried to return to his reading, but as often resumed his contemplation of the boy. At length it struck him as something more than shyness would account for the fact that he had not yet heard a word from the lips of the child, even when running after the cows. He must watch him more closely.

By now it was his dinnertime. Again he untied his handkerchief and gave Gibbie what he judged a fair share for his bulk—namely, about a third of the whole. Philosopher as he was, however, he could not help sighing a little when he got to the end of his diminished portion. But he was better than comforted when Gibbie offered him all that yet remained to him; and the smile with which Donal refused it made Gibbie as happy as a prince would like to be. What a day it had been for Gibbie! A whole human being, and some five and twenty four-legged creatures besides to take care of!

After the dinner, Donal gravitated to his book, and Gibbie resumed the executive. Some time had passed when Donal, glancing up, saw Gibbie lying flat on his chest, staring at something in the grass. He slid himself quietly nearer and discovered it was a daisy—one by itself alone; there were not many in the field. Like a mother leaning over her child Gibbie was gazing at it. The daisy was not a cold white one, neither was it a red one; it was just a perfect daisy.

"Can you read, boy?" asked Donal.

Gibbie shook his head.

"Can't you speak, man?"

Again Gibbie shook his head.

"Can you hear?"

Gibbie burst out laughing. He knew that he heard better than other people.

"Listen to this, then," said Donal.

He took his book from the grass, and in a chant read a Danish ballad as translated by Sir Walter Scott. Gibbie's eyes grew wider and wider as he listened; it seemed as if his soul were looking out of doors and windows at once—but a puzzled soul that understood nothing of what it saw. When Donal ceased, he remained open-mouthed and motionless for a time; then, drawing himself over the grass to Donal's feet, he raised his head and peeped above his knees at the book. A moment only he gazed and drew back with a hungry sigh; he had seen nothing in the book like what Donal had been drawing from it.

"Would you like to hear it again?" asked Donal.

Gibbie's face answered with a flash and Donal read the poem again. Gibbie's delight returned greater than before, for now something like a dawn began to appear among the cloudy words. Donal read it a third time and closed the book, for it was almost the hour for driving the cattle home.

How much Gibbie even then understood of the lovely old ballad it is impossible to say. The waking up of a human soul to know itself arouses so heavy a sense of marvel and inexplicable mystery. When by slow, filmy unveilings life grew clearer to Gibbie, and he not only knew but knew that he knew, his thoughts always went back to that day in the meadow with Donal Grant as the beginning of his knowledge of beautiful things in the world of man.

Donal rose and went, driving the cattle home, and Gibbie lay where he had again thrown himself upon the grass. When he lifted his head Donal and the cows had vanished.

Donal had looked all around as he left the meadow, and seeing the boy nowhere, had concluded he had gone to his people. The impression Gibbie had made upon him faded a little during the evening. For when he reached home and had watered them, he had to tie up the animals, each in its stall, and make them comfortable for the night; next, eat his own supper; then learn a proposition of Euclid and go to bed.

11   Apprenticeship

Hungering minds come of peasant people as often as of any and have appeared in Scotland as many times, I fancy, as in other nations. Cheap as education then was in Scotland, the parents of Donal Grant had never dreamed of sending a son to college. It was difficult for them to save even the few quarterly shillings that paid the fees of the parish schoolmaster.

After he left school, however, and got a place as herdkeeper, he fared better; for at the Mains he found a friend and helper in Fergus Duff, his master's second son, who was then at home from college. Partly that he was delicate in health, partly that he was something of a gentleman, he took no share with his father and elder brother in the work of the farm, although he was at the Mains from the beginning of April to the end of October. He would have been much more of a man if he had thought less of being a gentleman. He had taken a liking to Donal; having found in him a strong desire after every kind of knowledge, he had sought to enliven the tedium by imparting to him of the treasures he had gathered. They were not great and could never have carried Donal far, for he himself was only a respectable student. Happily, however, Donal needed but to have the outermost shell of a thing broken for him, and that Fergus could do. By and by Donal would begin breaking shells for himself.

But perhaps the best thing Fergus did for him was to lend him books. Donal had an altogether unappeasable hunger after every form of literature, and this hunger Fergus fed with the books of the house. To find himself now in the reversed relation of superior and teacher to the little outcast woke in Donal an altogether new and strange feeling; yet gratitude to his master had but turned itself around and had become tenderness to his pupil.

After Donal left him in the field, Gibbie lay on the grass, as happy as a child could well be. A loving hand laid on his feet or legs would have found them like ice; but where was the matter so long as he never thought of them? He could have eaten a dozen potatoes; but of what mighty consequence is hunger so long as it neither absorbs the thought nor causes faintness? The sun, however, was going down behind a great mountain, which cast a huge shadow, made of darkness and haunted with cold. Sliding across the river, over valley and field, nothing stayed its silent wave until it covered Gibbie with the blanket of the dark, under which he could not long forget that he was in a body to which cold is unfriendly. It was too cold that night to sleep in the fields when he knew where to find warmth. Like a fox into his hole, the child would creep into the corner where God had stored sleep for him; back he went to the barn, gently trotting, and wormed himself through the cathole.

The straw was gone! But he remembered the hay. And, happily, for he was tired, there stood the ladder against the loft. Up he went, nor turned aside to the cheese; but sleep was common property still. He groped his way forward through the dark loft until he found the hay, when at once he burrowed into it like a sandfish into the wet sand and slept until the stirring horses woke him.

He scrambled out on the top of the hay and looked down. The thing he would like best to do would be to look through the ceiling again and watch the woman at her work. Then, too, he would again smell the boiling porridge and the burning of the little sprinkles of meal that fell into the fire. Carefully he crept through the hole and softly round the shelf, whence he peeped once more down into the kitchen. His precautions had been so far unnecessary for, as yet, it lay unvisited, as witnessed by its disorder. Suddenly the thought came to Gibbie that here was a chance for him—here a path back to the world.

He got again upon the shelf and, with every precaution lest he should even touch a milkpan, descended by the lower shelves to the floor. There finding the door only latched, he

entered the kitchen and proceeded to do everything he had
seen the woman do, as nearly in her style as he could. He
swept the floor and dusted the seats, the windowsill and the
table with an apron he found left on a chair, then arranged
everything tidily and roused the rested fire. He had just concluded that the only way to get the great pot full of water
upon it would be to hang first the pot on the chain and then
fill it with the water, when his sharp ears caught sounds and
then heard approaching feet. He darted into the dairy, and in
a few seconds had clambered upon the ceiling and was lying
flat across the joists, with his eyes to the most commanding
crack he had discovered. He was anxious to know how his
service would be received. When Jean Mavor—she was the
farmer's half sister—opened the door, she stopped short and
stared; the kitchen was not as she had left it the night before!

"Hoot! I must have been walking in my sleep!" said
Jean aloud. "Or maybe that good laddie Donal Grant's been
giving me a helping hand. The lad's good enough to do anything."

Eagerly Gibbie now watched her motion and, bent
upon learning, nothing escaped him; he would do much better
next morning! At length the men came in to breakfast and he
thought to enjoy the sight; but alas! it wrought so with his
hunger as to make him feel sick, and he crept away out into
the cornyard where he sought the henhouse. But there was
no food there yet and he must not linger near; for if he were
discovered they would drive him away, and he would lose
Donal Grant. He had not seen him at breakfast, for indeed he
seldom during the summer had a meal except supper in the
house. Gibbie, therefore, as he could not eat, ran to the burn
and drank. He must go to Donal. The sight of him would help
him to bear his hunger.

The first indication Donal had of his proximity was
the rush of Hornie past him in flight out of the corn. Gibbie
was pursuing her with stones for lack of a stick. Thoroughly
ashamed of himself, Donal threw his book from him and ran
to meet Gibbie.

"You mustn't fling stones, creature," he said. "Haith,

it's not for me to find fault though," he added, "sitting reading books like the gowk I am, and letting the beasts run wild in the corn when I'm paid to keep them out of it!"

Gibbie's response was to set off at full speed for the place where Donal had been sitting. He was back in a moment with the book, which he pressed into Donal's hand, while from the other he withdrew his club. This he brandished aloft once or twice, then starting at a steady trot, speedily circled the herd and returned to his adopted master—only to start again, however, and attack Hornie whom he drove from the corn-side of the meadow right over the other; she was already afraid of him. After watching him for a time, Donal came to the conclusion that he himself could not do more. He therefore left all to Gibbie and did not once look up for a whole hour. Everything went just as it should; and not once, all that day, did Hornie again get a mouthful of the grain. It was rather a heavy morning for Gibbie, though, who had eaten nothing, for every time he came near Donal, he saw the handkerchief bulging in the grass, which a little girl had brought and left for him. But he was a rare one both at waiting and at going without.

At last, however, Donal grew hungry himself. He laid down his book, called out to Gibbie, "Creature, it's dinner-time," and took his bundle. Gibbie drew near with sparkling eyes. There was no selfishness in his hunger, for at the worst pass he had ever reached, he would have shared what he had with another; but he looked so eager that Donal perceived he was ravenous and made haste to undo the knots of the hand-kerchief which Mistress Jean appeared that day to have tied with more than ordinary vigor before she intrusted the bundle to the foreman's daughter. When the last knot yielded, he gazed with astonishment at the amount and variety of provisions disclosed.

"Losh!" he explained, "the mistress must have known there were two of us."

He little thought that what she had given him beyond the usual supply was an acknowledgment of services rendered by those same hands into which he now delivered a share, on the ground of other service altogether. It is not always, even where there is no mistake as to the person who deserved it, that the reward reaches the doer so directly.

Before the day was over, Donal gave his helper more and other pay for his service. Choosing a fit time when the cattle were well together and in good position, he took from his pocket a volume of ballads and said, "Sit down, creature. I'm going to read to you."

Gibbie dropped on his crossed legs like a lark to the ground and sat motionless. Donal, after deliberate search, began to read and Gibbie to listen; and it would be hard to determine which found the more pleasure in his part. For Donal had seldom had a listener—and never one so utterly absorbed.

When the hour came for the cattle to go home, Gibbie again remained behind, waiting until all should be still at the farm. He lay on the dyke brooding over what he had heard and wondering how it was that Donal got all those strange beautiful words and sounds and stories out of the book.

12   The Broonie

I must not linger over degrees and phases. Every morning Gibbie got into the kitchen in good time; and not only did he do more and more of the work, but he did it more and more to the satisfaction of Jean, until, short of the actual making of the porridge, he did everything antecedent to the men's breakfast. Without further question she attributed all the aid she received to the goodness of Donal Grant and continued to make acknowledgment of the same in both variety and quantity of victuals, whence as has been shown the real laborer received his due reward.

Until he had thoroughly mastered his work, Gibbie

persisted in regarding matters from his loophole in the ceiling. Having at length learned the art of making butter, he soon arrived at some degree of perfection in it. But when at last one morning he not only churned but washed and made it up entirely to Jean's satisfaction, she did begin to wonder how a mere boy could both have such perseverance and be so clever at a woman's work. For now she entered the kitchen every morning without a question of finding the fire burning, the water boiling, the place clean and tidy, the supper dishes well washed and disposed on shelf and rack; her own part was merely to see that proper cloths were handy to so thorough a user of them. She took no one into her confidence on the matter; it was enough, she judged, that she and Donal understood each other.

And now if Gibbie had contented himself with rendering this house service in return for the shelter of the barn and its hay, he might have enjoyed both longer; but from the position of his night quarters he came gradually to understand the work of the stable also. Before long the men, who were quite ignorant of anything similar taking place in the house, began to observe, more to their wonder than satisfaction, that one or other of their horses was generally groomed before his man came to him; that often there was hay in their racks which they had not given them; and that the master's white horse every morning showed signs of having had some attention paid him that could not be accounted for. The result was much talk and speculation, suspicion and offense; for all were jealous of their rights, their duty and their dignity in relation to their horses. No man was at liberty to do a thing to or for any but his own pair. Even the brightening of the harness brass, in which Gibbie sometimes indulged, was an offense. Many were the useless traps laid for the offender, many the futile attempts to surprise him. As Gibbie never did anything except for half an hour or so while the men were sound asleep or at breakfast, he escaped discovery.

All day he was with Donal and took from him the greater part of his labor; Donal had never had such time for reading. In return Donal gave him his dinner, and Gibbie could do very well upon one meal a day. Donal paid him also in poetry. It never came into his head, seeing Gibbie never spoke, to teach him to read. Donal soon gave up attempting to learn anything from him as to his place or people or history, for to all questions in that direction, Gibbie only looked grave and shook his head. As often, on the other hand, as Donal tried to learn where Gibbie spent the night, he received for answer only one of the little fellow's merriest laughs.

Nor was larger time for reading the sole benefit Gibbie conferred upon Donal. Such was the avidity and growing intelligence with which the little, naked town savage listened to what Donal read to him that his presence added to Donal's own live soul of thought and feeling. From listening to his own lips through Gibbie's ears, he not only understood many things better but, perceiving what things must puzzle Gibbie, came sometimes to his astonishment to see that, in fact, he did not understand them himself. Thus the bond between the boy and the child grew closer—even though Donal imagined now and then that Gibbie might be a creature of some speechless race other than human.

It was not all fine weather up there among the mountains in the beginning of summer. In the first week of June even, there was sleet and snow in the wind—the tears of the vanquished Winter, as he fled across the sea from Norway or Iceland. Then would Donal's heart be sore for Gibbie, when he saw his poor rags blown about like streamers in the wind. Donal had neither greatcoat, plaid, nor umbrella wherewith to shield Gibbie's raggedness. Once in great pity he pulled off his jacket and threw it on Gibbie's shoulders. But the shout of laughter that burst from the boy as he flung the jacket from him and rushed away into the middle of the feeding herd, a shout that came from no rudeness but from the very depths of delight stirred by the loving-kindness of the act, startled Donal out of his pity into brief anger. But Gibbie dived under the belly of a favorite cow and, peering out sideways from under her while the cow went on undisturbed, showed such an innocent countenance of merriment that the pride of Donal's hurt melted away and his laughter echoed Gibbie's.

Things had gone on in this way for several weeks when one morning the men came in to breakfast all out of temper together, complaining loudly of the person unknown who would persist in interfering with their work. They were the louder that their suspicions fluttered about Fergus, who was rather overbearing with them and therefore not a favorite. He was in reality not at all a likely person to bend back or defile hands over such labor, and their pitching upon him the object of their suspicion showed how much at a loss they were. Their only ground for suspecting him was that there was no other by any imagination they could suspect. Had he been in good favor with them, they would have thought no harm of most of the things they thought he did, especially as it eased their work; but he carried himself high, they said, doing nothing but ride over the farm and pick out every fault he could find—to show how sharp he was and look as if he could do better than any of them; and they fancied he carried an evil report to his father, and that this underhand work in the stable must be part of some sly scheme for bringing them into disgrace. And now at last had come the worst thing of all: Gibbie had discovered the cornbin, and having no notion but that everything in the stable was for the delectation of the horses, had been feeding them largely with oats—a delicacy with which, in the plenty of other provisions, they were very sparingly supplied; and the consequences had begun to show themselves in the increased unruliness of the more wayward among them. Gibbie had long given up resorting to the ceiling during their breakfast and remained in utter ignorance of the storm that was brewing because of him.

The same day brought things nearly to a crisis; for the overfed Snowball, proving too much for Fergus's horsemanship, came rushing home at a fierce gallop without him, having indeed left him in a ditch by the roadside. The remark thereupon made by the men in his hearing, that it was his own fault, led him to ask questions. He came gradually to know what they attributed to him, and was indignant at the imputation of such an employment of his mornings to one who had his studies to attend to, scarcely a wise line of defense where the truth would have been more credible as well as convincing—namely, that at the time when those works could alone be effected, he lay as lost a creature as ever sleep could make of a man.

In the evening Jean sought a word with Donal and expressed her surprise that he should be able to do everybody's work about the place, warning him it would be said he did it at the expense of his own. But what could he mean, she said, by wasting the good grain to put devilry into the horses? Donal stared in utter bewilderment. He knew perfectly that to the men suspicion of him was as impossible as to one of themselves. Did he not sleep in the same chamber with them?

Then came anew the question, utterly unanswerable now—who could it be that did not only all her morning work but, with a passion for labor insatiable, part of that of the men also? With the men, she knew her nephew better than to imagine for a moment it could be he. A good enough lad, she judged him, but not good enough for that. He was too fond of his own comfort to dream of helping other people! But now, having betrayed herself to Donal, she wisely went further and secured herself by placing full confidence in him. She laid open the whole matter, confessing that she had imagined her ministering angel to be Donal himself; now she had not even a conjecture after the person of her secret servant.

At length after a pause, her soul seemed to return into her deep-set grey eyes, and in a voice low and solemn and fraught with mystery, she said, "Donal, it's the broonie!"

Donal's mouth opened wide at the word. He had listened in his time to a multitude of strange tales and, Celtic in blood, had been inclined to believe many of them.

Jean Mavor came from a valley far in the Gormgarnet mountains, where in her youth she had heard yet stranger tales than had ever come to Donal's ears. Her brother, a hard-headed Highlander, would have laughed the notion to scorn. For the cowherd, however, as I say, the idea had no small attraction.

"Do you really think it, mem?" said Donal in wonder.

"Think what?" retorted Jean, instantly sharply jealous of being compromised.

"Do you really think there are such creatures as broonies, Mistress Jean?" said Donal.

"Who knows what there is and what there isn't?" returned Jean. She was not going to commit herself either way. Even had she imagined herself above believing such things, she would not have dared to say so. "But you hold your tongue, laddie," she went on, "and go to your work."

But either Mistress Jean's caution came too late and someone had overheard her suggestion or the idea was already abroad, for that very night it began to be reported upon the nearer farms that the Mains of Glashruach was haunted by a broonie who did all the work for both men and maids.

Quick at disappearing as Gibbie was, a little cunning on the part of Jean might soon have entrapped the broonie; but a considerable touch of fear was now added to her other motives for continuing to spend a couple of hours longer in bed than had formerly been her custom. So for yet a few days things went on much as usual; Gibbie saw no sign that his presence was suspected or that his doings were offensive.

One morning the long, thick mane of the horse Snowball was found carefully plaited up in innumerable locks. This was properly elf-work, but no fairies had been heard of on Daurside for many a long year. The broonie, on the other hand, was already in everyone's mouth—only a stray one, probably, that had wandered from some old valley away in the mountains. The rumor spread in long, slow ripples, till at last one of them struck the laird, where he sat at luncheon in the House of Glashruach.

13 The Ambush

Thomas Galbraith was by birth Thomas Durrant but had married an heiress by whom he came into possession of Glashruach and had, according to previous agreement, taken her name. When she died, he mourned her loss as well as he could, but was consoled by feeling himself now first master of both position and possession when the ladder by which he had attained them was removed. Had he been a little more sensitive still, he would have felt that the property was then his daughter's, and his only through her. But this he failed to consider.

Thoroughly respectable and a little devout, Mr. Galbraith was a good deal more of a Scotsman than a Christian. Growth was a doctrine unembodied in his creed; he turned from everything new.

To his servants and tenants he was, what he thought, just. In general expression he looked displeased but meant to look dignified. He had no turn for farming and therefore let out all his land, yet liked to interfere, and as much as possible kept a personal jurisdiction.

There was one thing, however, which if it did not throw the laird into a passion brought him nearer to the outer verge of displeasure than any other, and that was anything whatever to which he could affix the name of superstition.

He was seated with a game pie in front of him, over the top of which his daughter Ginevra was visible. The girl never sat nearer her father at meals than the whole length of the table, where she occupied her mother's place. She was a solemn-looking child of eight or nine, dressed in a brown merino frock of the plainest description. To the first glance she did not look a very interesting or attractive child; but looked at twice she was sure to draw the eyes a third time. Her father was never harsh to her, yet she looked rather frightened of him; but then he was cold, very cold. It troubled Ginevra greatly that when she asked herself whether she loved her father better than anybody else as she believed she ought, she became immediately doubtful whether she loved him at all.

She was eating porridge and milk. With spoon arrested in midpassage, she stopped suddenly and said, "Papa, what's a broonie?"

"What foolish person has been insinuating such contemptible superstition into your silly head?" he asked. "Tell me, child," he continued, "that I may put a stop to it at once."

"They say," said Ginevra, "there's a broonie at the Mains, who does all the work."

"What is the meaning of this, Joseph?" said Mr. Galbraith, turning from her to the butler with the air of rebuke, which was almost habitual to him.

"The meanin' o' what, sir?"

"I ask you, Joseph," answered the laird, "what this— this outbreak of superstition imports? You must be aware that nothing in the world could annoy me more than that Miss Galbraith should learn folly in her father's house. Pray acquaint me with the whole matter."

Joseph therewith proceeded to report what he had heard reported, which was in the main the truth, considerably exaggerated—that the work of the house was done overnight by invisible hands and the work of the stables too. In the latter, cantrips were played as well, some of the men talked of leaving the place, and Mr. Duff's own horse Snowball was nearly out of his mind with fear.

The laird clenched his teeth and for a whole minute said nothing. "It is one of the men themselves," he said at last. "Or some ill-designed neighbor," he added. "But I shall soon be at the bottom of it. Go to the Mains at once, Joseph, and ask young Fergus Duff to be so good as to stop over as soon as he conveniently can."

Fergus was pleased enough to be sent for by the laird, and soon told him all he knew from his aunt and the men, confessing that he himself had been too lazy of a morning to take any steps toward personal acquaintance with the facts.

But he added that as Mr. Galbraith took an interest in the matter, he would be only too happy to carry out any suggestion he might think proper to make on the subject.

"Fergus," returned the laird, "do you imagine things inanimate can of themselves change their relations in space?"

"Certainly not, sir," answered Fergus solemnly.

"Then, Fergus, let me assure you that to discover by what agency these apparent wonders are effected, you have merely to watch. If you fail, I will myself come to your assistance."

Fergus at once undertook to watch. But he went home not quite so comfortable as he had gone; for he did not altogether, notwithstanding his unbelief in the so-called supernatural, relish the approaching situation. Belief and unbelief are not always quite plainly distinguishable from each other, and fear is not always certain which of them is his mother. He was not the less resolved, however, to sit up all night if necessary. Not even to himself did he confess that he felt frightened, for he was a youth of nearly eighteen; but he could not quite hide from himself the fact that he anticipated no pleasure in the duty which lay before him.

For more reasons than one, Fergus judged it prudent to tell not even Auntie Jean of his intention; but waiting until the house was quiet, he stole softly from his room and repaired to the kitchen—where he sat down, took his book, and began to read. He read and read but no broonie came. His candle burned into the socket. He lighted another and read again. Still no broonie appeared and, hard and straight as was the wooden chair on which he sat, he began to doze. He began to feel very eerie as deeper and deeper grew the night around him. The night was dark—no moon and many clouds. Not a sound came from the close. The cattle, the horses, the pigs, the cocks and hens, the very cats and rats seemed asleep. There was not a rustle in the thatch, a creak in the couples. It was well, for the slightest noise would have been in great danger of scaring the household.

The hours passed slowly. Fergus dozed, read, and sat. When the grey of the dawn appeared, he said to himself he would lie down on the bench a while, he was so tired of sitting; he would not sleep. He lay down and in a moment was asleep. The light grew and grew, and the broonie came—a different broonie indeed from the one he had pictured. But as soon as he opened the door of the dairy, he was warned by the loud breathing of the sleeper and swiftly retreated. The same instant Fergus woke, stretched himself, saw it was broad daylight and, with his brain muddled by fatigue and sleep combined, crawled shivering to bed. Then in came the broonie again; and when Jean Mavor entered, there was her work done as usual.

Fergus was hours late for breakfast, and when he went into the commonroom, he found his aunt alone there.

"Well, Auntie," he said, "I think I scared your broonie!"

"Did you, man? Ay!—Then you did the work yourself to save your Auntie Jean's old bones?"

"No, no! I was too tired for that. And so would you have been yourself if you had been sitting up all night."

"Who did it, then?"

"Just yourself, I'm thinkin', Auntie."

"Never a finger of mine was laid on it, Fergus. If you scared one broonie, another came; for there's the work done, the same's ever!"

"Blast the creature!" cried Fergus.

"Whisht, whisht, laddie! He might be hearin' you this very minute."

"I beg your pardon, Auntie, but it's so very provoking!" returned Fergus, and therewith recounted the tale of his night's watch, omitting mention only of his feelings throughout the vigil.

As soon as he had had his breakfast, he went to carry his report to Glashruach.

The laird was vexed, and told him he must sleep well before night, and watch to better purpose.

The next night Fergus's terror returned in full force; but he watched thoroughly notwithstanding, and when his aunt entered she found him there, and her kitchen in a mess.

He had caught no broonie, it was true, but neither had a stroke of her work been done. The floor was unswept; not a dish had been washed; it was churning-day, but the cream stood in the jar in the dairy, not the butter in the pan on the kitchen dresser. Jean could not quite see the good or the gain of it. She had begun to feel like a lady, she said to herself, and now she must tuck up her sleeves and set to work as before.

"You must add cunning to courage, my young friend," said Mr. Galbraith after another conference; and the result was that Fergus went home resolved on yet another attempt.

He felt much inclined to associate Donal with him in his watch this time, but was too desirous of proving his courage both to himself and to the world to yield to the suggestion of his fear. He went to bed with a book immediately after the noonday meal, and rose in time for supper.

There was a large wooden press in the kitchen, standing out from the wall; this with the next wall made a little recess in which there was just room for a chair; and in that recess Fergus seated himself, in the easiest chair he could get into it. He then opened wide the door of the press, and it covered him entirely.

This night would have been the dreariest of all for him, the laird having insisted that he should watch in the dark had he not speedily fallen fast asleep, and slept all night—so well that he woke at the first noise Gibbie made.

It was a broad, clear morning, but his heart beat so loud and fast with apprehension and curiosity mingled that for a few moments Fergus dared not stir, but sat listening breathless to the movement beside him, nonetheless appalling that it was so quiet. Recovering himself a little, he cautiously moved the door of the press and peeped out.

He saw nothing so frightful as he had, in spite of himself, anticipated, but was not therefore, perhaps, the less astonished. The dread broonie of his idea shrunk to a tiny, ragged urchin with a wonderful head of hair, azure eyes, and deft hands, noiselessly bustling about on bare feet. He watched him at his leisure, watched him keenly, assured that any moment he could spring upon him.

As he watched, his wonder sank. As he continued to watch, an evil cloud of anger at the presumption began to gather in his mental atmosphere and was probably the cause of some movement by which his chair gave a loud creak. Without even looking round, Gibbie darted out. Instantly Fergus was after him. Gibbie rushed from the house and across the corner of the yard, and the next Fergus saw of him was the fluttering of his rags in the wind and the flashing of his white skin in the sun as he fled across the clover field. Gibbie was a better runner for his size than Fergus, and in better training too; but alas! Fergus's legs were nearly twice as long as Gibbie's. Fergus behind him was growing more and more angry as he gained upon him but felt his breath failing him. Just at the bridge to the iron gate to Glashruach he caught him at last, and sank on the parapet exhausted. The smile with which Gibbie, too much out of breath to laugh, confessed himself vanquished would have disarmed one more hard-hearted than Fergus had the fellow not lost his temper, and the answer Gibbie received to his smile was a box on the ear that bewildered him. Fergus began to ply him with questions; but no answer following, his wrath rose again, and again he boxed both his ears—without better result.

Then came the question, what was he to do with the redoubted broonie, now that he had him? He was ashamed to show himself as the captor of such a miserable culprit, but the little rascal deserved punishment, and the laird would require him at his hands. He turned upon his prisoner and told him he was an impudent rascal. Gibbie had recovered again and was able once more to smile a little. He had been guilty of burglary, said Fergus; and Gibbie smiled. He could be sent to prison for it, said Fergus; and Gibbie smiled—but this time a very grave smile. Fergus took him by the collar, which amounted to nearly a third part of the jacket, and shook him till he had half torn that third from the other two; then opened the gate and, holding him by the back of the neck, walked him up the drive, every now and then giving him a fierce shake that jarred Gibbie's teeth. Thus, over the old gravel, mossy and damp and grassy, between rowan and birch and pine and larch, looking every inch the outcast he was, did Sir Gilbert Galbraith approach the house of his ancestors for the first time.

14   Punishment

The house he was approaching had a little the look of a prison. Of the more ancient portion, the windows were very small, and every corner had a turret with a conical cap roof. Although he had received from Fergus such convincing proof that he was regarded as a culprit, Gibbie had no dread of evil awaiting him. The highest embodiment of the law with which he had acquaintance was the police, and from not one of them in all the city had he ever had a harsh word; his conscience was as void of offense as ever it had been, and the law consequently, notwithstanding the threats of Fergus, had for him no terrors.

The laird was an early riser, and therefore regarded the mere getting up early as a virtue, altogether irrespective of how the "time thus redeemed," as he called it, was spent. This morning, as it turned out, it would have been better spent in sleep. He was talking to his gamekeeper when Fergus appeared holding the dwindled broonie by the huge collar of his tatters. A more innocent-looking malefactor surely never appeared before awful Justice! Only he was in rags, and there are others besides dogs whose judgments go by appearance. Mr. Galbraith was one of them. He smiled a grim and ugly smile.

"So this is your vaunted broonie, Mr. Duff!" he said, and stood looking down upon Gibbie.

"It's all the broonie I could lay hands on, sir," answered Fergus. "I took him in the act."

"Boy," said the laird, rolling his eyes, more unsteady

than usual with indignation, in the direction of Gibbie, "what have you to say for yourself?"

Gibbie had nothing to say. He smiled, looking up fearlessly in the face of the magistrate, so awful in his own esteem.

"What is your name?" asked the laird, speaking yet more sternly.

Gibbie still smiled and was silent, looking straight into his questioner's eyes. He dreaded nothing from the laird. Fergus had beaten him, but Fergus he classed with the bigger boys in the city who had occasionally treated him roughly; this was a man, and men, except they were foreign sailors or drunk, were never unkind. He had no idea of his silence causing annoyance. Everybody in the city had known he could not answer; and now when Fergus and the laird persisted in questioning him, he thought they were making kindly game of him, and smiled the more. Nor was there much about Mr. Galbraith to rouse a suspicion of the contrary; for he made a great virtue of keeping his temper when most he caused other people to lose theirs.

"I see the young vagabond is as impertinent as he is vicious," he said at last, finding that to no interrogation could he draw forth any other response than a smile. "Here, Angus," he said, turning to the gamekeeper, "take him into the coachhouse and teach him a little behavior. A touch or two of the whip will find his tongue for him."

Angus seized the little gentleman by the neck as if he had been a polecat, and at arm's length walked him unresistingly into the coachhouse. There, with one vigorous tug, he tore the jacket from his back, and his only other garment, dependent thereupon by some device known only to Gibbie, fell from him. He stood in helpless nakedness smiling still; he had never done anything shameful, therefore had no acquaintance with shame. But when the scowling keeper approached him with a heavy cart whip in his hand, he cast his eyes down at his white sides, very white between his brown arms and brown legs, and then lifted them in a mute appeal, which somehow looked as if it were for somebody else, against what he could no longer fail to perceive the man's intent. But he had no notion of what the thing threatened amounted to. He had had few hard blows in his time and never felt a whip.

"You devil's child!" cried the fellow, clenching the cruel teeth of one who loved not his brother, "I'll let you know what comes of breaking into honest people's houses and taking things that are not your own!"

A vision of the gnawed cheese, which he had never touched since the ideas of its being property awoke in him, rose before Gibbie's mental eyes, and inwardly he bowed to the punishment. But the look he had fixed on Angus was not without effect, for the man was a father, though a severe one, and was not all a brute. He turned and changed the cart whip for a gig one with a broken shaft which lay near. It was well for himself that he did so, for the other would probably have killed Gibbie. When the blow fell the child shivered all over, his face turned white, and without uttering even a moan he doubled up and dropped senseless. A swollen cincture, like a red snake, had risen all round his waist, and from one spot in it the blood was oozing. It looked as if the lash had cut him in two.

The blow had stung Gibbie's heart and it had ceased to beat. But the gamekeeper understood vagrants! The young blackguard was only shaming!

"Up with you, you devil! or I'll scar you," he said from between his teeth, lifting the whip for a second blow.

Just as the stroke fell, marking him from the nape all down the spine, a piercing shriek assailed Angus's ears, and his arm, which had mechanically raised itself for a third blow, hung arrested.

The same moment in at the coachhouse door shot Ginevra, as white as Gibbie. She darted to where he lay and there stood over him, arms rigid and hands clenched hard, shivering as he had shivered and sending from her body shriek after shriek.

"Go away, missie!" cried Angus, who had respect for this child, though he had not yet learned to respect childhood; "he's a course creature and must have a whipping."

But Ginevra was deaf to his evil charming. She stopped her cries, however, to help Gibbie up, and took one of his hands to raise him. But his arm hung limp and motionless; she let it go; it dropped like a stick and again she began to shriek. Angus laid his hand on her shoulder. She turned on him and, opening her mouth wide, screamed at him like a wild animal, with all the hatred of mingled love and fear; then she threw herself on the boy, and covered his body with her own. Angus, stooping to remove her, saw Gibbie's face, and became uncomfortable.

"He's dead! He's dead! You've killed him, Angus! You're an evil man!" she cried fiercely. "I hate you. I'll tell on you. I'll tell my papa."

"Hoot, missie!" said Angus. "It was on your own papa's orders I gave him the whip, and he well deserved it, besides. And if you don't go away and be a good young lady, I'll give him more yet."

"I'll tell God!" shrieked Ginevra with fresh energy of defensive love and wrath.

Again he sought to remove her, but she clung so, with both legs and arms, to the insensible Gibbie that he could but lift both together and had to leave her alone.

"If you dare to touch him again, Angus, I'll bite you— bite you—bite you!" she screamed in a wild crescendo.

The laird and Fergus had walked away together, perhaps neither of them quite comfortable at the orders given, but the one too self-sufficient to recall them and the other too submissive to interfere. They heard the cries, nevertheless, and had they known them for Ginevra's would have rushed to the spot; but fierce emotion had utterly changed her voice. Ginevra's shrieks brought Gibbie to himself. Faintly he opened his eyes and stared, stupid with growing pain, at the tear-blurred face beside him. In the confusion of his thoughts, he fancied the pain he felt was Ginevra's, not his, and sought to comfort her, stroking her cheek with feeble hand and putting up his mouth to kiss her. But Angus, utterly scandalized at the proceeding, and restored to energy by seeing that the boy was alive, caught her up suddenly and carried her off—

struggling, writhing, and scratching like a cat.

The moment she thus disappeared, Gibbie began to apprehend that she was suffering for him, not he for her. His whole body bore testimony to frightful abuse. This was some horrible place inhabited by men such as those that killed Sambo! He must fly. But would they hurt the little girl? He thought not—she was at home. He started to spring to his feet but fell back almost powerless; then he tried more cautiously and got up wearily, for the pain and the terrible shock seemed to have taken the strength out of every limb. Once on his feet, he could scarcely stoop to pick up his remnant of trousers without again falling, and the effort made him groan with distress. He was in the act of trying in vain to stand on one foot, so as to get the other into the garment, when he fancied he heard the step of his executioner, doubtless returning to resume his torture. He dropped the rag and darted out the door, forgetting aches and stiffness and agony. All naked as he was, he fled like the wind, unseen of any eye.

He ran he knew not whither, feeling nothing but the desire first to get into some covert and then to run farther. His first rush was for the shrubbery, his next across the little park to the wood beyond. He did not feel the wind of his running on his bare skin. He did not feel the hunger that had made him so unable to bear the lash. On and on he ran. At length he came where a high wall joining some water formed a boundary. The water was a brook from the mountain, here widening and deepening into a still pool. He threw himself in and swam straight across; ever after that, swimming seemed to him as natural as walking.

Then first awoke a faint sense of safety; for on the other side he was knee deep in heather. He was on the wild hill, with miles on miles of cover! He would get right into the heather and lie with it all around and over him till the night came. Where he would go then he did not know. But it was all one, he could go anywhere. Donal must mind his cows, and the men must mind the horses, and Mistress Jean must mind her kitchen, but Sir Gibbie could go where he pleased. He would go up Daurside; but he would not go just at once; that man might be on the outlook for him.

Thus he communed with himself as he went over the knoll. On the other side he chose a tall patch of heather and crept under. How nice and warm and kind the heather felt, though it did hurt the weals dreadfully sometimes.

And now Sir Gibbie, though not much poorer than he had been, really possessed nothing separable from himself, except his hair and his nails. His sole other possession was a negative quantity—his hunger, namely, for he had not even a meal in his body; he had eaten nothing since the preceding noon. He was not nearly reduced to extremity yet though— this little heir of the world. In his body he had splendid health, in his heart a great courage, and in his soul an ever-throbbing love.

Poor Ginny was sent to bed for interfering with her father's orders; and what with the rage and horror and pity, an inexplicable feeling of hopelessness took possession of her, while her affection for her father was greatly, perhaps for this world irretrievably, injured by that morning's experience.

Fergus told his aunt what had taken place and made much game of her broonie. But the more Jean thought about the affair, the less she liked it. It was she upon whom it all came! What did it matter who or what her broonie was? What had they whipped the creature for? What harm had he done? If indeed he was a little ragged urchin, the thing was only the more inexplicable! He had taken nothing! She had never missed so much as a barley scone! The cream had always brought her the right quantity of butter! Not even a bannock, so far as she knew, was ever gone from the press, nor an egg from the bossy where they lay heaped! There was more to it than she could understand! Her nephew's mighty feat, so far from explaining anything, had only sealed up the mystery. She could not help cherishing a shadowy hope that, when things had grown quiet, he would again reveal his presence by his work, if not by his visible person. It was mortifying to think that he had gone as he came, and she had never set eyes upon him.

Donal Grant, missing his "creature" that day for the

first time, heard enough when he came home to satisfy him that he had been acting the broonie in the house and the stable as well as in the field, incredible as it might well appear that such a child should have had even mere strength for what he did. Then first also, after Donal had thus lost him, he began to understand his worth, and to see how much he owed him. While he had imagined himself kind to the urchin, the urchin had been laying him under endless obligation through his gentleness and his absolute unselfishness.

15   Refuge

It was a lovely Saturday evening on Glashgar. The few flowers about the small turf cottage scented the air in the hot western sun. The heather was not in bloom yet, and there were no trees; but there were rocks and stones and a brawling burn that half surrounded a little field of oats, one of potatoes, and a small spot with a few stocks of cabbage and kale. On the borders grew some bushes of double daisies, primroses, and carnations. These Janet tended as part of her household while her husband saw to the oats and potatoes. Robert had charge of the few sheep on the mountain which belonged to the farmer at the Mains, and for his trouble had the cottage and the land, most of which he himself had reclaimed.

They were never in any want, and never had any money except what their children brought them out of their small wages. But that was plenty for their every need; nor had they the faintest feeling that they were persons to be pitied. It was very cold up there in winter, to be sure, and they both suffered from rheumatism; but they had no debt, no fear, much love, and a large hope for what lay on the other side of death. As to the rheumatism, that was necessary, Janet said, to teach them patience, for they had no other trouble.

They were indeed growing old, but neither had begun to feel age a burden yet; and when it should prove such, they had a daughter prepared to give up service and come home to help them. Their thoughts about themselves were nearly lost in their thoughts about each other, their children, and their friends. Janet's main care was her old man, and Robert turned to Janet as the one stay of his life, next to the God in whom he trusted. While Janet prayed at home, his closet was the mountainside. All day, from the mountain and sky, from the sheep and his dog, from winter storms, spring sun and winds, summer warmth and glow, and more than all from the presence and influence of his wife, came to him somehow spiritual nourishment and vital growth. He loved life, but if he had been asked why, he might not have found a ready answer. He loved his wife—just because she was Janet.

The sun was now far down his western arc as Janet finished cleaning her cottage and gazed out toward the sunset; and as she gazed into the darkness, suddenly there emerged from it and staggered toward her—was it an angel? was it a specter? Did her old eyes deceive her? It seemed a child—reeling, and spreading out hands that groped. She covered her eyes for a moment, for it might be a vision in the sun, and looked again. It was indeed a naked child! and was she still so dazzled by the red sun as to see red where red was none?—or were those indeed blood-red streaks on his white skin? Straight now, though slow, he came toward her. It was the same child who had come and gone so strangely before! He held out his hands to her and fell on his face at her feet like one dead. Then with a horror of pitiful amazement, she saw a great cross marked in two cruel stripes on his back.

She stood half-stunned, regarding for one moment motionless the prostrate child and his wounds. The next, she lifted him in her arms and, holding him tenderly to her mother-heart, carried him into the house. There she laid him on his side in her bed, covered him gently over, and hastened to the little byre at the end of the cottage to get him some warm milk. When she returned, he had already lifted his heavy eyelids and was looking wearily about the place. She set down the milk and went to the bedside. Gibbie put up his arms, threw them around her neck, and clung to her as if she had been his mother. And from that moment she was his mother.

"What have they done to ye, my bairn?" she said, in tones of loving pity.

No reply came back—only a smile of absolute content. For what were stripes and nakedness and hunger to Gibbie now that he had a mother to love! Gibbie's necessity was to love. But here was more; here was Love offering herself to him! She raised him with one arm and held the bowl to his mouth, and he drank. When she laid him down again, he turned on his side, off his scored back, and in a moment was fast asleep. She left to make some gruel for him against his waking; and then proceeded to lay the supper for her expected children. The clean yellow-white table of soft, smooth fir needed no cloth—only horn spoons and wooden cups.

At length a hand came to the latch, and mother and daughter greeted as mother and daughter only can; then came a son, and mother and son greeted as mother and son only can. They kept on arriving singly to the number of six— two daughters and four sons, the youngest some little time after the rest. Each, as he or she came, Janet took to the bed, and showed her seventh child where he slept. Each time she showed him, she turned down the bedclothes and revealed the little smitten back. The women wept. The young men were furious, each after his fashion.

"God curse the rascal that did it!" cried one of them, clenching his teeth and quite forgetting himself in the rage of the moment.

"Laddie, take back the word," said his mother calmly. "If you don't forgive your enemies, you'll not be forgiven yourself."

The sixth of the family now entered, and his mother led him up to the bed.

"The Lord preserve us!" cried Donal Grant, "it's the creature!—And is this the way they've treated him! The quietest creature and the willingest!"

Donal began to choke.

"You know him, then, laddie?" said his mother.

"Well enough," answered Donal. "He's been with me and the cattle now, every day for weeks."

With that he hurried into the story of his acquaintance with Gibbie and the fable of the broonie. Janet desired them to say nothing about the boy in the valley but let him be forgotten by his enemies till he grew able to take care of himself. Besides, she said, their father might get into trouble with the master and the laird if it were known they had him.

Donal vowed to himself that if Fergus had had a hand in the abuse, he would never speak a civil word to him again.

He turned toward the bed and there were Gibbie's azure eyes wide open and fixed upon him.

"Eh, creature!" he cried, and darting to the bed, he took Gibbie's face between his hands and said, in a voice to which pity and sympathy gave a tone like his mother's, "What devil was it that beat you like that? I wish I had the trimmin' of him!"

Gibbie smiled.

"Has the beatin' taken the tongue from him?" asked the mother.

"No, no," answered Donal; "he's been like that ever since I've known him. I've never heard a word from the mouth of him."

"He'll be one of the deaf and dumb," said Janet.

"He's not deaf, Mother; that I know well. But dumb he must be, I'm thinkin'.—Creature," he continued, stooping over the boy, "if you hear what I'm sayin', take hold of my nose."

Thereupon, with a laugh like that of an amused infant, Gibbie raised his hand, and with thumb and forefinger gently pinched Donal's nose, at which they all burst out laughing with joy. It was as if they had found an angel's baby in the bushes and had been afraid he was an idiot but were now relieved. Away went Janet and brought him his gruel. It was with no small difficulty and not without a moan or two that

Gibbie sat up in the bed to take it. He took the wooden bowl and began to eat; and the look he cast on Janet seemed to say he had never tasted such delicious food. Indeed, he never had; and the poor cottage, where once more he was a stranger taken in, appeared to Gibbie a place of wondrous wealth.

Janet brought out a garment of her own and aired it at the fire. It had no lace at the neck or cuffs, no embroidery down the front. But when she put it on him, amid the tearful laughter of the women, and had tied it around his waist, it made a dress most becoming in their eyes, and gave Gibbie an indescribable pleasure from its whiteness and its coolness to his inflamed skin.

They had just finished clothing him thus when the goodman came home, and the mother's narration had to be given afresh, with Donal's notes explanatory and completive. As the latter reported the doings of the imagined broonie and the commotion they had caused at the Mains and along Daurside, Gibbie's countenance flashed with pleasure and fun; and at last he broke into such a peal of laughter as had never, for pure merriment, been heard before so high on Glashgar. All joined involuntarily in the laugh—even the old man who had been listening with his grey eyebrows knit. When at last his wife showed him the child's back, he lifted his two hands and moved them slowly up and down, as in pitiful appeal for man against man to the Sire of the race.

They sat down to their homely meal. Simplest things will carry the result of honest attention as plainly as more elaborate dishes. In the judgment of all her guests, the porridge was such as none could make but mother, the milk such as none but mother's cow could yield, the cakes such as she only could bake.

Gibbie sat in the bed like a king on his throne, gazing on his kingdom. Gibbie could not, at that period of his history, have invented a heaven more to his mind, and as often as one of them turned eyes toward the bed, his face shone with merry gratitude.

It was before long almost time for the sons and daughters to go down the hill again and leave the cottage and the

blessed old parents and the harbored child to the night, the
mountain silence, and living God. The sun had long been
down; but far away in the north the faint, thin fringe of his
light garment was still visible.

"Now, lads and lassies, before we have worship, run,
every one of you," said the mother, "and pick some heather
to make a bed for the wee man—in the nook there, at the head
of ours. He'll sleep fine there, and no harm will come near
him."

She was obeyed instantly. The heather was pulled and
set together upright as it grew, only much closer, so that the
tops made a dense surface. They boxed them in below with
a board or two and bound them together above with a blanket
over the top, and a white sheet over that was large enough to
be doubled and receive Gibbie between its folds. Then another blanket was added, and the bed, a perfect one, was
ready. The eldest of the daughters took Gibbie in her arms
and, tenderly careful over his hurts, lifted him from the old
folks' bed and placed him in his own—one more luxurious,
for heather makes a still better stratum for repose than oat
chaff—and Gibbie sank into it with a sigh that was but a
smile grown vocal.

Then Donal, as the youngest, got down the big Bible
and laid it before his father. The old man put on his specta-
cles, took the book, and found the passage that fell, in continuous process, to that evening.

After the reading followed a prayer. By the time the
prayer was over, Gibbie was fast asleep again. What it all
meant he had not an idea; and the sound lulled him. When he
woke next, from the aching of his stripes, the cottage was
dark. The old people were fast asleep. A hairy thing lay by
his side which, without the least fear, he examined and found
to be a dog; whereupon he fell fast asleep again, if possible,
happier than ever. And while the cottage was thus quiet, the
brothers and sisters were still tramping along the moonlight
paths of Daurside. They had all set out together, but at one
point after another there had been a parting, and now they

were on six different roads, each drawing nearer to the labor of the next week.

16   A New Son

At first opportunity Donal questioned Fergus as to his share in the ill-usage of Gibbie. Fergus treated the inquiry as an impertinent interference, and mounted his high horse at once. What right had his father's herdboy to question him as to his conduct? He put it so to him and in nearly just as many words.

Thereupon answered Donal, "It's just this, you see, Fergus: You've been very good to me and I'm more obliged to you than I can say. But it would be dishonest for me to take books from you, and ask you questions I can't make out myself and then go on despisin' you in my heart for cruelty and wrong. What was the creature punished for? Tell me that. According to your aunt's account, he had taken nothing and had done nothing but good."

"Why didn't he speak up then and defend himself, and not be so confounded obstinate?" returned Fergus. "I couldn't get him to utter a single word. As for his punishment, it was by the laird's orders that Angus MacPholp took the whip to him. I had nothing to do with it." Fergus did not consider the punishment he himself had given him as worth mentioning.

"Well, I'll be a man someday, and then Angus will have to settle with me!" said Donal through his clenched teeth. "Man, Fergus! the creature's as dumb as a worm. I don't believe that he ever spoke a word in his life."

This cut Fergus to the heart, for he was far from being without generosity or pity. I fear, however, from what I know of Fergus afterward that now, instead of seeking about to make some amends, he turned the strength that should have gone in that direction to the justifying of himself to himself in what he had done. Anyhow, he was far too proud to confess to Donal that he had done wrong—too much offended at being rebuked by one he counted so immeasurably his inferior to do the right thing his rebuke set before him. What did the mighty business matter! The little rascal was nothing but a tramp; and if he didn't deserve his punishment this time, he had deserved it a hundred times without having it, and would ten thousand times again.

Ginevra was hardly the same child after the experience of that terrible morning. At no time very much at home with her father, something had now come between them, which all her struggles to love him as before were unavailing to remove. The father was too stupid, too unsympathetic, to take note of that look of fear that crossed her face if ever he addressed her suddenly.

With a cold spot in his heart where once had dwelt some genuine regard for Donal, Fergus went back to college. Donal went on herding the cattle, cudgeling Hornie, and reading what books he could lay his hands on; alas, there was no supply through Fergus anymore! The previous year, before he took his leave, he had been careful to see Donal provided with at least books for study; but this time he left him to shift for himself. He was small because he was proud, spiteful because he was conceited.

In the meantime, Gibbie slept and waked and slept again, night after night, with the loveliest days between, at the cottage on Glashgar. The morning after his arrival, the first thing he was aware of was Janet's face beaming over him with a look in her eye more like worship than benevolence. Her husband was gone, and she was about to milk the cow and was anxious lest, while she was away, Gibbie should disappear as before. But the light that rushed into his eyes was in full response to that which kindled the light in hers, and her misgiving vanished; he could not love her like that and leave her. She gave him his breakfast of porridge and milk, and went to her cow.

When she came back she found everything tidy in the

cottage, the floor swept, every dish washed and set aside; and Gibbie was examining an old shoe of Robert's to see whether he could not mend it. Janet proceeded at once with joy to the construction of a garment she had been devising for him. Taking a bluewinsey petticoat of her own, drawing it in round his waist, and tying it over the chemise which was his only garment, she found as she had expected, that its hem reached his feet: she partly divided it up the middle, before and behind, and had but to back-stitch two short seams, and there was a pair of sailor-like trousers, as tidy as comfortable! Gibbie was delighted with them. Then Janet thought about a cap; but considering him a moment critically and seeing how his hair stood out like thatch eaves round his head, she betook herself instead to her New Testament.

Gibbie stood by as she read in silence, gazing with delight, for he thought it must be a book of ballads like Donal's that she was reading. But Janet found his presence and his gaze discomposing. To worship freely one must be alone or else with fellow worshipers. And reading and worshiping were often so mingled with Janet as to form but one mental consciousness. She looked up therefore from her book.

"Can you read, laddie?" she said.

Gibbie shook his head.

"Sit down then, and I'll read to you."

Gibbie obeyed more than willingly, and thus had his first lesson in the chief thing worth learning. I cannot tell how or what were the slow stages by which his mind budded and swelled until the knowledge of God burst into flower. I cannot tell the shape of the door by which the Lord entered into that house and took possession of it. I cannot even tell in what shape He appeared in Gibbie's thoughts. For Janet never suspected how utter was Gibbie's ignorance. She never dreamed that he did not know what was generally said about Jesus Christ.

So, teaching him only that which she loved, not that which she had been taught, Janet read to Gibbie of Jesus, and talked to him of Jesus, until at length his whole soul was full of the Man, of His doings, of His words, of His thoughts, of

His life. Almost before he knew, he was trying to fashion his life after that of the Master.

Janet had no inclination to trouble her own head, or Gibbie's heart, with what men call the plan of salvation. It was enough to her to find that he followed her Master.

17 "Gibbie"

From that very next day after he was received into the cottage on Glashgar, Gibbie as a matter or course took upon himself any work his hand could find to do, and Janet averred to her husband that never had any of her daughters been more useful to her. At the same time, however, she insisted that Robert should take the boy out with him. She would not have him do woman's work, especially work for which she herself was perfectly able. She had not come to her years, she said, to learn idleness; and the boy would save Robert many a weary step among the hills.

"He can't speak to the dog," objected Robert, giving utterance to the first difficulty that suggested itself.

"The dog can't speak himself," returned Janet, "and the wonder is that he can understand; who knows but he may come closer to the one that's speechless like himself! Give the creature a chance, and I bet he'll make himself plain to the dog. You just try him. You tell him to tell the dog something and see what will come of it."

Robert made the experiment and it proved satisfactory. As soon as he had received Robert's orders, Gibbie claimed Oscar's attention. The dog looked up in his face, noted every glance and gesture, and, partly from sympathetic instinct, partly from observation of the state of affairs in respect of the sheep, divined with certainty what was the duty required of him, and was off like a shot.

"The two dumb creatures understand one another better than I understand either of them," said Robert to his wife when they came home.

And now indeed it was a blessed time for Gibbie. It had been pleasant down in the valley, with the cattle and Donal and foul weather sometimes; but now it was the full glow of summer; the sweet, keen air of the mountain bathed him as he ran. Gibbie was one of the meek and inherited the earth. He was of the poet-kind also and, now that he was a shepherd, saw everything with a shepherd's eyes.

It was not long before the town-bred child grew to love the heavens almost as dearly as the earth. He would gaze and gaze at the clouds as they came and went. Watching them and the wind, weighing the heat and the cold and marking many indications, some of them known perhaps only to himself, he understood the signs of the earthly times at length nearly as well as an insect or a swallow and far better than long-experienced old Robert. The mountain was Gibbie's very home; yet to see him far up on it, in the red glow of the setting sun, with his dog, as obedient as himself, hanging upon his every signal, one could have fancied him a shepherd boy come down from the plains of heaven to look after a lost lamb. Often, when the two old people were in bed and asleep, Gibbie would be out watching the moon rise.

Then there was the delight, fresh every week, of the Saturday gathering of the brothers and sisters, whom Gibbie could hardly have loved more had they been of his own immediate kin. Dearest of all was Donal, whose greeting, "Well, creature," was heavenly to Gibbie's ears. Donal would have had him go down and spend a day every now and then with him and the cattle, but Janet would not hear of it until the foolish tale of the broonie should have quite blown over.

"Eh, but I wish," she added as she said so, "I could find out something about his folk, or even where he came from or what they called him! Never a word has the creature spoken!"

"You should teach him to read, Mother," said Donal.

"How would I do that, laddie? I would have to teach

him to speak first," returned Janet.

"Let him come down to me and I'll try my hand, then," said Donal.

Notwithstanding, Janet persisted in her refusal—for the present. But Donal's words set her thinking of the matter, how she might teach him to read; and at last the idea dawned upon her to substitute writing for speech.

She showed Gibbie the letters, naming each several times and going over them repeatedly. Then she gave him Donal's school slate and said, "Now, make an *A*, creature."

Gibbie did so, and well too; she found that already he knew about half the letters.

"He's no fool!" she said to herself in triumph.

The other half soon followed; and she then began to show him words. She was not very severe about the spelling, if only it was plain he knew the word.

One day, a few weeks after Gibbie had begun to read by himself, Janet became aware that he was sitting on his stool, in what had come to be called the creature's corner, more than usually absorbed in some attempt with slate and pencil. She went near and peeped over his shoulder. At the top of the slate he had written the word *give,* then the word *giving,* and below them, *gib,* then *gibing;* upon these followed *gib* again, and he was now plainly meditating something further. Suddenly he seemed to find what he wanted, for in haste, almost as if he feared it might escape him, he added a *y,* making the word *giby*—then first lifted his head and looked round, evidently seeking her. She laid her hand on his head. He jumped up with one of his most radiant smiles and, holding out the slate to her, pointed with his pencil to the word he had just completed. She did not know it for a word but sounded it, making the *g* soft. He shook his head sharply, and laid the point of his pencil upon the *g* of the *give* written above. Janet had been his teacher too long not to see what he meant, and immediately pronounced the word as he would have it. Upon this he began a wild dance, but sobering suddenly, sat down, and was instantly again absorbed in further attempt. It lasted so long that Janet resumed her previous household occupation. At length he rose, and with thoughtful, doubtful contemplation of what he had done, brought her the slate. There, under the foregone success, he had written the words, *galatians* and *breath,* and under them, *gal-breath.* She read them all, and at the last, witnessing to his success by pronouncing them to his satisfaction, he began another dance, which again he ended abruptly, to draw her attention once more to the slate. He pointed to the *giby* first, and the *galbreath* next, and she read them together. This time he did not dance but seemed waiting some result.

The idea was dawning upon Janet that he meant himself; but she was thrown off by the cognomen's correspondence with that of the laird, which suggested that the boy had been merely attempting the name of the great man of that district. With this in her mind, and doubtfully feeling her way, she essayed the tentative of setting him right in the Christian name, and said: "Thomas—Thomas Galbraith." Gibbie shook his head as before, and again resumed his seat. Presently he brought her the slate, with all the rest rubbed out, and these words standing alone—*sir giby galbreath.* Janet read them aloud, whereupon Gibbie began dancing once more in triumph; he had, he hoped, for the first time in his life, conveyed a fact through words.

"That's what they call you, is it?" said Janet, looking motherly at him: "Sir Gibbie Galbraith?"

Gibbie nodded vehemently.

"It'll be some nickname the boys have given him," said Janet to herself, but continued to gaze at him, in questioning doubt of her own solution. She could not recall having ever heard of a Sir in the laird's family; but ghosts of things forgotten kept rising formless and thin in the sky of her memory. Had she never heard of a Sir Somebody Galbraith somewhere? And still she stared at the child, trying to grasp what she could not even see. By this time Gibbie was standing quite still, staring at her in return. He could not think what made her stare so at him.

"Who called you that?" said Janet at length, pointing to the slate.

Gibbie took the slate, dropped upon his seat and, after considerable cogitation and effort, brought her the words "Gibyse Fapher." Janet for a moment was puzzled, but when she thought of correcting the *p* with a *t,* Gibbie entirely approved.

"Who was your father, creature?" she asked.

Gibbie, after a longer pause, and more evident labor than hitherto, brought her the enigmatical word "Assotr," which, with the Sir running about in her head, quite defeated Janet.

Perceiving his failure, he jumped upon a chair and, reaching after one of Robert's Sunday shoes on the shelf, took it between his knees and began a pantomime of the making or mending of the same; it was clear to Janet he must have been familiar with the process collectively called shoemaking. And therewith she recognized the word on the slate—a sutor. She smiled to herself at the association of man and trade, and concluded that the Sir at least was a nickname. And yet whether from the presence of some rudiment of an old memory, or from something about the boy that belonged to a higher style than his present showing, her mind kept swaying in an uncertainty whose very object eluded her.

"What would you like us to call you, then, creature?" she asked, anxious to meet the child's own idea of himself.

He pointed to giby.

"Well, Gibbie," responded Janet—and at the word, now for the first time addressed by her to himself, he began dancing more wildly than ever, and ended with standing motionless on one leg; now first and at last he was fully recognized for what he was!—"Well, Gibbie, I'll call you what you think fit," said Janet. "And now go your way, Gibbie, and see that Crummie's not too far out of sight."

From that hour Gibbie had his name from the whole family—his Christian name only, however, Robert and Janet having agreed it would be wise to avoid whatever might possibly bring the boy again under the notice of the laird. The latter half of his name they laid aside for him, as parents do a dangerous or over-valuable gift to a child.

18 The Beast-Loon o' Glashgar

Almost from the first moment of his being domiciled on Glashgar what with the good food, the fine exercise, the exquisite air, and his great happiness, Gibbie began to grow; and he took to growing so fast that his legs soon shot far out of his winsey garment. His wiry limbs grew larger without losing their firmness or elasticity; his chest, the effort in running up hill constantly alternated with the relief of running down, rapidly expanded and his lungs grew hardy as well as powerful. He became at length such in wind and muscle that he could run down a wayward sheep almost as well as Oscar. And his nerve grew also with his body and strength till his coolness and courage were splendid. Never, when the tide of his affairs ran most in the shallows, had Gibbie had much acquaintance with fears, but now he had forgotten the taste of them and would have encountered a wild highland bull alone on the mountains as readily as tie the cow Crummie up in her stall.

One afternoon, Donal, having got a half-holiday by the help of a friend and the favor of Mistress Jean, came home to see his mother, and having greeted her set out to find Gibbie. He had gone a long way, looking and calling without success, and had come in sight of a certain tiny loch that filled a hollow of the mountain. The little lake, though small in surface, was truly of unknown depth and had elements of dread about it, telling upon far less active imaginations than Donal's. While he stood gazing at it, almost afraid to go nearer, a great splash that echoed from the steep rocks surrounding it brought his heart into his mouth. Immediately followed a loud barking in which he recognized the voice of Oscar. Before he had well begun to think what it could mean, Gibbie appeared on the opposite side of the loch, high above its level, on the top of the rocks forming its basin. He began instantly a rapid descent toward the water, where the rocks were so steep and footing so precarious that Oscar wisely remained at the top and made no attempt to follow him.

Presently the dog caught sight of Donal, where he stood on a lower level, whence the water was comparatively easy of access, and starting off at full speed joined him with much demonstration of welcome. But he received little notice from Donal, whose gaze was fixed, with much wonder and more fear, on the descending Gibbie. Some twenty feet from the surface of the loch, he reached a point whence clearly in Donal's judgment there was no possibility of farther descent. But Donal was never more mistaken; for that instant Gibbie flashed from the face of the rock head foremost, like a fishing bird, into the lake. Donal gave a cry and ran to the edge of the water accompanied by Oscar, who all the time had showed no anxiety but had stood wagging his tail. When they reached the loch, there was Gibbie already but a few yards from the only possible landing place, swimming with one hand, while in the other arm he held a baby lamb, its head lying quite still on his shoulder. Then Donal first began to perceive that "the creature" was growing into an athlete.

When he landed he gave Donal a merry laugh of welcome, but without stopping flew up the hill to take the lamb to its mother. Fresh from the icy water, he ran so fast that it was all Donal could do to keep up with him.

Every time Donal came home, he would bring some book of verse with him and, leading Gibbie to some hollow, shady or sheltered as the time required, would there read to him ballads, or songs, or verse as mood or provision might suggest.

I wonder how much Gibbie was indebted to constrained silence during all these years. That he lost by it, no one will doubt; that he gained also, a few will admit. I cannot doubt it bore an important part in the fostering of the visionary thoughts and feelings and actions now growing inside him. While Donal read, rejoicing in the music of sound,

Gibbie was doing something besides: He was listening with the same ears, and trying to see with the same eyes which he brought to bear upon the things Janet taught him out of the Book. Whether Donal read from a thumbed old edition, or some new tale or poem from the Edinburgh press, Gibbie was always placing what he heard by the side of what he knew, asking himself what Jesus would have done, or what He would require of a disciple.

When he sank foiled from any endeavor to understand how a man was to behave in certain circumstances, he always took refuge in doing something—and doing it better than before; leaped the more eagerly if Robert called him, spoke the more gently to Oscar, turned the sheep more careful not to scare them—as if by instinct he perceived that the only hope of understanding lies in doing. He would run to do the thing he had learned yesterday, when as yet he could find no answer to the question of today. Thus, as the weeks of solitude and thought glided by, the reality of Christ grew upon him, till in the very rocks and heather and the faces of the sheep he felt His presence everywhere. He fancied He came down every now and then to see how things were going in the lower part of His kingdom; and that when He did so, He made use of Glashgar and its rocks for His stair.

When the winter came with its frost and snow, Gibbie saved Robert much suffering. At first Robert was unwilling to let him go out alone in stormy weather; but Janet believed that the child doing the old man's work would be specially protected. He did not suffer from the cold; for, a sheep having died toward the end of the first autumn, Robert, in view of Gibbie's coming necessity, had begged of his master the skin and dressed it with the wool upon it. Of this, between the three of them, they made a coat for him, so that he roamed the hill like a savage in a garment of skin.

Before very long, it became, of course, well known about the country that Mr. Duff's crofters upon Glashgar had taken in and were bringing up a foundling—some said an innocent, some said a wild boy—who helped Robert with his sheep and Janet with her cow, but could not speak a word of either Gaelic or English. By and by strange stories came to be told of his exploits, representing him as gifted with bodily powers as much surpassing the common as his mental faculties were assumed to be under the ordinary standard. The rumor concerning him swelled as well as spread until, toward the end of his second year on Glashgar, the notion of Gibbie in the imaginations of the children of Daurside was that of an almost supernatural being who had dwelt upon, or rather who had haunted Glashgar from time immemorial and of whom they had been hearing all their lives. Although they had never heard anything bad of him, only that he was wild, wore a hairy skin, could do more than any other boy dared attempt, was dumb, and yet sheep and dogs and cattle could understand him perfectly; and this was more than enough to envelop the idea of him in a mist of dread. When the twilight began to gather about the cottages and farmhouses for miles up and down the river, the very mention of "the beast-loon o' Glashgar" was enough to send many of the children scouring like startled hares into the house.

Gibbie little thought what clouds of foolish fancies rising from the valleys below had, by their distorting vapors, made of him an object of terror to those whom at the very first sight he would have loved and served. Among these, perhaps the most afraid of him were the children of the gamekeeper, for they lived on the very foot of the haunted hill, near the bridge and gate of Glashruach; and the laird himself happened one day to be witness of their fear. He inquired the cause, and yet again was his enlightened soul vexed by the persistency with which the shadows of superstition still hung about his lands. Had he been half as philosophical as he fancied himself, he might have seen that there was not necessarily a single film of superstition involved in the belief that a savage roamed a mountain—which was all that Mistress MacPholp, depriving the rumor of its richer coloring, ventured to impart as the cause of her children's perturbation.

But anything a hairsbreadth out of the common was a thing hated of Thomas Galbraith's soul; and whatever another believed which he did not choose to believe, he set down at once as superstition. He held therefore immediate communication with his gamekeeper on the subject. It had not occurred either to master or man that the offensive being whose doubtful existence caused the scandal was the same toward whom they had once been guilty of such brutality. The same afternoon the laird questioned his tenant of the Mains concerning his cottars, and he was assured that better or more respectable people were not in all the region of Gormgarnet.

When Robert became aware of Gibbie's gifts of other kinds than those revealed to himself by his good shepherding, he began to turn it over in his mind whether they ought not to send the boy to school that he might learn the things he was so much more than ordinarily capable of learning.

"Let him go down to the Mains and herd with Donal," said Robert to Janet. "He knows a lot more than you or me or Gibbie; and when he's learned all that Donal can show him, it'll be time to think what next."

"Well," answered Janet, "no one can say but that's sense, Robert; and though I'm loath to let the laddie go, for your sake more than my own, let him go to Donal. I hope, between the two, they won't let the cattle among the corn."

"The corn's most all cut now," replied Robert. "But he needn't go every day. He can give one day to the learning, and the next to thinking about it among the sheep. And any day you want to keep him, you can keep him; for it won't be as if he went to school."

Gibbie was delighted with the proposal.

"Only," said Robert, in final warning, "don't let them take you, Gibbie, and score your back again, my creature: and don't answer anybody when they ask what you're called, anything more than just Gibbie."

The boy laughed and nodded and, as Janet said, the boy's laugh was as good as the best man's word.

Now came a happy time for the two boys. Donal began at once to teach Gibbie arithmetic. When they had had enough of that for a day, he read Scottish history to him; and when they had done what seemed their duty by that, then came the best of the feast—whatever tales or poetry Donal had laid his hands upon.

Once they were startled by seeing the gamekeeper enter the field. The moment he saw him, Gibbie laid himself flat on the ground ready to spring to his feet and run. The man, however, did not come near them.

19   The Gamekeeper

The second winter came, and with the first frost Gibbie resumed his sheepskin coat and the brogues and leggings which he had made for himself of deerhide tanned with the hair. It pleased the two old people to see him so warmly clad. Very soon the stories about him were all stirred up afresh and new rumors added. This one and that of the children declared they had caught sight of the beast-loon, running about the rocks like a goat; and one day a boy of Angus's own, who had been a good way up the mountain, came home nearly dead with terror saying the beast-loon had chased him a long way. He did not add that he had been throwing stones at the sheep, not perceiving anyone in charge of them. So one fine morning in December, having nothing particular to attend to, Angus shouldered his double-barrelled gun and set out for a walk over Glashgar in the hope of coming upon the savage that terrified the children. He must be off; that was settled. Where Angus was in authority, the outlandish was not to be suffered. The sun shone bright, and a keen wind was blowing.

About noon he came in sight of a few sheep in a sheltered spot, where were little patches of coarse grass among the heather. On a stone a few yards above them sat Gibbie, not reading, as he would be half the time now, but busied with a set of Pan's pipes—which, under Donal's direction, he had made for himself—drawing from them experimental sounds, and feeling after the possibility of a melody. He was so much occupied that he did not see Angus approach, who now stood for a moment or two regarding him. He was hirsute as Esau, his head crowned with its own plentiful crop (even in winter he wore no cap), his body covered with the wool of the sheep, and his legs and feet with the hide of the deer, the hair as in nature, outward. The deerskin Angus knew for what it was from afar, concluding it the spoil of the only crime of which he recognized the enormity, whereas it was in truth part of a skin he himself had sold to a saddler in the next village. He boiled over with wrath and strode nearer, grinding his teeth. Gibbie looked up, knew him and starting to his feet ran to the hill. Angus, leveling his gun, shouted to him to stop, but Gibbie only ran the harder and not once looked round. Idiotic with rage, Angus fired. One of his barrels was loaded with shot, the other, with ball. Meaning to use the shot barrel, he pulled the wrong trigger and liberated the bullet. It went through the calf of Gibbie's right leg and he fell. It had, however, passed between two muscles without injuring either greatly, and had severed no artery.

The next moment Gibbie was on his feet again and running. He did not yet feel pain. Happily he was not very far from home and he made for it as fast as he could—preceded by Oscar, who, having once by accident been shot himself, had a mortal terror of guns. Maimed as Gibbie was, he could yet run a good deal faster up the hill than the rascal who followed him. But long before he reached the cottage, the pain had arrived, and the nearer he got to it the worse it grew. In spite of the anguish, however, he held on with determination; to be seized by Angus and dragged down to Glashruach would be far worse.

Robert Grant, suffering from rheumatism, was at home that day. He was seated with his pipe in his mouth and Janet was just taking the potatoes for their dinner off the fire when the door flew open, and in stumbled Gibbie and fell on the floor. The old man threw his pipe from him, and rose trembling, but Janet was before him. She dropped down on her knees beside the boy, and put her arm under his head. He was white and motionless.

"Eh, Robert!" she cried. "He's bleedin'!"

The same moment they heard quick, heavy steps approaching. At once Robert divined the truth and a great wrath banished rheumatism and age together. Like a boy he sprang to the shelf whence his yet powerful hand came back armed with a huge, rusty old broadsword that had seen service in its day. Two or three fierce tugs at the holt proved the blade immovable in the sheath, and the steps being now almost at the door, he clubbed the weapon, grasping it by the sheathed blade. Holding it with the edge downward so that the blow he meant to deal should fall from the round of the basket hilt, he heaved it aloft, the rage of a hundred ancestors welling up in his usually peaceful breast. His red eyes flashed and the few hairs that were left him stood erect on his head like the mane of a roused lion. Before Angus had his second foot over the threshold, down came the helmet-like hilt with a dull crash on his head, and he staggered against the wall.

"Take that, Angus MacPholp!" panted Robert through his clenched teeth, following the blow with another from his fist that prostrated the enemy. Again he heaved his weapon and, standing over him where he lay more than half-stunned, said in a hoarse voice, "By the great God my maker, Angus MacPholp, if you try to get up, I'll come down on you again!— Here, Oscar!—Watch him and take him by the throat if he moves a finger."

The gun dropped from Angus's hand, and Robert, keeping his eye on Angus, secured it.

"It's loaded," muttered Angus.

"Rest still, then," returned Robert, pointing the weapon at his head.

"It'll be murder," said Angus, and made a movement to lay hold of the barrel.

"Hold him down, Oscar!" cried Robert. The dog's paws were instantly on his chest and his teeth grinning within an inch of his face. "It would be but blood for blood, Angus MacPholp," he went on. "Your hour's come, my man. That child is not the first blood of man you've shed, and it's time the Scripture was fulfilled and the hand of man shed yours."

"You're not going to kill me, Rob Grant?" growled the fellow in growing fright.

"I'm going to see whether the sheriff won't be persuaded to hang you," answered the shepherd. "This must be put a stop to—Quiet! or I'll brain you, and save him the trouble!—Here, Janet, bring your pot of potatoes. I'm going to empty the gun. If he dares to move, just give him the whole boiling lot in the face; only take care and hold off the dog."

So saying he carried the weapon to the door and, in terror lest he might through wrath or the pressure of dire necessity use it against his foe, emptied its second barrel into the earth and leaned it up against the wall outside.

Janet obeyed her husband so far as to stand over Angus with the potato pot; how far she would have carried her obedience had he attempted to rise may remain a question.

When Robert returned and relieved her guard, Janet went back to Gibbie whom she had drawn toward the fire. In a minute or two more he was able to crawl to his bed in the corner, and then Janet proceeded to examine his wound.

By this time his leg was much swollen, but the wound had almost stopped bleeding, and it was plain there was no bullet in it, for there were two orifices. She washed it carefully and bound it up. Then Gibbie raised his head and looked somewhat anxiously around the room.

"You're lookin' for Angus?" said Janet; "he's yonder upon the floor. Don't be frightened; your father and Oscar have him safe enough."

"Here, Janet!" cried her husband. "If you're through with the child, I must be going."

"Hoot, Robert! You're not going to leave Gibbie and me in the house with the murderin' man!" returned Janet.

"Indeed I am, lass! Just run and bring the line that you hang the duds on while they're drying, and we'll tie the hands and feet of him."

Janet obeyed and went. Angus, who had been quiet enough for the last ten minutes, meditating and watching, began to swear furiously; but Robert paid no more heed than if he had not heard him. He stood calm and grim at his head with the clubbed sword heaved over his shoulder. When Janet came back, by her husband's directions she passed the rope repeatedly round the keeper's ankles, then several times between them, drawing the bouts tightly together. Again and again, as she tied it, did Angus meditate a sudden spring, but the determined look of Robert caused him to hesitate until it was altogether too late. When they began to bind his hands, however, he turned desperate and struck at both, cursing and raging.

"If you're not quiet, you'll taste the dog's teeth," said Robert. Angus reflected that he would have a better chance when he was left alone with Janet, and yielded. "Truth!" Robert went on as he continued his task, "I have no pity left for you, Angus MacPholp.—Now, Janet, bring a bundle of straw from the stall and lay it under his head. I must be away and get word to the sheriff. Scotland's come to a pretty end when they shoot men with guns as if they were creatures to be skinned and eaten. He may well be a keeper of game, for he's as poor a keeper of brother as old Cain himself. But," he concluded, tying the last knot hard, "we'll do what we can to keep the keeper."

So saying he put the bannock in his pocket, flung his broad blue bonnet upon his head, took his stick and, ordering Oscar to remain at home and watch the prisoner, set out for a walk of five miles as if he had never known such a thing as rheumatism. He must find another magistrate than the laird; he would not trust him where his own gamekeeper Angus MacPholp was concerned.

"Keep your eye upon him, Janet," he said, turning in the doorway. "Don't let him out of your sight before I come back with the constable. I'll be back in about three hours."

With these words he turned finally, and disappeared.

Lying thus trapped in the den of the beast-loon, the mortification of Angus at being taken and bound by an old man, a woman, and a collie dog was extreme. He went over the whole affair again and again in his mind, ever with a fresh burst of fury. It was in vain he excused himself on the ground that the attack had been so sudden and treacherous, and the precautions taken so complete. He had proved himself a fool, and the whole country would ring with mockery of him! He had sense enough, too, to know that he was in a serious as well as ludicrous predicament; he had scarcely courage enough to contemplate the possible result.

If he could but get his hands free, it would be easy to kill Oscar and disable Janet. For the idiot, he counted him nothing. He had better wait, however, until there should be no boiling liquid ready to her hand.

Janet set out the dinner, peeled some potatoes and, approaching Angus, would have fed him. In place of accepting her ministrations, he fell to abusing her with the worst language he could find. She withdrew without a word, and sat down to her own dinner; but finding the torrent of vituperation kept flowing, she rose again and, going to the door, fetched a great jug of cold water from the pail that always stood there. Coming behind her prisoner, she emptied it over his face. He gave a horrid yell, taking the douche for a boiling one.

"You don't need to cry out like that at good, cold water," said Janet. "But you'll just abstain from any more such words in my hearin', or you'll get the same every time you break out." As she spoke, she knelt and wiped his face and head with her apron.

A fresh oath rushed to Angus's lips, but the fear of a second jugful made him suppress it, and Janet sat down again to her dinner. She could scarcely eat a mouthful, however, for pity of the rascal beside her at whom she kept looking wistfully without daring again to offer him anything.

While she sat thus, she caught the swift, investigating look he cast on the cords that bound his hands, and then at the fire. She perceived at once what was passing in his mind. Rising she went quickly to the byre and returned immediately with a chain they used for tethering the cow. The end of it she slipped deftly round his neck and made it fast, putting the little bar through a link.

111

"Are you going to hang me, you she-devil?" he cried, making a futile attempt to grasp the chain with his bound hands.

"You'll be wanting a drop more of cold water, I'm thinkin'," said Janet.

She stretched the chain to its length, and with a great stone drove the sharp iron stake at the other end of it into the clay floor.

Gibbie had fallen asleep, but he now woke and she gave him his dinner, then took her Bible. Gibbie had lain down again, and she thought he was asleep.

Angus grew more and more uncomfortable, both in body and in mind. He knew he was hated throughout the country and had hitherto rather enjoyed the knowledge; but now he judged that the popular feeling, by no means a mere prejudice, would tell against him in a trial. He knew also that the magistrate to whom Robert had betaken himself was not overly friendly with his master and certainly would not listen to any intercession from him. At length, what with pain, hunger, and fear, his pride began to yield. After an hour had passed in utter silence, he condescended to parley.

"Janet Grant," he said, "let me go, and I'll trouble you and yours no more."

"You think me some fool to listen to you?" suggested Janet.

"I'll swear any lawful oath that you want to lay on me," protested Angus, "that I'll do whatever you please to require of me."

"I don't doubt but that you would swear; but what next?" said Janet.

"What next but you'll loose my hands?" rejoined Angus.

"Don't even mention it," replied Janet; "for as you know, I'm under authority, and you yourself heard my man tell me to take every precaution not to let you go."

"Was ever a man," protested Angus, "made such a fool of by a pair of old cottars like you and Robert Grant!"

"With the help of the Lord, by means of the dog," supplemented Janet.

"Let me go, woman! I'll harm nobody. The poor idiot's not much the worse, and I'll take more care when I shoot another time."

"Wiser folks than me must see to that," said Janet.

"Hoots, woman! it was nothing but an accident."

"I don't know; but we'll have to see what Gibbie says."

"What! his word's good for nothing."

"For a penny or a thousand pounds."

"My wife will be out of her wits," pleaded Angus.

"Would you like a drink of milk?" asked Janet rising.

"I would that," he answered.

She filled her little teapot with milk, and he drank it from the spout, hoping she was on the point of giving way.

"Now," she said, when he had finished his drink, "you just make the best of it, Angus. Anyway, it's a good lesson in patience to you, and that you haven't had very often, I'm thinkin'. Robert will be here before long."

With these words she set down the teapot and went out; it was time to milk the cow.

In a little while Gibbie rose, tried to walk but failed, and getting down on his hands and knees crawled out after her. Angus caught a glimpse of his face as he crept past him, and then first recognized the boy he had lashed. Not compunction but an occasional pang of dread lest he should have been the cause of his death had served so to fix Gibbie's face in his memory that now he had a near view of him, pale with suffering and loss of blood and therefore more like his former self, Angus knew him beyond a doubt. With a great shoot of terror he concluded that the idiot had been lying there silently gloating over his revenge, waiting only till Janet should be out of sight, and was now gone after some instrument wherewith to take it. He pulled and tugged at his bonds, but only to find escape absolutely hopeless. In gathering horror, he lay motionless at last, but strained his hearing toward every sound.

The byre was just on the other side of the turf wall

against which was the head of Gibbie's bed, and through the wall Gibbie had heard Janet's voice. He crawled to the end of the cottage so silently that she heard no sound of his approach. He would not go into the byre, for that might disturb her; she would have to look up to know that it was only Gibbie. He would listen at the door. He found it wide open and, peeping in, saw Crummie chewing away and Janet on her knees.

"O Lord, if you would but say what you would have done! The man's done me no ill, except he's hurt your bonnie Gibbie. It's Gibbie that has to forgive him. But my man told me not to let him up. I'm willing enough to let him go, but he's Robert's prisoner and Gibbie's enemy. He's not my prisoner nor my enemy and I don't think I have the right. And who knows but he might go shooting more folk yet 'cause I let him go."

Here her voice ceased and she fell a-moaning.

Her trouble was echoed in dim pain from Gibbie's soul. That the prophetess who knew everything should be thus abandoned to dire perplexity was a dreadful, a bewildering, fact. But now first he understood the real state of the affair in the purport of the old man's absence; also how he was himself potently concerned in the business. If the offense had been committed against Gibbie, then with Gibbie lay the power, therefore the duty, of forgiveness. Few things were easier to him than to love his enemies, and his merit in obeying the commandment was small indeed. No sooner had Janet ceased than he was on his way back to the cottage; on its floor lay one who had to be waited upon with forgiveness.

Wearied with futile struggles, Angus found himself compelled to abide his fate and was lying quite still when Gibbie reentered. The boy thought he was asleep, but on the contrary he was watching his every motion, full of dread. Gibbie went hopping upon one foot to the hole in the wall where Janet kept the only knife she had. It was not there. He glanced around but could not see it. There was no time to lose. Gibbie looked around again for a moment, as if in doubt, then darted upon the tongs and thrust them into the fire, caught up the asthmatic old bellows and began to blow the peats. Angus saw the first action, heard the second, and a hideous dismay clutched his very heart. The savage fool was about to take his revenge in pinches with the red hot tongs! Manhood held him silent until he saw him take the implement of torture from the fire, glowing not red but white hot, when he uttered such a terrific yell that Gibbie dropped the tongs but caught them up again instantly and made a great hop to Angus. If Janet had heard that yell and came in, all would be spoiled.

But the faithless keeper began to struggle so fiercely, writhing with every contortion and kicking with every inch left possible to him, that Gibbie hardly dared attempt anything for dread of burning him. With a sudden thought Gibbie sprang to the door and locked it so that Janet should not get in, and Angus, hearing the bolt, was the more convinced that his purpose was cruel so struggled and yelled all the more, with his eyes fixed on the glowing tongs now fast cooling in Gibbie's hand.

In the meantime, Janet in her perplexity had, quite forgetful of the poor cow's necessities, abandoned Crummie and wandered down the path so that she heard nothing.

Gibbie thrust the tongs again into the fire and, while blowing it, bethought him that it might give Angus confidence if he removed the chain from his neck. But to Angus the action seemed only preparatory to taking him by the throat with the horrible implement. In his agony and wild endeavor to frustrate the supposed intent, he struggled harder than ever. But now Gibbie was undoing the rope fastened round the chest. This Angus did not perceive, and when it came suddenly loose in the midst of one of his fierce, straining contortions, the result was that he threw his body right over his head and lay on his face for a moment confused. Gibbie saw his advantage. He snatched his clumsy tool out of the fire, seated himself on the corresponding part of Angus's person, and seizing with the tongs the rope between his feet held on to both in spite of his heaves and kicks. In the few moments that passed while Gibbie burned through a round of the rope, Angus imagined a considerable number of pangs;

but when Gibbie rose and hopped away, he discovered that his feet were at liberty and scrambled up, his head dizzy and his body reeling. Gibbie looked up at him with a smile, and Angus did not even box his ears. Holding by the wall, Gibbie limped to the door and opened it. With a nod meant for thanks, the gamekeeper stepped out, took up his gun from where it leaned against the wall and hurried away down the hill. A moment sooner and he would have met Janet; but she had just entered the byre again to milk poor Crummie.

When she came into the cottage, she stared with astonishment to see no Angus on the floor. Gibbie, who had lain down again in such pain, made sign that he had let him go; whereupon such a look of relief came over her countenance that he was filled with fresh gladness, and was, if possible, more satisfied still with what he had done.

It was late before Robert returned—alone, weary and disappointed. The magistrate was away from home; he had waited for him as long as he dared; but at length, both because of his wife's unpleasant position and the danger to himself if he longer delayed his journey across the mountain, seeing it threatened a storm and there was no moon, he set out. That he too was relieved to find no Angus there he did not attempt to conceal. The next day he went to see him and told him that, to please Gibbie, he had consented to say nothing more about the affair. Angus could not help being sullen, but he judged it wise to behave as well as he could, kept his temper therefore, and said he was sorry he had been so hasty, but that Robert had punished him pretty well, for it would be weeks before he recovered from the blow on the head he had given him. So they parted on tolerable terms and there was no further persecution of Gibbie from that quarter.

20   The Beast-Boy

That winter the old people were greater tried with rheumatism; for not only were the frosts severe but there was much rain between. Their children did all in their power to minister to their wants, and Gibbie was nurse as well as shepherd.

Gibbie still occupied his heather bed on the floor, and it was part of his business to keep up a good fire on the hearth; happily, peats were plentiful.

For weeks he had been picking out tunes on his panpipes; also, he had lately discovered that, although he could not articulate, he could produce tones, and had taught himself to imitate the pipes. Now to his delight he had found that the noises he made were recognized as song by his father and mother. From that time he was often heard crooning to himself.

Change, meantime, was in progress elsewhere, as well upon the foot as high on the side of Glashgar. Thomas Galbraith of Glashruach, Esquire, was not kept from folly by his hatred for what he called superstition; he had long fallen into what will ultimately prove the most degrading superstition of all—the worship of Mammon—and was rapidly sinking from deep to lower deep. Such was the folly of the man that he risked what he loved best in the world by investing in Welsh gold mines.

The property of Glashruach was a good one but not nearly so large as it had been, and he was anxious to restore it to its former dimensions. To increase his money that he might increase his property, he took to speculation, but had never had much success until that same year when he disposed of certain shares at a large profit—nothing troubled by the conviction that the man who bought them (in ignorance of many a fact which the laird knew) must in all probability be ruined by them. He counted this success and it gave him confidence to speculate further.

In the spring, affairs began to look rather bad for him, and in the month of May he considered himself compelled to go to London. He had a faith in his own business faculty quite as foolish as any superstition in Gormgarnet. There he fell into the hands of a certain man—a fellow who used his influence and facilities as member of Parliament in promoting bubble companies. He was close to another man, likewise of principles that love the shade; and between them they had no difficulty in making a tool of Thomas Galbraith, as chairman of a certain aggregate of iniquity.

In the course of that winter, one of Donal's sisters was engaged by the housekeeper at Glashruach to wait upon Miss Galbraith. Ginevra was still a silent, simple, unconsciously retiring and therewith dignified girl in whom childhood and womanhood had begun to interchange hues. Happy they in whom neither had a final victory! Happy also all who have such women to love! At one moment Ginevra would draw herself up with involuntary recoil from doubtful approach; the next, Ginny would burst out in a merry laugh at something in which only a child could have perceived the mirth-causing element. The people about the place loved her, but from the stillness on the general surface of her behavior, the faraway feeling she gave them, and the impossibility of divining how she was thinking except she chose to unburden herself, they were all a little afraid of her as well.

In the mind of her new maid, however, there was no strife, and the desire to be acceptable to her awoke at once and grew rapidly in her heart. She was the youngest of Janet's girls, about four years older than Donal, not clever but as sweet as honest and full of divine service. Always ready to think others better than herself, the moment she saw the still face of Ginevra, she took her for a little saint and accepted her as a queen whose will to her should be law. Ginevra, on her part, was taken with the healthy hue and honest eyes of the girl, and felt no dislike to her touching her hair nor lost her temper when she was awkward and pulled it. Before the winter was over the bond between them was strong.

One principal duty required of Nicie was to accompany her mistress every fine day to the manse, a mile and a half from Glashruach where Ginevra took instruction in the morning hours from the daughter of the parish clergyman. One morning they found, on reaching the manse, that the minister was very unwell and that in consequence Miss Machar could not attend to Ginevra; they turned, therefore, to walk home again. Now the manse, upon another root of Glashgar, was nearer than Glashruach to Nicie's home, and many a time as she came and went did she lift longing eyes to the ridge that hid it from her view. This morning Ginevra observed that every other moment Nicie was looking up the side of the mountain as if she saw something unusual upon it—occasionally, indeed, when the winding of the road turned their backs to it, stopping and turning round to gaze.

"What is the matter with you, Nicie?" she asked. "What are you looking at up there?"

"I'm wonderin' what my mother is doing," answered Nicie; "she's up there."

"Up there!" exclaimed Ginny and, turning, stared at the mountain too, expecting to perceive Nicie's mother somewhere upon the face of it.

"No, no, missie. You can't see her," said the girl; "she's not in sight. She's over beyond there. But if we were where we could see two or three sheep against the sky, we could see the house where she and my father live."

"How I should like to see your father and mother, Nicie!" exclaimed Ginevra.

"Well, I'm sure they would be right glad to see you, missie, any time you would like to go and see them."

"Why shouldn't we go now, Nicie? It's not a dangerous place, is it?"

"No, missie. Glashgar's as quiet and well-behaved a mountain as any in all the country," answered Nicie, laughing. "It's poor like my family and hasn't much to spare, but the sheep get a few nibbles upon her here and there; and my mother manages to keep a cow and get plenty of milk for her tea."

"Come then, Nicie. We have plenty of time. Nobody wants either you or me, and we shall get home before anyone misses us."

Nicie was glad enough to consent; they turned at once to the hill and began climbing. But Nicie did not know this part of it nearly so well as that which lay between Glashruach and the cottage, and after they had climbed some distance, often stopping and turning to look down on the valley below, the prospect of which, with its streams and river, kept still widening and changing as they ascended, they arrived at a place where the path grew very doubtful and she could not tell in which of two directions they ought to go.

"I'll take this way, and you take that, Nicie," said Ginevra, "and if I find there is no path my way, I will come back to yours; and if you find there is no path your way, you will come back to mine."

It was a childish proposal and one to which Nicie should not have consented, but she was little more than a child herself. Advancing a short distance in doubt, and the path reappearing quite plainly, she sat down, expecting her little mistress to return directly. No thought of anxiety crossed her mind. How should such a thought come in broad sunlight, on a mountainside, in the first of summer, and with the long day before them? There, sitting in peace, Nicie fell into a maidenly reverie, and so there Nicie sat for a long time, half dreaming in the great light without once really thinking about anything. All at once she came to herself; some latent fear had exploded in her heart. Yes! What could have become of her little mistress? She jumped to her feet and shouted, "Missie! Missie Galbraith! Ginny!" but no answer came back. The mountain was as still as at midnight. She ran to the spot where they had parted and along the other path; it was plainer than that where she had been so idly forgetting herself. She hurried on, wildly calling as she ran.

In the meantime, Ginevra, having found the path indubitable and imagining it led straight to the door of Nicie's mother's cottage and that Nicie would be after her in a moment, thinking also to have a bit of fun with her, set off dancing and running so fast that by the time Nicie came to herself, she was a good mile from her. What a delight it was to be thus alone upon the great mountain—with the earth banished so far below and the great rocky heap climbing and leading and climbing up and up toward the sky!

But the path was after all a mere sheep track and led her at length into a lonely hollow in the hillside, with a swampy peat bog at the bottom of it. She stopped. The place looked unpleasant, reminding her of how she always felt when she came unexpectedly upon Angus MacPholp. She would go no farther alone; she would wait till Nicie overtook her.

In her haste and anxiety, however, Nicie had struck into another sheep track, and was now higher up the hill; so that Ginny could see no living thing nearer than in the valley below. Never in her life before had she felt that she was alone. She had often felt lonely, but she had always known where to find the bodily presence of somebody. Now she might cry and scream the whole day and nobody answer! Her heart swelled into her throat, then sank away, leaving a wide hollow. It was so eerie! But Nicie would soon come, and then all would be well.

She sat down on a stone where she could see the path she had come a long way back. But never and never did any Nicie appear. At last she began to cry.

"O God, help me home again!" cried Ginevra, and stood up in her great loneliness to return.

The same instant she spied, seated upon a rock a little way off but close to her path, the beast-boy. There could be no mistake. He was just as she had heard him described by the children at the gamekeeper's cottage. That was his hair sticking all out from his head, though the sun in it made it look like a crown of gold or a shining mist. Those were his bare arms, and that was dreadful indeed! Bare legs and feet she was used to; but bare arms! Worst of all, making it absolutely certain he was the beast-boy, he was playing upon a curious kind of whistling thing, making dreadfully sweet music to entice her nearer that he might catch her and tear her to pieces! Was this the answer that God sent to the prayers she had offered in her sore need—the beast-boy?

Most girls would have screamed, but such was not Ginny's natural mode of meeting a difficulty. With fear she was far more likely to choke than to cry out. So she sat down again and stared at him. Perhaps he would go away when he found he could not entice her. He did not move but kept playing on his curious instrument. Perhaps by returning into the hollow she could make a circuit and so pass him lower down the hill. She rose at once and ran.

Now Gibbie had seen her long before she had seen him, but from experience was afraid of frightening her. He had therefore drawn gradually near, and sat as if unaware of her presence. Treating her as he would a bird with which he wanted to make better acquaintance, he would have her get accustomed to the look of him before he made advances. But when he saw her run in the direction of the swamp, knowing what a dangerous place it was, he was terrified; he sprang to his feet and darted off to get between her and the danger. She heard him coming like the wind at her back and, whether from bewilderment or that she did intend throwing herself into the water to escape him, instead of pursuing her former design, she made straight for the swamp. As she approached the place, there he was on the edge of a great hole half full of water as if he had been sitting there for an hour! Was he going to drown her in that hole?

She turned again and ran toward the descent of the mountain. But ere there Gibbie feared a certain precipitous spot; and besides, there was no path in that direction. So Ginevra had not run far before again she saw him right in her way. She threw herself on the ground in despair and hid her face. After thus hunting her as a cat might a mouse, or a lion a man, what could she look for but that he would pounce upon her and tear her to pieces? Fearfully expectant of the horrible grasp, she lay breathless. At length to her ears came a strange sweet voice of singing—such a sound as she had never heard before. It seemed to come from far away. The sound grew and grew, and came nearer and nearer. But although it was song, she could distinguish no vowel-melody in it, nothing but a tone-melody—a crooning, as it were, ever upon one vowel in a minor key. It came quite near at length, and yet even then had something of the faraway sound left in it. It came close, and ceased suddenly. She opened her eyes and looked up. Over her stood the beast-boy, gazing down upon her! From under a great crown of reddish gold looked out two eyes of heaven's own blue, and through the eyes looked out something that dwells behind the sky.

She lay motionless, flat on the ground, her face turned sideways upon her hands. Then a curious feeling began to wake in her of having seen him before—somewhere, ever so long ago, and that sight of him as well as this had to do with misery, with something that made a stain that would not come out. Yes—it was the very face, only larger, and still sweeter, of the little, naked child whom Angus had so cruelly lashed! That was ages ago but she had not forgotten, and never could forget either the child's back or the lovely, innocent white face that he turned round upon her. If it was indeed him, perhaps he would remember her. In any case, she was now certain he would not hurt her.

Then rose the very sun himself in Gibbie's eyes and flashed a full response of daylight—a smile that no woman, girl, or matron could mistrust. Timidly, yet trustingly, Ginevra took one hand from under her cheek and stretched it up to him. He clasped it gently. She moved, and he helped her to rise.

"I've lost Nicie," she said.

Gibbie nodded, but did not look concerned.

"Nicie is my maid," said Ginevra.

Gibbie nodded several times. He knew who Nicie was rather better than her mistress.

"I left her away back there, a long, long time ago, and she has never come to me," she said.

Gibbie gave a shrill, loud whistle that startled her. In a few seconds, from somewhere unseen, a dog came bounding to him over stones and heather. How he spoke to the dog, or what he told him to do, she had not an idea; but the next instant Oscar was rushing along the path she had come and was presently out of sight. So full of life was Gibbie, so quick and decided was his every motion, so full of expression his every glance and smile, that she had not yet begun to wonder he had not spoken; indeed, she was hardly yet aware of the fact. She knew him now for a mortal but, just as it had been with Donal and his mother, he continued to affect her as a creature of some higher world come down on a mission of goodwill to men.

Gibbie took her hand and led her toward the path she had left; she yielded without a movement of question. But he did not lead her far in that direction; he turned to the left up the mountain. It grew wilder as they ascended. But the air was so thin and invigorating, the changes so curious and interesting as now they skirted the edge of a precipitous rock, now scrambled up the steepest of paths by the help of the heather that nearly closed over it; and the reaction of relief from the terror she had suffered was so exciting that she never for a moment felt tired. Then they went down the side of a little burn—a torrent when the snow was dissolving, and even now a good stream. It was the same one, as she learned afterward, to whose song under her window she listened every night in bed. They crossed the burn and climbed the opposite bank. Then Gibbie pointed, and there was the cottage; and Nicie was coming up the path to it with Oscar bounding before her! The dog was merry, but Nicie was weeping bitterly. They were a good way off, with another larger burn between; but Gibbie whistled and Oscar came flying to him. Nicie looked up, gave a cry, and like a sheep to her lost lamb came running.

"Oh, missie!" she said, breathless, as she reached the opposite bank of the burn, and her tone had more than a touch of sorrowful reproach in it, "What made you run away?"

"There was a path, Nicie, and I thought you would come after me."

"I was a goose, missie; but I'm glad I've got you. Come along and see my mother."

"Yes, Nicie. We'll tell her all about it. You see, I haven't got a mother to tell, so I will tell yours."

Never before had Ginny spent such a happy day, drunk such milk as Crummie's, or eaten such cakes as Janet's. She saw no more of Gibbie; the moment she was safe, he and Oscar were off again to the sheep, for Robert was busy cutting peats that day and Gibbie was in sole charge. Eager to know about him, Ginevra gathered all that Janet could tell of his story, and in return told the little she had seen of it, which was the one dreadful point.

"Is he a good boy, Mistress Grant?" she asked.

"One of the best boys I ever knew," answered Janet.

Ginny gave a little sigh, and wished she were good.

"When did you see Donal?" asked Janet of Nicie.

"Not since I was here last," answered Nicie.

"I was thinkin'," returned her mother, "you should be able to see him now from the back of the big house; for he was telling me he was with the cattle in the new meadow upon the Lorrie bank."

"Oh, is he there?" said Nicie. "Maybe I can get a sight of him. He came to the kitchen door, but Mistress MacFarlane would not let him in. She would have no loons comin' about the place, she said. I said that he was my brother, and she said that was nothing to her. I told her that all my brothers were known to be good lads; but she told me to hold my tongue. I could have given her a box on the ear—I was that angry with her!"

"She'll be sorry for it some day," said Janet with a quiet smile; "and what someone's sure to be sorry for, you might as well forgive them at once."

"How do you know, Mother, that she will be sorry for it?" asked Nicie, not very willing to forgive Mistress Mac-Farlane.

" 'Cause the Master says we will have to pay the uttermost farthing. There's nobody to be left off. We must all do right by our neighbors."

Ginevra went home with a good many things to think about.

21   The Lorrie Meadow

It was high time, according to agricultural economics, that Donal Grant should be promoted a step in the ranks of labor. A youth like him was fit for horses and their work, and looked idle in a field with cattle. But Donal was not ambitious, at least in that direction. He was more and more in love with books and learning and the music of thought and word; and he well knew that no one doing a man's work upon a farm could have much time left for study. Therefore, with his parents' approval, he continued to fill the humbler office and receive the scantier wages belonging to it.

The day following their adventure on Glashgar, Nicie, being in the grounds with her little mistress, proposed in the afternoon that they should look whether they could see her brother down in the meadow of which her mother had spoken. Ginevra willingly agreed, and they took their way through the shrubbery to the bank of the little river—the largest tributary of the Daur from the roots of Glashgar.

"There he is!" cried Nicie.

"I see him," responded Ginny, "—with his cows all about the meadow."

Donal sat a little way from the river reading.

"He's at his book!" said Nicie.

"I wonder what book it is," said Ginny.

"That would be hard to say," answered Nicie. "Donal reads a lot of books—more, his mother says, than she doubts he can get the good out of."

"I should like to ask Donal what book he's got," said Ginny.

"I'll cry to him and you can ask," said Nicie:— "Donal!—Donal!"

Donal looked up and, seeing his sister, came running to the bank of the stream.

"Couldn't you come over, Donal?" said Nicie. "Here's Miss Galbraith who wants to ask you a question."

Donal was across in a moment, for here the water was nowhere over a foot or two in depth.

"Oh, Donal! You've wet your feet!" cried Ginevra.

Donal laughed.

"What harm will that do me, mem?"

"None, I hope," said Ginny; "but it might, you know."

"I might have been drowned," said Donal.

"Nicie," said Ginny with dignity, "your brother is laughing at me."

"No, no, mem," said Donal apologetically. "I was only so glad to see you and Nicie that I forgot my manners."

"Then," returned Ginny, quite satisfied, "would you mind telling me what book you were reading?"

"It's a book of ballads," answered Donal. "I'll read one of them to you if you like, mem."

"I should like very much," responded Ginny. "I've read all my own books till I'm tired of them, and I don't like Papa's books."

"I'll read you a little bit then and see if you like it. Here's a nice spot among the daisies."

She dropped at once on the little gowany bed, gathered her frock about her ankles, and said, "Sit down, Nicie. It's so kind of Donal to read something to us! I wonder what it's going to be."

Donal began an old ballad but then before it was finished had to rush through the burn without leave-taking, for Hornie was attempting a trespass; and the two girls, thinking it was time to go home, rose and climbed to the house at their leisure.

The next morning, not more than the gentlest hint was necessary to make Nicie remark that perhaps if they went down again to the Lorrie, Donal might come and bring the book. But when they reached the bank and looked across, they saw him occupied with Gibbie. The two had their heads close together over a slate upon which now the one, now the other, seemed to be drawing. This went on and on and they never looked up. Ginny would have gone home and come again in the afternoon, but Nicie called Donal. He sprang to his feet and came to them, followed by Gibbie. Donal crossed the burn, but Gibbie remained on the other side. When presently Donal took his book of ballads from his pocket and the little company seated themselves, Gibbie stood with his back to them and his eyes on the cattle. That morning they were not interrupted. Donal read to them for a whole hour.

After this, Ginevra went frequently with Nicie to see her mother, and learned much of the best from her. Often also they went down to the Lorrie and had an interview with Donal, which was longer or shorter as Gibbie was there or not to release him.

Ginny's life was now far happier than it had ever been. New channels of thought and feeling were opened, new questions were started, new interests awaked; so that instead of losing by Miss Machar's continued inability to teach her, she was learning far more than her former teacher could give her, learning it too with the pleasure which invariably accompanies true learning.

Though Ginevra was little more than a child, Donal felt from the first the charm of her society; and she by no means received without giving, for his mental development was greatly expedited thereby. Few weeks passed before he was her humble squire, devoted to her with all the chivalry of a youth for a girl whom he supposed as much his superior in kind as she is in worldly position. His sole advantage, in his own judgment, and that which alone procured him the privilege of her society was that he was older and therefore knew a little more.

He now first found himself capable of making verses—such as they were; and one day with his book before him he ventured to repeat, as if he read them from the book, the following. They halted a little, no doubt, in rhythm, neither were perfect, but for a beginning they had promise. Gibbie, who had thrown himself down on the other bank and lay listening, at once detected the change in the tone of his utterance, and before Donal ceased had concluded that he was not reading them but that they were his own.

> Rin, burnie! clatter;
>   To the sea win:
> Gien I was a watter,
>   Sae wad I rin.
>
> Blaw, win', caller, clean!
>   Here an' hyne awa':
> Gien I was a win',
>   Wadna I blaw!
>
> Shine, auld sun,
>   Shine strang an' fine:
> Gien I was the sun's son,
>   Herty I wad shine.

Hardly had he ended when Gibbie's pipe began from the opposite side of the water, and true to time and cadence and feeling, followed with just the one air to suit the song—from which Donal, to his comfort, understood that one at least of his audience had received his lilt. But Ginevra had not received it and, being therefore of her own mind and not of the song's, was critical.

At that very moment Hornie caused a diversion, and Gibbie understood what Donal was feeling too well to make even a pretense of going after her. I must to his praise record the fact that, instead of wreaking his mortification on the cow, Donal spared her several blows out of gratitude for the deliverance her misbehavior had wrought him. He was in no haste to return to his audience. To have his first poem thus rejected was killing. She was but a child who had so unkindly criticized it, but she was the child he wanted to please; and for a few moments life itself seemed scarcely worth having. He called himself a fool and resolved never to read another poem to a girl so long as he lived. By the time he had again walked through the burn, however, he was calm and comparatively wise and knew what to say.

"Do you hear yonder stream after you go to bed, mem?" he asked Ginevra as he climbed the bank, pointing a little lower down the stream to the mountain brook which there joined it.

"Always," she answered. "It runs right under my window."

"What kind of noise does it make?" he asked again.

"It's different at different times," she answered. "It sings and chatters in summer, and growls and cries and grumbles in winter, or after rain up in Glashgar."

"Do you think the stream's any happier in the summer, mem?"

"No, Donal; the burn has no life in it and so can't be happier one time than another."

"But when you're lying listening to the stream, did you never imagine yourself running down with it—down to the sea?"

"No, Donal; I always fancy myself going up the mountain where it comes from, and running about wild there in the wind, when all the time I know I'm safe and warm in bed.... Are you vexed with me, Donal?"

"No, no, mem. You're too good and pretty," answered Donal, "to be a vex to anybody."

Ginevra was silent. She could not quite understand Donal, and of this she was the more convinced when she saw the beautiful eyes of Gibbie fixed in admiration upon him.

The way Donal kept his vow never to read another poem of his own to a girl was to proceed that very night to make another for that express purpose as he lay awake in the darkness.

I doubt whether Ginevra understood this song better than the first, but she was now more careful of criticizing; and when by degrees it dawned upon Ginevra that Donal was the maker of certain of these verses he read, she grew half afraid of him and began to regard him with big eyes. He moved from a herdboy, an unintelligible person, to a poet, therefore a wonder.

22   Father and Daughter

By degrees Gibbie had come to be well known about the Mains and Glashruach. Angus's only recognition of him was a scowl in return for his smile; but, as I have said, he gave him no further annoyance, and the tales about the beast-loon were dying out from Daurside. Jean Mavor was a special friend to him; for she knew now well enough who had been her broonie and made him welcome as often as he showed himself with Donal.

In the autumn Mr. Galbraith returned to Glashruach but did not remain long. He was kinder than usual to Ginevra. Before he went he said to her that as Mr. Machar had sunk into a condition requiring his daughter's constant attention, he would find her an English governess as soon as he reached London. Meantime she must keep up her studies by herself as well as she could. Probably he forgot all about it, for the governess was not heard of at Glashruach, and things fell into their old way. There was no spiritual traffic between the father and daughter; consequently Ginevra never said anything about Donal or Gibbie or her friendship for Nicie. He had himself to blame altogether; he had made it impossible for her to talk to him. But it was well he remained in ignorance and so did not put a stop to the best education she could have at this time of her life—such as neither he nor any friend of his could have given her.

It was interrupted, however, by the arrival of the winter—a wild time in that region. To such feet as Ginevra's the cottage on Glashgar was for months almost inaccessible. More than once the Daur was frozen thick. Not a glimpse did

Ginevra get all this time of Donal or of Gibbie.

At last like one of its own flowers in its own bosom, the spring began again to wake in God's thought of His world. The snow, like all other deaths, had to melt and run, leaving room for hope. Then the summer woke smiling and the two youths and the two maidens met yet again on Lorrie bank. The four were a year older, a year nearer trouble, and a year nearer getting out of it. Ginevra was more of a woman, Donal more of a poet, Nicie as nice and much the same, and Gibbie, if possible, more a foundling of the universe than ever. He was growing steadily. The mountain was a grand nursery for him and the result, both physical and spiritual, corresponded. Janet revered him as much as he revered her; the first impression he made upon her had never worn off—had only changed its color a little. More important even than a knowledge of the truth is a readiness to receive it; and Janet saw from the first that Gibbie's ignorance at its worst was but room vacant for the truth.

In the summer Mr. Galbraith reappeared unannounced at Glashruach, so changed that, startled at the sight of him, Ginevra stopped midway in her advance to greet him. The long, thin man was now haggard and worn; he looked sour and suspicious. He was annoyed that his daughter should recognize an alteration in him and, turning away, took no further notice of her presence. Ginevra knew from experience that the sight of tears would enrage him and with all her might repressed those she felt beginning to rise. She went up to him timidly and took the hand that hung by his side. He did not repel her but he left it hanging lifeless and returned with it no pressure upon her—which was much worse.

"Is anything the matter, Papa?" she asked with trembling voice.

"I am not aware that I have been in the habit of communicating with you on the subject of my affairs," he answered; "nor am I likely to begin to do so, where my return after so long an absence seems to give so little satisfaction."

"Oh, Papa! I was frightened to see you looking so ill."

"Such a remark upon my personal appearance is but

a poor recognition of my labors for your benefit, I venture to think, Ginny," he said.

He was at the moment contemplating, as a necessity, the sale of every foot of the property her mother had brought him. Nothing less would serve to keep up his credit and gain time to disguise more than one failing scheme. Everything had of late been going badly. He had lost a good deal of his confidence and self-satisfaction; but he had gained no humility instead.

The servants found more change in him than Ginevra did. He found fault with everyone, so that even Joseph dared hardly open his mouth and said he must give warning. The day after his arrival he spent the morning with Angus walking over certain fields much desired, he knew, of a neighboring proprietor. Inwardly calculating the utmost he could venture to ask for them with a chance of selling, he scolded Ginevra severely on his return because she had not had lunch but had waited for him. A little reflection might have shown him she dared not take it without him. Naturally, therefore, she could not now eat because of a certain sensation in her throat. The instant he saw she was not eating, he ordered her out of the room; he would have no such airs in his family! By the end of the week such a sense of estrangement possessed Ginevra that she would turn on the stair and run up again if she heard her father's voice below.

In this evil mood he learned from someone (all his life Donal believed it was Fergus) a hint concerning the relations between his daughter and his tenant's herdboy. To describe the laird's feelings at the bare fact that such a hint was possible would be more labor than the result would repay.— What! his own flesh and blood, the heiress of Glashruach derive pleasure from the boorish talk of such a companion! It could not be true; the mere thought filled him with indignation! He was overwhelmed with a righteous disgust.

He watched and waited and more than once pretended to go away from home. At last one morning from the larchwood, he saw the unnatural girl seated with her maid on the bank of the river, the herdboy reading to them, and on the other side the dumb idiot lying listening. Mr. Galbraith was almost beside himself. In a loud voice of bare command, he called to her to come to him. With a glance of terror at Nicie, she rose and they went up through the larches together.

I will not spend my efforts upon a reproduction of the verbal torrent of wrath with which the father assailed his shrinking, delicate, honest-minded woman-child. As for Nicie, he dismissed her on the spot. She had to depart without even a good-bye from Ginevra, and went home weeping.

23 The Earthquake and the Storm

Ever since he became a dweller in the air of Glashgar and mindful of his first visit thereto and his grand experience on that occasion, Gibbie had been in the habit—as often as he saw reason to expect a thunderstorm—of ascending the mountain and there on the crest of the granite peak to await the arrival of the tumult.

Toward the evening of a wondrously fine day in the beginning of August, a perfect day of summer in her matronly beauty, it began to rain. All the next day the slopes and stairs of Glashgar were swept with heavy showers, driven slanting in strong gusts of wind from the northwest.

Gibbie drove his sheep to the refuge of a pen on the lower slope of a valley that ran at right angles to the wind. He then went home and, having told Robert what he had done and eaten his supper, set out in the early falling light to ascend the mountain. A great thunderstorm was at hand and was calling him. It was almost dark before he reached the top, but he knew the surface of Glashgar nearly as well as the floor of the cottage. Just as he had fought his way to the crest of the peak in the face of one of the fiercest of the blasts, a sudden rush of fire made the heavens like the smoke-filled vault of an oven, and at once the thunder followed in a succession of single, sharp explosions without any roll between. The mountain shook with the windy shocks, but the first of the thunderstorm was the worst, and it soon passed. The wind and the rain continued, and the darkness was filled with the rush of water wildly tearing down the sides of the mountain. Thus heaven and earth held communication in torrents all the night. To the ears and heart of Gibbie their noises were a mass of broken music. Every spring and autumn the floods came, and he knew them, and they were welcome to him in their seasons.

It required some care to find his way down through the darkness and the waters to the cottage, but as he was neither in fear nor in haste, he was in little danger. His hands and feet could pick out the path where his eyes were useless. When at length he reached his bed, it was not for a long time to sleep, but to lie awake and listen to the raging of the wind all about and above and below the cottage and the rushing of the streams down past it on every side.

He woke and it was morning. He rose and, dressing hastily, opened the door. What a picture of grey storm rose outspread before him! The wind fiercely invaded the cottage, thick charged with waterdrops. Stepping out he shut the door in haste lest it should blow upon the old people in bed and wake them. He could not see far on any side for the rain that fell and the mist and steam that arose, upon which the wind seemed to have no power; but wherever he did see, there water was running down. Up the mountain he went—he could hardly have told why. It was a wild, hopeless scene—as if God had turned His face away from the world and all nature was therefore drowned in tears. Gibbie stood gazing and thinking.

That moment Glashgar gave a great heave under him, then rocked and shook from side to side a little and settled down still and steady. The next instant came an explosion followed by a frightful roaring and hurling, as of mingled water and stones. On the side of the mountain beneath him he saw what through the mist looked like a cloud of smoke or dust rising to a height. He darted toward it. As he drew nearer, the cloud seemed to condense, and presently he saw plainly enough that it was a great column of water shooting up and out from the face of the hill. The mountain was cracked, and through the crack and down the hill a river was shooting a sheer cataract, raving and tearing and carrying stones and rocks with it like foam.

Suddenly Gibbie, in the midst of his astonishment and delight, noted the path of the new stream, and from his knowledge of the face of the mountain perceived that its course was direct for the cottage. Down the hill he shot after it.

The torrent had already worn for itself a channel. What earth there was it had swept clean away to the rock, and the loose stones it had thrown aside or hurled with it in its headlong course. But as Gibbie bounded along, following it with a speed almost equal to its own, he was checked in the midst of his haste by the sight, a few yards away, of another like terror—another torrent issuing from the side of the hill and rushing to swell the valley stream. Another and another he saw, with growing wonder as he ran. Two of them joined the one he was following, and he had to cross them as he could; the others he saw near and farther off. Now and then a huge boulder would go rolling, leaping, bounding down the hill before him, and just in time he escaped one that came springing after him as if it were a living thing that wanted to devour him. Nor was Glashgar the only torrent-bearing mountain of Gormgarnet that day, though the rain prevented Gibbie from seeing anything of what the rest of them were doing.

Gibbie at length forsook the bank of the new torrent to take the nearest way home. When he came near, to his amazement there stood the little house unharmed, but right next to it the garden ground was gone. He darted through the drizzle and spray, reached the door, and lifted the hatch. The same moment he heard Janet's voice in joyful greeting.

"Now, now! Come away, laddie," she said. "Who would have thought we would have had to leap the rock to get out of the water? But we're waitin' on you to go.—Come, Robert, we're off down the hill to the Mains."

She stood in the middle of the room in her best gown as if she had been going to church.

Robert rose from the edge of the bed, staff in hand, ready too. He also was in his Sunday clothes. Oscar, who could make no change of attire, wagged his tail when he saw him rise and got out of his way. The water, creeping in from all corners, threatened soon to render the place uninhabitable.

"Now, Gibbie," she said, "you go and loosen Crummie. But you'll have to lead her. She won't be able to see in such a wind as this, and there will be no plain road before her."

Gibbie shot round the corner to the byre, whence through all the roar every now and then they had heard the cavernous mooing of Crummie, piteous and low. He found a stream a foot deep running between her fore and hind legs and did not wonder that she wanted to be on the move. Speedily he loosed her and, fastening the chain-tether to her halter, led her out. She was terrified at sight of the falling water, and they had some trouble in getting her through it, but presently she was making the descent as carefully and successfully as any of them.

It was a heavy undertaking for the two old folk to walk all the way to the Mains and in such a state of the elements; but where there is no choice, we do well to make no difficulty. Janet was half-troubled that her mountain should have failed her. Robert plodded on in silence, and Gibbie was in great glee, singing after his fashion all the way, though now and then half-choked by the fierceness of the wind round some corner of rock, filled as it was with raindrops that stung like hailstones.

At length they reached the valley road. The water that ran in the bottom was the Lorrie. Three days ago it was a lively little stream. Now it had filled and far overflowed its banks to become a swift river. When they approached the bridge, however, by which they must cross the Lorrie to reach the Mains, their worst trouble lay before them. For the enemy, with whose reinforcements they had all the time been descending, showed himself ever in greater strength the farther they advanced; and here the road was flooded for a long way on both sides of the bridge. There was therefore a good deal of wading to be done. But the road was an embankment, there was little current, and in safety at last they ascended the rising ground on which the farm building stood. When they reached the yard, they sent Gibbie to find shelter for Crummie, and themselves went up to the house.

"The Lord preserve us!" cried Jean Mavor with uplifted hands when she saw them enter the kitchen.

"He'll do that, mem," returned Janet with a smile.

"But what can He do? If you're driven out of the hill, what's to become of the houses in the meadows? I'd like to know that!"

"The water's not up to your door yet," remarked Janet.

"God forbid!" retorted Jean.—"But, eh, you're wet!"

"Wet's not the word," said Robert, trying to laugh but failing from sheer exhaustion.

The farmer, hearing their voices, came into the kitchen.

"Hoot, Rob!" he said roughly as he entered, "I thought you had more sense! What's brought you here at such a time?"

"Fell necessity, sir," answered Robert.

"Necessity!" retorted the farmer. "Were you out of meal?"

"Out of dry meal, I don't doubt, by this time," replied Robert.

"Hoots! I wish we were in a like necessity—well up on the hill instead of down here upon the river-meadow. It's just clean ridiculous. You should have known better at your age, Rob. You should have thought twice, man."

"Indeed, sir," answered Robert, "there was little time to think, with the Glashgar burstin', and the water comin' in our house. You don't think Janet and me would be two such old fools as to put on our Sunday clothes to swim in if we thought to see things as we left them when we got back!"

"Haith! if the water was running into your house, man, it *was* time to leave."

The old people went to change their clothes for some Jean provided, and in the meantime she made up her fire and prepared some breakfast for them.

"And where's your dummie?" she asked, as they re-entered the kitchen.

"He had poor Crummie to look after," answered Janet; "but he might have been in by this time."

"He'll be with Donal in the stall, no doubt," said Jean; "he's a little shy about comin' in without an invitation." She went to the door and called with a loud voice across the yard through the wind and the clashing torrents: "Donal, send the dummie in to his breakfast!"

"He's gone back to his sheep!" cried Donal in reply.

"Preserve us!—the creature will be lost!" exclaimed Jean.

"That's less likely than any man about the place," said Donal, half-angry with his mistress for calling his friend dummie. "Gibbie knows better what he's about than any two that thinks him a fool because he can't let out such stuff and nonsense as they can't keep in."

Jean went back to the kitchen only half reassured concerning her broonie, and far from contented with his absence. But she was glad to find that neither Janet nor Robert appeared alarmed at the news.

"I wish the creature had had some breakfast," she said.

"He had a little oatcake in his pocket," answered Janet.

"Hoots!" returned Jean.

When they had eaten their breakfast, Robert took his pipe to the barn, saying there was not much danger of fire that day; Janet washed up the dishes and sat down to her Book; and Jean went out and in, attending to many things.

24 The Flood

Meantime the rain fell, the wind blew, and the water rose. Little could be done beyond feeding the animals, threshing a little corn in the barn, and twisting straw ropes for the thatch of the ricks for the coming harvest—if indeed there was a harvest, for already not a few of last year's ricks from farther up the country were floating past the Mains, down the Daur to the sea. The sight was a dreadful one to the farmers' eyes. From the Mains, to right and left as far as the bases of the hills instead of fields was water, yellow brown—here in still expanse or slow progress, there sweeping along in fierce current. The quieter parts of it were dotted with trees, divided by hedges, shaded with ears of corn; upon the swifter parts floated objects of all kinds.

Mr. Duff went wandering restlessly from one spot to another, finding nothing to do. In the gloaming, which fell the sooner that a rain blanket miles thick wrapped the earth up from the sun, he came across from the barn and, entering the kitchen, dropped weary with hopelessness on a chair.

From being nearly in the center of its own land, the farmsteading of the Mains was at a considerable distance from any other. But there were two or three cottages upon the land; and as the evening drew on, another aged pair, who lived in one only a few hundred yards from the house, made their appearance. They were soon followed by the wife of the foreman with her children, who lived farther off. Quickly the night closed in and Gibbie was not come. Robert was growing very uneasy; Janet kept comforting and reassuring him.

"There's one thing," said the old man: "Oscar's with him."

"Oscar's not with him," said Donal. "The dog came to me in the stable long after Gibbie was gone; he was lookin' for him."

Robert gave a great sigh but said nothing.

Janet did not sleep a wink that night: she had so many to pray for. Not Gibbie only, but every one of her family was in peril from the waters, all being employed along the valley of the Daur.

The dawn appeared—but the farm had vanished. Not even heads of growing corn were anywhere more to be seen. The loss would be severe, and John Duff's heart sank within him. The sheep which had been in the mown cloverfield that sloped to the burn were now all in the cornyard, and the water was there with them. If the rise did not soon cease, every rick would be afloat. There was little current, however, and not half the danger there would have been had the houses stood a few hundred yards in any direction from where they were.

"Have some breakfast, John," said his sister.

"Let them take it that hungers," he answered.

"Take it, or you'll not have the strength to be worth savin'," said Jean.

Thereupon he fell to it and ate, if not with appetite then with will that was wondrous.

The flood still grew, still the rain poured, and Gibbie did not come. Indeed, no one any longer expected him, whatever might have become of him. Except by boat the Mains was inaccessible now, they thought. Soon after breakfast, notwithstanding, a strange woman came to the door. Jean, who opened it to her knock, stood and stared speechless. It was a grey-haired woman, with a more disreputable look than her weather-flouted condition would account for.

"Grand weather for the ducks!" she said.

"Where do you come from?" returned Jean, who did not relish the freedom of her address.

"From over there," she answered.

"And how did you get here?"

"Upon my two legs."

Jean looked this way and that over the watery waste and again stared at the woman in growing bewilderment.

"Your legs must be longer than they look then,

woman," said Jean, glancing at the lower part of the stranger's person.

The woman only laughed—a laugh without any laughter in it.

"Well, what do you want, now that you are here?" continued Jean with severity. "You didn't come to the Mains to tell them what kind of weather it is!"

"I came to wherever I could get," answered the woman, "and for my part, that's nothing to nobody now—though it's not as it once was—there might be more of me for the better of it. And so if you could give me a glass of whiskey—"

"You'll get no whiskey here," interrupted Jean with determination.

The woman gave a sigh and half turned away as if she would depart. But however she might have come, it was plainly impossible she could depart.

"Woman," said Jean, "know that I care nothing about you, and I don't like you, or the look of you; and if it were a fine summer night, I'd close my door in your face. But I dare not do that against my neighbor; so you can come in and sit down—my mind's spoken. You'll get what will hold the life in you, and a little bit of straw in the barn. Only you must keep quiet, for the goodman doesn't like tramps."

"Tramps here, tramps there!" exclaimed the woman, starting into high displeasure; "I would have you know I'm an honest woman, and no tramp!"

"You shouldn't look so much like one then," said Jean coolly. "But come in, and I'll say nothing so long as you behave."

The woman followed her, took the seat pointed out to her by the fire, and ate the cakes and milk handed her without a word of thanks. But she seemed to grow better tempered as she ate. On the other side of the fire sat Janet, knitting away busily with a look of ease and leisure. She said nothing but now and then cast a kindly glance out of her grey eyes at the woman.

With the first of the light, some of the men on the farm

had set out to look for Gibbie, well knowing it would be a hard matter to reach Glashgar. About nine they returned, having found it impossible. One of them, caught in a current and swept into a hole, had barely escaped with his life. But they were unanimous that the dummie was better off in any cave on Glashgar than he would be in the best bedroom at the Mains if things went on as they threatened.

Robert had all the morning kept on going to the barn and back again to the kitchen, consumed with anxiety about the son of his old age. But the barn began to be flooded, and he had to limit his prayer-walk to the space between the door of the house and the chair where Janet sat—knitting busily and praying amidst the rush of the seaward torrents, the mad howling and screeching of the wind, and the lowing of the cattle.

"Is Gibbie worse off, Robert, in this water upon Glashgar, than the disciples in the boat on the Sea of Galilee when the Master didn't come to them? Take heart, man."

"You're right, Janet," answered Robert.

"Gibbie will probably be here when you least look for him," said Janet.

Neither of them caught the gleam that lighted the face of the strange woman at those last words of Janet. She looked up at her with the sharpest of glances, but the same instant compelled her countenance to resume its former expression of indifference, and under that became watchful of everything said and done.

Still the rain fell and the wind blew; the torrents came tearing down from the hills and shot madly into the rivers; the rivers ran into the valleys and deepened the lakes that filled them. On every side of the Mains, from the foot of Glashgar to Gormdhu, all was one yellow and red sea, with numberless roaring currents. It burrowed holes, opened long-deserted channels; here deposited inches of rich mold, there yards of sand and gravel; here it was carrying away fertile ground, leaving behind only bare rock or shingle where the corn had been waving; there it was scooping out the bed of a new lake. Houses were torn to pieces and their contents, as from broken boxes, sent wandering on the brown waste. Huge trees passed as if shot down an Alpine slide, cottages and bridges of stone giving way before them. Wooden mills, thatched roofs, great mill wheels went dipping and swaying and hobbling down. From the upper windows of the Mains, looking toward the chief current, they saw a drift of everything that would float—everything belonging to farms and dwellings. Chairs and tables, chests, carts, saddles, tubs of linen, beds and blankets, workbenches, harrows, girnels, planes, cheeses, churns, spinning wheels, cradles, iron pots, wheelbarrows—all these and many other things hurried past as they gazed.

The water was now in the stable and cowhouses and barn. A few minutes more and it would be creeping into the kitchen. The Daub and its tributary, the Lorrie, were about to merge their last difference on the floor of Jean's parlor. Worst of all, a rapid current had set in across the farther end of the stable, which no one had as yet observed.

Jean bustled about her work as usual and would accept no help from any of her guests in preparing dinner.

"There's one thing, Mother," said Donal, entering the kitchen covered with mud, a rabbit in one hand and a large salmon in the other, "we're not likely to starve, with salmon in the bushes and rabbits in the trees!"

Donal was being questioned by his master when the strange woman said, addressing no one in particular, "I doubt the gable of the stable will stand more than another half hour."

"It must fall then," said the farmer.

"Hoots!" said the woman, "don't talk that way, sir. You might at least give the poor beasts a chance."

"How would you do that?" said Jean. "If you cut them loose, they would but take to the water in fear and drown that much sooner."

"No, no, Jean," interposed the farmer, "they would take care of themselves to the last, and get to the driest spot possible, just as you would yourself."

"Allowing," said the stranger, "I would rather drown

swimming than tied by the head. But you have a place to put them ... What kind of floor is up the stairs there?"

"Ow, good enough floors," answered the farmer. "But it's the walls, woman, not the floor we have to be concerned about in this weather."

"If the joists be strong and well set into the walls, why shouldn't you take the horses up the stairs to your bedrooms? It'll be all to the good of the walls, for the weight of the beasts will be upon them to hold them down, and the whole house against the water. And if I were you, I would put the best of the cattle in the parlor and the kitchen here."

Mr. Duff broke into a strange laughter.

"Would you take up the carpets first, woman?" he said.

"I would," she answered; "that goes without sayin'— if there was time; but I tell you there is none; and you'll buy two or three carpets for the price of one horse."

"Haith! the woman's right," he cried, suddenly waking up to the sense of the proposal, and shot from the house.

All the women, Jean making no exception to any help now, rushed to carry the beds and blankets to the garret.

Just as Mr. Duff entered the stable from the nearer end, the opposite gable fell out with a great splash, letting in the wide level vision of turbidly raging waters, fading into the obscurity of the wind-driven rain. While he stared aghast, a great tree struck the wall like a battering ram so that the stable shook. The horses, which had been for some time moving uneasily, were now quite scared. There was not a moment to be lost. Duff shouted for his men; one or two came running; and in less than a minute more those in the house heard the iron-shod feet splashing and stamping through the water, as one after another the horses were brought across the yard to the door of the house. Mr. Duff led by the halter his favorite Snowball, who was a good deal excited, plunging and rearing so that it was all he could do to hold him. He had ordered the men to take the others first, thinking he would follow more quietly. But the moment Snowball heard the first thundering of hoofs on the stairs, he went out of his senses with terror, broke from his master, and went plunging back to the stable.

Duff darted after him, but was only in time to see him rush from the farther end into the swift current, where he was at once out of his depth. Instantly caught and hurried, rolling over and over, the horse disappeared from his master's sight.

He ran back into the house and up to the highest window. From that he caught sight of him a long way down, swimming. Once or twice he saw him turned heels over head. But alas! it was in the direction of the Daur, which would soon, his master did not doubt, sweep his carcass into the North Sea. With troubled heart he strained his sight after him as long as he could distinguish his lessening head, but it got among some wreck and, unable to tell anymore whether he saw it or not, he returned to his men with his eyes full of tears.

25 Glashruach

As soon as Gibbie had found a stall for Crummie and thrown a great dinner before her, he turned and sped back the way he had come. There was no time to lose if he still would have the bridge to cross the Lorrie—and his was indeed the last foot that ever touched it. Guiding himself by well-known points, for he knew the country perhaps better than any man born and bred in it, he made straight for Glashgar, itself hid in the rain. Now wading, now swimming, now walking along the top of a wall, Gibbie held stoutly on. And at length, clear of the level water and with only the torrents to mind, he set off up the hill. It was not so hard a struggle to cross the water, but he had still to get to the other side of several torrents far more dangerous than any current he had been in. Again and again he had to ascend a long distance before he found a possible place to cross, but he reached the fold at last.

It was a little valley opening on that where lay the

tarn. Swollen to a lake, the waters of it were now at the very gate of the pen. Left where they were, the sheep would probably be drowned; if not, they would be starved. But if he let them go, they would keep out of the water and find for themselves what food and shelter were to be had. He opened the gate, drove them out and a little way up the hill, and left them.

By this time it was about two o'clock, and Gibbie was very hungry. He had enough of the water for one day, however, and was not inclined to return to the Mains. If the cottage were still standing—and it might be—he would find plenty to eat there. He turned toward it. Great was his pleasure when, after another long struggle, he perceived that not only was the cottage there but the torrent was gone. Either the flow from the mountain had ceased or the course of the water had been diverted.

When he reached home, he swept out the water that lay on the floor, took the driest peats he could find, succeeded in lighting a large fire, and made himself some water-brose.

His hunger appeased, he sat resting in Robert's chair, gradually drying. Falling asleep, he slept for an hour or so. When he woke, he took his New Testament and began to read. He read until he came to these words: "Hereby perceive we the love of God, because he laid down his life for us, and we ought to lay down our lives for the brethren."

Gibbie said to himself, "Here am I sittin' with my fire and my soup and my Bible, and all the world below Glashgar lying in a flood! I can't lay down my life to save their souls; so I must save for them what I can—it may be but a hen or a calf."

The Bible was back in its place and Gibbie out of the door the same moment. He had not an idea what he was going to do. All he yet understood was that he must go down the hill to be where things might have to be done—and before darkness fell. He must go where there were people.

His first definitely directive thought was that his nearest neighbors were likely enough to be in trouble—"the folk at the main house." He would go straight there.

Glashruach stood on one of the roots of the Glashgar

where the mountain settles down into the valley of the Daur. Immediately outside its principal gate ran the Glashburn; on the other side of the house, within the grounds, ran a smaller hill stream, already mentioned as passing close under Ginevra's window. Both these fell into the Lorrie. Between them the mountain sloped gently up for some little distance clothed with forest. On the side of the smaller burn, however, the side opposite the house, the ground rose abruptly. Straight from the mountain between the two streams Gibbie approached the house, through larches and pines, raging and roaring in the wind. Below him was a wide, swift, fiercely rushing river, where water was none before! No, he made no mistake; there was the rest of the road, the end of it next to the house! That was a great piece of it that fell frothing into the river and vanished! Bridge and gate and wall were gone utterly. The burn had swallowed them and now, foaming with madness, was roaring along a great way within the grounds and rapidly drawing nearer to the house, tearing to pieces and devouring all that defended it. Not with all he had that day seen and gone through had Gibbie until now gathered any notion of the force of the rushing water.

He darted down the hill.

Mr. Galbraith had gone again, leaving Ginevra to the care of Mistress MacFarlane, the housekeeper. At this moment, however, they were not alone, for on the other side of the fire sat Angus, not thither attracted by any friendship for the housekeeper but by the glass of whiskey which he sipped as he talked. Many a flood had Angus seen and some that had done frightful damage, but never one that had caused him anxiety; and although this was worse than any of the rest, he had not yet a notion how bad it really was.

In her room, Ginevra wandered listlessly to the window and stood there gazing out on the wild confusion—the burn roaring below, the trees opposite ready to be torn to pieces by the wind, and the valley beneath covered with stormy water. The tumult was so loud that she did not hear a gentle knock at her door. As she turned away she saw it softly open and there, to her astonishment, stood Gibbie, come, she imagined, to seek shelter because their cottage had been blown down.

"You mustn't come here, Gibbie," she said, advancing. "Go down to the kitchen, to Mistress MacFarlane. She will see to what you want."

Gibbie made eager signs to her to go with him. She concluded that he wanted her to accompany him to the kitchen and speak for him; but knowing that would only enrage her keeper with them both, she shook her head and went back to the window. The moment she looked out, she gave a cry, and stood staring. Gibbie had followed her, softly as swiftly, and looking out also saw good cause indeed for her astonishment: the channel of the raging burn was all but dry! Instantly he understood what it meant.

In his impotence to persuade, he caught the girl in his arms and rushed with her from the room. She had faith enough in him by this time not to struggle or scream. He shot down the stair with her and out of the front door. Her weight was nothing to his excited strength. The moment they issued, and she saw the Glashburn raving along through the lawn with little more than the breadth of the drive between it and the house, she saw the necessity of escape, though she did not perceive half the dire necessity for haste. Every few moments, a great gush would dash out twelve or fifteen yards over the gravel and sink again, carrying many feet of the bank with it and widening by so much the raging channel.

"Put me down, Gibbie," she said; "I will run as fast as you like."

He obeyed at once.

"Oh," she cried, "Mistress MacFarlane!—I wonder if she knows. Run and knock at the kitchen window."

Gibbie darted off, gave three loud hurried taps on the window, came flying back, took Ginevra's hand in his, drew her on till she was at her full speed, turned sharp to the left round the corner of the house, and shot down to the empty channel of the burn. As they crossed it, even to the inexperienced eyes of the girl it was plain what had caused the phenomenon. A short distance up the stream, the whole facing of its lofty right bank had slipped down into its channel. Not a tree, not a shrub, not a bed of moss was to be seen; all was bare, wet rock. Any moment the barrier might give way and the water resume its course. They made haste, therefore, to climb the opposite bank. In places it was very steep, and the soil slipped so that often it seemed on its way with them to the bottom, while the wind threatened to uproot the trees to which they clung. It was with a fierce scramble they gained the top. Then the sight was a grand one.

The arrested water swirled and beat and foamed against the landslide, then rushed to the left, through the wood, over bushes and stones, a raging river, the wind tearing off the tops of its waves, to the Glashburn, into which it plunged, swelling yet higher its huge volume. Rapidly it cut for itself a new channel. Every moment a tree fell and shot with it like a rocket. Looking up its course, they saw it come down the hillside a white streak, and burst into boiling brown and roar at their feet. The wind nearly swept them from their place; but they clung to the great stones and saw the airy torrent fill itself with branches and leaves and lumps of foam. Then first Ginevra became fully aware of the danger in which the house from which Gibbie had rescued her was standing.

"But where's Mistress MacFarlane?" she said. "Oh, Gibbie! We mustn't leave her."

He replied by pointing down to the bed of the stream; she and Angus were crossing. Ginevra was satisfied when she saw the gamekeeper with her, and they set out as fast as they could go, ascending the mountain. Gibbie was eager to have her in warmth and safety before it was dark.

It was an undertaking hard for any girl, especially such for one unaccustomed to exertion. But the excitement of battling with the storm, the joy of adventure, and the pleasure of feeling her own strength sustained her well for a long time. She never lost her courage, and Gibbie, though he could not hearten her with words, was so ready with smile and laugh, so fearless, so free from anxiety while doing everything he could think of to lessen her toil and pain, that she hardly felt in his silence any lack. It was getting dark when they reached the only spot where he judged it possible to cross the Glash-burn. He carried her over and then it was all downhill to the cottage. Once inside it, Ginevra threw herself into Robert's chair and laughed, then cried, then laughed again.

Gibbie blew up the peats, made a good fire, and put on water to boil; then opened Janet's drawers and having signified to his companion to take what she could find, went to the cowhouse, threw himself on a heap of wet straw, worn out, and had enough to do to keep himself from falling asleep.

A little rested, he rose and reentered the cottage, when a merry laugh from both of them went ringing out into the storm; the little lady was dressed in Janet's workday garments and making porridge. She looked very funny. Gibbie found plenty of milk in the dairy under the rock, and they ate their supper together in gladness. Then Gibbie prepared the bed in the little closet for his guest, and she slept as if she had not slept for a week.

Gibbie woke with the first of the dawn. The rain still fell—descending in spoonfuls rather than drops; the wind kept shaping itself into long, hopeless howls, rising to shrill yells that went drifting away over the land, and then howling again. There must be more for Gibbie to do! He must go again to the foot of the mountain and see if there was anybody to help. They might even be in trouble at the Mains, who could tell!

Ginevra woke, rose, made herself as tidy as she could, and left her closet. Gibbie was not in the cottage. She blew up the fire, and finding the pot ready beside it with clean water, she set it on to boil. Gibbie did not come. The water boiled. She took it off but, being hungry, put it on again. Several times she took it off and put it on again. Gibbie never came. She made herself some porridge at last. Everything necessary was upon the table, and as she poured the gruel into the wooden dish for the purpose, she noticed a slate beside it with something written upon it. The words were, "I will cum back as soon as I cann."

She was alone, then! It was dreadful; but she was too hungry to think about it. She ate her porridge and then began to cry. It was very unkind of Gibbie to leave her, she said to herself. But, then, he was a sort of angel and doubtless had to go and help somebody else. There was a little pile of books on the table which he must have left for her. She began examining them, and soon found something to interest her so that an hour or two passed quickly. But Gibbie did not return and the day went wearily. She cried now and then, made great efforts to be patient, succeeded pretty well for a while, and cried again.

Still Gibbie did not come. Before the day was over, she had had a good lesson in praying. For here she was, one who had never yet acted on her own responsibility, alone on a bare mountainside, in the heart of a storm which seemed as if it would never cease. And not a creature knew where she was but the dumb boy, and he had left her!

The noises were terrible. Through the general roar of wind and water and rain, every now and then came a sharper sound, like a report or crack, followed by a strange thunder, it seemed. They were the noises of stones carried down by the streams, grinding against each other, and dashing stone against stone; and of rocks falling and rolling, and bounding against their fast-rooted neighbors. When it began to grow dark, her misery seemed more than she could bear; but then, happily, she grew sleepy and slept the darkness away.

With the new light came new promise and fresh hope. It no longer rained so fiercely; the wind had fallen; and the streams did not run so furious a race down the sides of the mountain. She ran to the burn, got some water to wash herself—she could not spare the clear water, of which there was some still left in Janet's pails—and put on her own clothes, which were now quite dry. Then she got herself some breakfast, and after that tried to say her prayers.

26   Angus MacPholp

Gibbie sped down the hill through a worse rain than ever. Going down his own side of the Glashburn, the nearest path to the valley, the gamekeeper's cottage was the first dwelling on his way.

It had been with great difficulty (for even Angus did not know the mountain so well as Gibbie) that the gamekeeper reached it with the housekeeper the night before. All night Angus watched, peering into the darkness, but saw nothing except three lights that burned above the water—one of them, he thought, at the Mains. The other two went out in the darkness. When the morning came, there was the Glashburn, meeting the Lorrie in his garden. But the cottage was well built and fit to stand a good siege. In a few minutes they were isolated, with the current of the Glashburn on one side and that of the Lorrie in front. When he saw the water come in at the front and back doors at once, Angus ordered his family up the stair.

As Gibbie came down the hill, he heard Mrs. Mac-Pholp screaming in agony, and he ran at full speed toward the cottage. The gamekeeper was in the raging water trying to rescue a favorite dog. About thirty yards from the house, the current bore Angus straight into a large elder tree. He got into the middle of it and there remained, trembling. Gibbie, however, did not see him at first; plunging in, he swam round to the front of the cottage to learn what was the matter. There the wife's gesticulations directed his eyes to her drowning husband.

But what was he to do? He could swim to the tree well enough and, he thought, back again, but how was that to be made of service to Angus? If he had a line, and there must be plenty of lines in the cottage, he could send him the end of it. He caught hold of the eaves and scrambled onto the roof. But in the folly and faithlessness of her despair, the woman would not let him enter. She struck at him from the window, crying, "You'll not come in here with my husband drowning yonder! Go to him, you coward!"

Never had poor Gibbie so much missed the use of speech.

On the slope of the roof he could do little to force an entrance, therefore threw himself off it to seek another and betook himself to the thin windows below. Through that of Angus's room he caught sight of a floating anker cask. It was the very thing! And there on the walls hung a quantity of nets and cordage! But how to get in? It was a sash-window and of course swollen with the wet, therefore not to be opened; and there was not a square in it large enough to let him through. He swam to the other side, crept softly onto the roof and over the ridge. But a broken slate betrayed him. The woman saw him, rushed to the fireplace, caught up the poker, and darted back to defend the window.

"You'll not come in here, I tell you," she screeched, "with my man stickin' in yonder tree!"

Gibbie advanced. She made a blow at him with the poker. He caught it, wrenched it from her grasp, and threw himself from the roof. The next moment they heard the poker at work, smashing the window.

"He'll be in and murder us all!" cried the mother and ran to the stair, while the children screamed with terror.

But the water was far too deep for her. She returned to the attic, barricaded the door, and went again to the window to watch her drowning husband.

Gibbie was inside in a moment and seizing the cask proceeded to attach to it a strong line. Satisfied at length, he floated out his barrel and followed with the line in his hand to aid its direction if necessary. It struck the tree. With a yell of joy Angus laid hold of it and, hauling the line taut and feeling it secure, committed himself at once to the water. He held by the barrel and swam with his legs while Gibbie, away to the side with a hold on the rope, was swimming his hardest to draw him out of the current. But a weary man was Angus when at length he reached the house. It was all he could do to get himself in at the window and crawl up the stair. At the top of it he fell benumbed on the floor.

By the time the repentant and grateful Mistress MacPholp thought of Gibbie, not a trace of him was to be seen. While they looked for him in the water and on the land, Gibbie was again in the room below carrying out a fresh thought. He emptied the cask, into which a good deal of water had got, then corked the bunghole tight, laced the cask up in a piece of net, attached the line to the net, and wound it about the cask by rolling the latter round and round. He took the cask between his hands, and pushed from the window straight into the current of the Glashburn. In a moment it had swept him to the Lorrie. By the greater rapidity of the former, he got easily across the heavier current of the latter and was presently in water comparatively still, swimming quietly toward the Mains. Not a human being was visible and but a few house roofs and tops of trees showing like low bushes. He drew near the Mains.

What was that cry from far away? Surely it must be that of a horse in danger! It brought a lusty equine response from the farm. Where could horses be with such a depth of water about the place? Then began a great lowing of cattle. But again came the cry of the horse from afar and Gibbie, this time recognizing the voice as Snowball's, forgot the rest. The cry came again and again so that he was satisfied in what direction he must look. He seemed to see white against the brown water, far away to the left. It might be Snowball on the turnpike road, which thereabout ran along the top of a high embankment. He rolled the line about the barrel and pushed vigorously for what might be the horse.

It took him a weary hour—in so many currents was he caught, one after the other, all straining to carry him far below the object he wanted to reach. When at length he scrambled on the embankment beside the poor, shivering, perishing creature, the horse gave a low neigh of delight; he did not know Gibbie, but he was a human being. He was quite cowed and submissive, and Gibbie at once set about his rescue. He tied the end of the line to the remnant of the halter on his head. Encouraged by the pressure of the halter, the horse followed, and they made for the Mains. It was a long journey, and Gibbie had not breath enough to sing to Snowball, but he made what noise he could, and they got slowly along.

27   The Raft

Mistress Croale was not the last who arrived at the Mains. Just after the loss of Snowball, a woman came floating into the farmyard on a raft with her four little children seated around her, holding the skirt of her gown above her head and out between her hands for a sail. She had made the raft herself by tying some bars of a paling together and crossing them with what other bits of wood she could find. Nobody knew her. She had come down the Lorrie.

The strangers were mostly in Fergus's bedroom; the horses were all in their owner's; and the cattle were in the remaining rooms. Bursts of talk among the women were followed by fits of silence. Who could tell how long the flood might last! or indeed whether the house might not be undermined before morning, or be struck by one of those big things of which so many floated by and give way with one terrible crash. Mr. Duff, while preserving a tolerable calm exterior, was nearly at his wits' end. He would stand for half an hour together with his hands in his pockets, looking motionless out of a window, murmuring now and then to himself, "This is clean ridiculous!" But when anything had to be done, he was active enough. Mistress Croale sat in a corner, very quiet and looking not a little cowed. There was altogether more water than she liked. Now and then she lifted her lurid black eyes to Janet, who stood at one of the windows, knitting away at her master's stocking and casting many a calm glance at the brown waters and the strange drift that covered them.

"If only Gibbie was here!" said Janet now and again.

"You have more than once made mention of one connected with you by the name of Gibbie," said Mistress Croale.

"Ay," answered Janet, "and what may be your interest in him?"

"Oh, nothing," returned Mistress Croale. "I knew one of that name long ago that was lost sight of."

"There's Gibbies here and Gibbies there," remarked Janet, probing her.

"But there's not many wee Sir Gibbies, or the world would not be so doomed."

Janet was arrested in her turn. Could the fierce, repellent woman be the mother of her gracious Gibbie? Could she be, and look so lost? But the loss of him had lost her perhaps. Anyhow, God was his Father, whoever was the mother of him.

"How did you come to lose your child, woman?" she asked.

But Mistress Croale was careful also, and had her reasons.

"He ran from the bloody hand," she said enigmatically.

Janet recalled how Gibbie came to her scored by the hand of cruelty.

"How did he come by the bonnie nickname?" she asked at length.

"Nickname?" retorted Mistress Croale fiercely. "His own name and title by law and right, as sure as ever there was a King James that first put his hand to makin' of baronets!—as it's often I have heard Sir George, the father of him, tell the same."

She ceased abruptly, annoyed with herself it seemed for having said so much.

"You wouldn't be the lady yourself, would you, mem?" suggested Janet in her gentlest voice.

Mistress Croale made her no answer. Perhaps she thought of the days when she alone of women did the simplest of woman's offices for Sir George.

"It's long since you lost him?" asked Janet after a pause.

"Ay," she answered, gruffly and discourteously in a tone intended to quench interrogation.

But Janet persisted.

"Would you know him again if you saw him?"

"Know him? I would know him if he had grown to be a grandfather. 'Know him,' said she! Whoever knew him as I did, child that he was, and wouldn't know him if he were dead and an angel made of him!—But well I know, it's little difference that would make!"

She rose in her excitement and, going to the other window, stood gazing vacantly out upon the rushing sea. To Janet it was plain she knew more about Gibbie than she was inclined to tell, and it gave her a momentary sting of apprehension.

"What was it about him that you knew so well?" she asked in a tone of indifference, as if speaking only through the meshes of her work.

"I'll know those who ask before I tell," she replied sullenly. But the next instant she screamed aloud, "Lord God Almighty! yon's him! yon's himself!"—and stretching out her arms, dashed a hand through a pane, letting in an eddying swirl of wind and water, while the blood streamed unheeded from her wrist.

The same moment Jean entered the room. She heard both the cry and the sound of the breaking glass.

"What set off the beggar-wife!" she exclaimed.

Mistress Croale took no heed. She stood now staring from the window still as a statue except for the panting motion of her sides. At the other window stood Janet, gazing also, with blessed face. For there, like a triton of a sea horse, came Gibbie through the water on Snowball swimming wearily.

He caught sight of Janet at the window and straightaway his countenance was radiant with smiles. Mistress Croale gave a shuddering sigh, drew back from her window, and betook herself again to her dark corner. Jean went to Janet's broonie, saving from the waters the lost and lamented Snowball. She shouted to her brother.

"John! John! here's your Snowball . . . here's your Snowball!"

John ran to her call and, beside himself with joy when he saw his favorite come swimming along, threw the window wide and began to bawl the most unnecessary directions and encouragements, as if the exploit had been brought thus far toward a happy conclusion solely through him. From all the windows Gibbie was welcomed with shouts and cheers and congratulations.

"Lord preserve us!" cried Mr. Duff, recognizing the rider at last, "it's Rob Grant's innocent! Who would have thought it!"

"Take him round the door . . . Where did you find him?—You would best get him in at the window on to the stair . . . He must be hungry.—You'll be wet, I'm thinkin'! . . . Come up the stair, and tell us all about it." A score of such conflicting shouts assailed Gibbie as he approached, and he replied to them all simply with a wide smile.

When they arrived at the door, they found a difficulty awaiting them. The water was now so high that Snowball's head rose above the lintel; and though all animals can swim, they do not all know how to dive. A tumult of suggestions immediately broke out. But Donal had already thrown himself from a window with a rope and swung to Gibbie's assistance; the two understood each other and, heeding nothing the rest were saying, held their own communications. In a minute the rope was fastened round Snowball's body and the end of it drawn between his forelegs and through the ring of his headstall. Donal swam with it to his mother on the stair with the request that as soon as she saw Snowball's head under the water, she would pull with all her might and draw him in at the door. Donal then swam back and threw his arms round Snowball's neck from below, while the same moment Gibbie cast his whole weight on it from above. The horse was over head and ears in an instant and through the door in another. With snorting nostrils and blazing eyes, his head rose in the passage, and in terror he struck out for the stair. As he scrambled heavily up from the water, his master and Robert seized him and with much petting and patting and gentling, though there was little enough difficulty in managing him now, conducted him into the bedroom to the rest of the horses. There he was welcomed by his companions and immediately began devouring the hay upon his master's bedstead. Gibbie came close behind him, was seized by Janet at the top of the stair, embraced like one come alive from the grave, and led dripping as he was into the room where the women were.

The farmer looked back from the door as he was leaving the room. Gibbie was performing a wild circular dance of which Janet was the center, throwing his limbs about like the toy the children call a Jumping Jack; this ended suddenly in a motionless ecstasy upon one leg. Having regarded for a moment the rescuer of Snowball with astonishment, John Duff turned away. It did not occur to him that it was the joy of having saved that caused Gibbie's merriment thus to overflow.

For all the excitement Mistress Croale had shown at first view of Gibbie, she sat still in her dusky corner, made no movement toward him nor did anything to attract his attention, only kept her eyes fixed upon him; and Janet in her mingled joy and pain forgot her altogether. When at length it recurred to her that she was in the room, she cast a somewhat anxious glance toward the place she had occupied all day. It was empty; and Janet was perplexed to think how she had gone unseen.

At suppertime Mistress Croale was missing altogether. Nobody could with certainty say when he had last seen her. The house was searched from top to bottom, and the conclusion arrived at was that she must have fallen from some window and been drowned—only, surely she would at least have uttered one cry! Examining certain of the windows to know whether she might not have left some sign of such an exit, the farmer discovered that the raft was gone which brought the woman and her children.

"Losh!" cried another man, "yonder will be her I saw an hour ago."

"You gowk!" said his master. "How could she go so far without going to the bottom?"

"On the raft, sir," answered the man. "I took her for a dog on a door. The wife must be a witch!"

John Duff stared at the man with his mouth open, and for half a minute all were dumb. The thing was incredible, yet hardly to be controverted. The woman was gone, the raft was gone, and something strange that might be the two together had been observed about the time when she ceased to be observed in the house.

Mr. Duff said the luck changed with the return of Snowball—his sister said, with the departure of the beggar-wife. Before dark the rain had ceased, and it became evident that the water had not risen for the last half hour. In two hours more it had sunk a quarter of an inch.

Gibbie threw himself on the floor beside his mother's chair; she covered him with her grey cloak; and he fell fast asleep. At dawn, he awoke with a start. He had dreamed that Ginevra was in trouble. He made Janet understand that he would return to guide them home as soon as the way was practicable, and set out at once to find a way.

The water fell rapidly. Almost as soon as it was morning, the people at the Mains could begin doing a little toward restoration.

In the afternoon, Gibbie reappeared at the Mains, and Robert and Janet set out at once to go home with him. It was a long journey for them—he had to take them so many rounds. They rested at several houses, and saw much misery on their way. It was night before they arrived at the cottage. They found it warm and clean and tidy; Ginevra had, like a true lady, swept the house that gave her shelter. For Ginevra it was heavenly bliss to hear their approaching footsteps; and before she left them she had thoroughly learned that the poorest place where the atmosphere is love is more homely and, by consequence, more heavenly than the most beautiful, even where law and order are elements supreme.

As to the strange woman's evident knowledge concerning Gibbie, Janet could do nothing but wait—fearing rather than hoping; but she had got so far above time and chance that nothing really troubled her, and she could wait quietly.

28   Mr. Sclater

It may be remembered that Rev. Clement Sclater, upon Gibbie's disappearance from the city, felt great interest in his fate. From such questions as started about the boy himself, he gathered all the information at which he could arrive concerning his family and history. That done, he proceeded to attempt interesting in his unknown fortunes those relatives of Gibbie's mother whose existence and residences he had discovered. In this, however, he had met with no success.

At the house where she was born, there was now no one but a second cousin, to whom her elder brother, dying unmarried, had left the small estate of the Withrops along with the family contempt for her husband, and for her because of him. So said the cousin to Mr. Sclater. As to the orphan, he said, to speak honestly, the more entirely he disappeared, the better he would consider it. The younger brother who had taken to business was the senior partner in a large ship-building firm at Greenock.

William Fuller Withrop was a bachelor, and reputed rich. What Mr. Sclater heard of him did not arouse brilliant hopes. To leave no stone unturned, however, he wrote to Mr. Withrop. The answer he received was that the sister, concerning whose child he had applied to him, had never been anything but a trouble to the family, and it could hardly be expected of him to show any lively interest in her offspring.

Thus failing, Mr. Sclater said to himself he had done all that could be required of him.

One morning some years later, as he sat at breakfast with his wife, reading the morning paper, his eye fell upon a paragraph announcing the sudden death of a well-known William Fuller Withrop, of the eminent ship-building firm of Greenock. He had left no will but an estate of some two hundred thousand pounds.

The minister thereupon sprang from his chair and ran straight from the house to the top step of his lawyer's door.

From his lawyer he would have gone at once to Mistress Croale, but he had not an idea where she might even be heard of. For some years now she had made her living, one poor enough, by hawking small household necessities.

On her next return to the Daurfoot, as the part of the city was called where now she was most at home, she had heard the astounding and welcome news that Gibbie had fallen heir to a large property and that the reward of one hundred pounds had been proclaimed to anyone giving such information as should lead to the discovery of Sir Gilbert Galbraith, commonly known as "wee Sir Gibbie." A description of him was added, and Mistress Croale saw the necessity of haste to any hope of advantage. She had nothing to guide her beyond the fact of Sir George's habit of referring to the property on Daurside, and the assurance that with the said habit Gibbie must have been as familiar as herself.

With this initiative, as she must begin somewhere and could prosecute her business anywhere, she filled her basket and set out at once for Daurside. There, after a good deal of wandering hither and thither, she had made the desired discovery unexpectedly and marvelously, and left behind her in the valley the reputation of having been on more familiar terms with the flood and the causes of it than was possible to any but one who kept company worse than human.

29 Mr. Galbraith

The next morning, Janet felt herself duty-bound to make inquiry concerning those interested in Miss Galbraith. She made the best of her way with Gibbie to Glashruach but found it a ruin in a wilderness. Acres of trees and shrubbery had disappeared and a hollow waste of sand and gravel was in their place. What was left of the house stood on the edge of a red, gravelly precipice of fifty feet in height. At the foot lay the stones of the kitchen wing in which had been the room whence Gibbie carried Ginevra. The newer part of the house was gone from its very roots; the ancient portion, all innovations wiped from it, stood grim, desolated, marred and defiant as of old. Not a sign of life was about the place; the very birds had fled. With difficulty they crossed the burn to the gamekeeper's cottage. But they saw only a little girl who told them her father had gone to find the laird, that her mother was ill in bed, and Mistress MacFarlane on her way to her own people.

"My dear missie," said Janet, when they got home, "you must write to your father, or he'll be out of his wits about you."

Ginevra wrote therefore to the duke's and to the laird's usual address in London as well; but he was on his way from the one place to the other when Angus overtook him, and received neither letter.

Now came to the girl a few such days of delight, of freedom, of life as she had never even dreamed of. She roamed Glashgar with Gibbie, kindest and most interesting of companions. Wherever his sheep went, she went too, and to many places besides—some of them such strange, wild, terrible places as would have terrified her without him.

What a boy he was! He never hurt anything and nothing ever seemed to hurt him. And what a number of things he knew! He showed her things on the mountain, things in the sky, things in the pools and streams wherever they went. He did better than tell her about them; he made her see them, and then the things themselves told her. She was not always certain she saw just what he wanted her to see, but she always saw something that made her glad with knowledge. He had a New Testament Janet had given him which he carried in his pocket; and when she joined him, for he was always out with his sheep hours before she was up, she would generally find him seated on a stone or lying in the heather with the little book in his hand. The moment he saw her, he would spring merrily up to welcome her.

On the fourth day, the rain, which had been coming and going, finally cleared off, the sun was again glorious, and the farmers began to hope a little for the drying and ripening of some portion of their crops. Then first Ginevra asked Gibbie to take her down to Glashruach; she wanted to see the ruin they had described to her.

When she came near she neither wept nor wailed. So utterly altered was the look of everything that had she come upon it unexpectedly, she would not have recognized either place or house. They went up to a door. She seemed never to have seen it; but when they entered, she knew it as one from the hall into a passage which, with what it led to being gone, the inner had become an outer door. A quantity of sand was heaped up in the hall, and the wainscot was wet and swelled and bulging. They went into the dining room. It was a miserable sight. The thick carpet was sodden—spongy like a bed of moss after heavy rains; the leather chairs looked diseased; the color was all gone from the table; the paper hung loose from the walls.

She ascended the old stone stair which led to her father's rooms above, went into his study, and there not a hair was out of its place. She walked toward the window to look across to where once had been her own chamber. But as she approached it, there, behind the curtain, she saw her father, motionless, looking out. She turned pale and stood. Even at such a time had she known he was in the house, she would not have dared set her foot in that room. Gibbie, who had followed and entered behind her, perceived her hesitation, saw and recognized the back of the laird, knew that she was afraid of her father, and stood also waiting, he knew not for what.

Becoming aware of a presence, the laird half turned; seeing Gibbie, he imagined he had supposed the place deserted and entered in a prowling way. With stately offense the man asked what he wanted there, and waved his dismissal. Then he first saw the other, standing white-faced with eyes fixed upon him. He turned pale also, and stood staring at her. For one instant of unreasoning weakness, he imagined he saw a ghost. It was but one moment but it might have been more had not Ginevra walked slowly up to him saying in a trembling voice, as if she expected the blame of all that had happened, "I couldn't help it, Papa." He took her in his arms and kissed her. She clung to him, trembling now with pleasure as well as apprehension. But the end came sooner than she feared. For when the father rose erect from her embrace, there, to his amazement, still stood the odd-looking, outlandish intruder, smiling with the most impertinent interest!

"Go away, boy. You have nothing to do here," said the laird.

"Oh, Papa!" cried Ginevra, clasping her hands, "that's Gibbie! He saved my life. I should have drowned but for him."

The laird was both proud and stupid, therefore more than ordinarily slow to understand what he was unprepared to hear.

"I am much obliged to him," he said haughtily; "but there is no occasion for him to wait."

At this point his sluggish mind began to recall something.—Why, this was the very boy he saw in the meadow with her that morning!—He turned fiercely upon him where Gibbie lingered, either hoping for a word of adieu from Ginevra or unwilling to go while she was uncomfortable.

"Leave the house instantly," he said, "or I will knock you down."

"Oh, Papa!" moaned Ginevra wildly. "Don't speak so

to Gibbie. He is a good boy. It was he that Angus whipped so cruelly—long ago. I have never been able to forget it."

Her father was confounded at her presumption. How dared she expostulate with him! She had grown a bold, bad girl! Good heavens! Evil communications!

"If he does not get out of this house directly," he cried, "I will have him whipped again! Angus!"

He shouted the name, and its echo came back in a wild tone, altogether strange to Ginevra. She seemed struggling in the meshes of an evil dream. Involuntarily she uttered a cry of terror and distress. Gibbie was at her side instantly, putting out his hand to comfort her. She was just laying hers on his arm, scarcely knowing what she did, when her father seized him and dashed him to the other side of the room. He went staggering backward, vainly trying to recover himself, and fell, his head striking against the wall. The same instant Angus entered, saw nothing of Gibbie where he lay and approached his master. Gibbie had recovered and risen. He saw now that he could be of no service to Ginevra, and that his presence only made things worse for her. But he saw also that she was unhappy about him, and that must not be. He broke into such a merry laugh—and it had need to be merry, for it had to do the work of many words of reassurance—that she could scarcely refrain from a half-hysterical response as he walked from the room. The moment he was out of the house, he began to sing; and for many minutes, as he walked up the gulf hollowed by the Glashburn, Ginevra could hear the strange, other-world voice, and knew it was meant to hold communion with her and comfort her.

"What do you know of that fellow, Angus?" demanded his master.

"He's the very devil himself, sir," muttered Angus.

"You will see that he is sent off the property at once—and for good, Angus," said the laird. "His insolence is insufferable. The scoundrel!"

On the pretext of following Gibbie, Angus was only too glad to leave the room. Then Mr. Galbraith turned upon his daughter.

"So, Ginny," he said, "that is the sort of companion you choose when left to yourself! A low, beggarly, insolent scamp! Scarcely the equal of the brutes he had the charge of!"

"They're sheep, Papa!" pleaded Ginevra, in a wail that rose almost to a scream.

"I do believe the girl is an idiot!" said her father and turned from her contemptuously.

"I think I am, Papa," she sobbed. "Don't mind me. Let me go away, and I will never trouble you anymore." She would go to the mountain, she thought, and be a shepherdess with Gibbie.

Her father took her roughly by the arm, pushed her into a closet, locked the door, went and had his luncheon and, in the afternoon, took her by coach to the principal hotel in the city, whence the next morning he sent out early to find a school where he might leave her and his responsibility with her.

When Gibbie knew himself beyond the hearing of Ginevra, his song died away and he went home sad. The gentle girl had stepped at once from the day into the dark, and he was troubled for her.

When he reached home, he found his mother in serious talk with a stranger. The tears were in her eyes and had been running down her cheeks, but she was calm and dignified as usual.

"Here he comes!" she said as he entered. "The will of the Lord be done—now and forevermore! I'm at His bidding—and so is Gibbie."

It was Mr. Sclater. The witch had sailed her raft well.

30 The City Again

One bright afternoon toward the close of the autumn, a company of schoolgirls, two-and-two in long file, was walking in orderly manner, a female grenadier at its head. Among the faces was one very different from the rest, a countenance almost solemn and a little sad. The other girls were looking on this side and that, eager to catch sight of anything to trouble the monotony of the daily walk; but the eyes of this one were cast down.

Suddenly came a rush, a confusion, a fluttering of the doves—whence or how none seemed to know—a gentle shriek from several of the girls, and there suddenly was an odd-looking lad who had got hold of one of the dainty, gloved hands and stood, without a word, gazing in rapturous delight.

"Go away, boy! What do you mean by such impertinence?" cried the outraged Miss Kimble, poking his chest with her parasol. Such a strange-looking creature! He could not be in his sound senses. In the meantime she had failed to observe that, after the first start, the girl stood quite still and was now looking in the lad's face, apparently forgetting to draw her hand from his. The next moment, with hasty yet dignified step, came the familiar form of their own minister, the Rev. Clement Sclater, who with reproof in his countenance, which was red with annoyance and haste, laid his hands on the lad's shoulders to draw him from the prey on which he had pounced.

"Remember, you are not on a hillside but in a respectable street," said the reverend gentleman.

The youth turned his head over his shoulder, not otherwise changing his attitude, and looking at him with some bewilderment. Then the young lady spoke.

"Gibbie and I are old friends," she said, and reaching up laid her free hand on his shoulder as if to protect him—

for the vision of an old horror came rushing back on the mind of Ginevra.

Gibbie had darted from his companion's side some hundred yards off. The cap which Mr. Sclater had insisted on his wearing had fallen as he ran, and he had never missed it. His hair stood out on all sides of his head, and the sun behind him shone in it like a glory, just as when first he appeared to Ginevra in the peat-moss like an angel standing over her.

"Miss Galbraith!" said Miss Kimble, in the tone that indicates nostrils distended, "I am astonished at you! What an example to the school! I never knew you to misbehave yourself before! Take your hand from this—this—very strange-looking person's shoulder directly!"

Ginevra obeyed, but Gibbie stood as before.

"Remove your hand, boy, instantly!" cried Miss Kimble, growing more and more angry and began knocking him with her parasol, which apparently Gibbie took for a joke, for he laughed aloud.

"Pray do not alarm yourself, ma'am," said Mr. Sclater, slowly recovering his breath; he was not yet quite sure of Gibbie, or confident how best he was to be managed; "this young ... gentleman is Sir Gilbert Galbraith, my ward. Sir Gilbert, this lady is Miss Kimble."

"Oh!" said the lady, who had ceased her battery and stood bewildered and embarrassed—the more that by this time the girls had all gathered round, staring and wondering.

Ginevra's eyes too had filled with wonder; she cast them down, and a strange smile began to play about her mouth. All at once she was in the middle of a fairy tale and had not a notion what was coming next. Her dumb shepherd boy a baronet!—and, more wonderful still, a Galbraith! She must be dreaming in the wide street! The last she had seen of him was as he was driven from the house by her father, when he had just saved her life. That was but a few weeks ago, and here he was called Sir Gilbert Galbraith! It was a delicious bit of wonder.

"Oh!" said Miss Kimble a second time, recovering herself a little, "I see! A relative, Miss Galbraith! I did not un-

derstand. That of course sets everything right—at least—
even then—the open street, you know! You will understand,
Mr. Sclater. I beg your pardon, Sir Gilbert. I hope I did not
hurt you with my parasol!"

Gibbie laughed aloud.

"Thank you," said Miss Kimble, confused and an-
noyed with herself for behaving so, especially before her girls.
"I should be sorry to have hurt you. Going to college, I presume, Sir Gilbert?"

Gibbie looked at Mr. Sclater.

"He is going to study with me for a while first," answered the minister.

"I am glad to hear it. He could not do better," said Miss
Kimble. "Come, girls."

And with friendly farewells she moved on, her train
after her.

———————

Mr. Sclater had behaved judiciously and taken gentle
pains to satisfy the old couple that they must part with Gibbie. One of the neighboring clergy knew Mr. Sclater well, and
with him paid the old people a visit to help dismiss any lin-
gering doubt that he was the boy's legally appointed guardian. To their own common sense, indeed, it became plain that,
except some such story was true, there could be nothing to
induce him to come after Gibbie or desire to take charge of
the outcast. But they did not feel thoroughly satisfied until
Mr. Sclater brought Fergus Duff to the cottage, to testify to
him as being what he indicated. It was a sore trial, but among
the griefs of losing him, no fear of his forgetting them was
included. Mr. Sclater's main difficulty was with Gibbie himself. At first he laughed at the absurdity of his going away
from his father and mother and the sheep. They told him he
was Sir Gilbert Galbraith. He answered on his slate, as well
as by signs which Janet at least understood perfectly, that he
had told them so and had been so all the time, "and what
difference does it make?" he added. Mr. Sclater told him he
was—or would be, at least, he took care to add, when he came

of age—a rich man as well as a baronet.

"Writch men," wrote Gibbie, "do as they like, and Ise stay."

Mr. Sclater told him it was only poor boys who could do as they pleased, for the law looked after boys like him so that, when it came into their hands, they might be capable of using their money properly. Almost persuaded at length that he had no choice, that he could no longer be his own master until he was twenty-one, he turned and looked at Janet, his eyes brimful of tears. She gave him a little nod. He rose and went out, climbed the crest of Glashgar, and did not return to the cottage till midnight.

In the morning appeared on his countenance signs of unusual resolve. Amid the many thoughts he had had the night before had come the question: What would he do with the money when he had it? First of all, he thought about what he could do for Janet and Robert and every one of their family. And naturally the first thing that occurred to him was to give Donal money to go to college like Fergus Duff. In that he knew he made no mistake. Had not Donal said twenty times he would not mind being a herdboy all his life if only he could go to college first? But then he began to think what a long time it was before he would be twenty-one, and what a number of things might come and go before then. Donal might by that time have a wife and children, and he could not leave them to go to college! Why should not Mr. Sclater manage somehow that Donal should go at once? Some other rich person could lend them the money, and he would pay it, with interest, when he got his. Before he went to bed he got his slate, and wrote the following: "my dear minister, If you will teak Donal too, and lett him go to the kolledg, I will go with you as seens ye like; butt if ye will not, I will runn away."

When Mr. Sclater, who had a bed at the gamekeeper's, appeared the next morning, anxious to conclude the business and get things in motion for their departure, Gibbie handed him the slate the moment he entered the cottage. While the minister read, he stood watching him.

Now Mr. Sclater was a prudent man and always

looked ahead; therefore, apparently he took a long time to read Gibbie's very clear, although unscholarly, communication. Before answering it, he must settle the probability of what Mrs. Sclater would think of the proposal to take two savages into her house together, where also doubtless the presence of this Donal would greatly interfere with the process of making a gentleman of Gibbie. Unable to satisfy himself, he raised his head at length, unconsciously shaking it as he did so. That instant Gibbie was out of the house. Mr. Sclater, perceiving the blunder he had made, hurried after him, but he was already out of sight. Returning in some dismay, he handed the slate to Janet, who with sad, resigned countenance was baking. She rubbed the oatmeal dough from her hands, took the slate and read with a smile.

"You must not take Gibbie for a young colt, Mister Sclater, and think to break him in," she said, after a thoughtful pause, "or you'll have to learn your mistake. There's not enough of himself in him for you to get a grip of him by that handle. He knows what he will have and he'll get it, as sure as it'll be right. As for Donal, Donal's my own, and I shall say nothing. Sit down, sir; you'll not see Gibbie again today."

"Is there no means of getting at him, my good woman?" said Mr. Sclater, miserable at the prospect of a day utterly wasted.

"I could give you sight of him, I daresay, but what better would you be for that? If you had all the lawyers of Edinburgh at your back, you wouldn't touch Gibbie on Glashgar."

"But you could persuade him, I am sure, Mistress Grant. You have only to call him in your own way, and he would come at once."

"What would you have me persuade him of, sir? To anything that's right, Gibbie wants no persuading; and for this that's between you, the laddies are just like brothers, and I have no right to interfere with what the one would do for the other. Things seem to me reasonable enough."

"What sort of lad is this son of yours? The boy seems much attached to him!"

"He's a laddie that's been given over to his books ever since I taught him to read myself," Janet answered. "But he'll be here tonight, I'm thinkin', to see the last of Gibbie, and you can judge for yourself."

It required but a brief examination of Donal that evening to satisfy Mr. Sclater that he was more than prepared for the university.

As to Donal's going to Mr. Sclater's house, Janet soon relieved him.

"No, no, sir," she said; "it would be to learn ways that wouldn't be fitting for a poor lad like him."

"It would be much safer for him," said Mr. Sclater.

"If I couldn't trust my Donal to his own company and the hunger for better, I would begin to doubt who made the world," said his mother; and Donal's face flushed with pleasure at her confidence. "No, he must get a garret room somewhere in the town, and there hold to his books. And you'll let Gibbie go and see him when he has time to spare. There must be many a decent woman that would be pleased to take him in."

Mr. Sclater foresaw no little trouble in his new responsibility but consoled himself that he would have more money at his command and in the end would sit, as it were, at the fountainhead of large wealth. Already, with his wife's property, he was a man of consideration; but he had a great respect for money, and much overrated its value as a means of doing even what he called good.

When Rev. Sclater and Gibbie met Miss Kimble and her "young ladies," the two had just arrived from Glashgar and were on their way from the coach office to the minister's house in Daur Street.

31 Daur Street

Gibbie was in a dream of mingled past and future when his conductor stopped at a large and important-looking house, with a flight of granite steps up to the door. Gibbie had never been inside such a house in his life. He gave a glance around, thought it a big place, and followed Mr. Sclater up the stair with the free, mounting step of the Glashgar shepherd. Forgetful and unconscious, he walked into the drawing room with his bonnet on his head. Mrs. Sclater rose when they entered and he approached her with a smile. She shook hands with him in a doubtful kind of way.

"How do you do, Sir Gilbert?" she said. "Only ladies are allowed to wear their caps in the drawing room, you know," she added, in a tone of courteous half rebuke.

What she meant by the drawing room, Gibbie had not an idea. He looked at her head, and saw no cap; she had nothing on it but a quantity of beautiful black hair. Then suddenly he remembered his bonnet; he knew well enough bonnets had to be taken off in house or cottage. He had never done so because he had never worn a bonnet. But it was with a smile of amusement only that he now took it off.

Gibbie had not been educated in the relative grandeur of things of this world, and he regarded the things he now saw just as things, without the smallest notion of any power in them to confer superiority by being possessed. Man was the one sacred thing to Gibbie. Amidst the mere upholstery of houses and hearts, amidst the common life of the common crowd, he was what he had learned to be among the nobility and in the palace of Glashgar.

Mrs. Sclater was a well-bred woman, superior in the small duties and graces of social life. She did not much care to "play the mother to a bear cub," she said to her friends, with a good-humored laugh. "Just think," she added, "with such a childhood as the poor boy had, what a mass of vulgarity must be lying in that uncultivated brain of his! It is no small mercy, as Mr. Sclater says, that our ears at least are safe. Poor boy!" Her husband was confident that if anybody could, his wife would make a gentleman of Sir Gilbert; and he ought to know, for she had done a good deal of polishing upon him.

Mrs. Sclater's first piece of business the following morning was to take Gibbie to the most fashionable tailor in the city and have him measured for such clothes as she judged suitable for a gentleman's son. Gibbie seemed as much at home with the handsome lady as if she had been his own mother, and walked by her side with a step and air as free as the wind from Glashgar. But the new clothes felt anything but comfortable. Gibbie could endure cold or wet or hunger, he had borne pain upon occasion with complete submission; but the tight armholes of his jacket could hardly be such a decree of Providence as it was rebellion to interfere with.

Mrs. Sclater soon began to find that even in regard to social externals she could never have had a readier pupil. He watched her so closely, and with such an appreciation of the difference in things of the kind between her and her husband, that for a short period he was in danger of falling into habits of movement and manipulation too dainty for a man, a fault nonetheless objectionable in the eyes of his instructee that she, on her own part, carried the feminine a little beyond the limits of the natural. But here also she found him so readily set right that she imagined she was going to do anything with him she pleased and was not a little proud of her conquest and the power she had over the young savage.

She had yet to discover that Gibbie had his own ideas too, that it was the general noble teachableness and affection of his nature that had brought about so speedy an understanding between them in everything wherein he saw she could show him the better way, but that nowhere else would he feel bound or inclined to follow her injunctions. Much and strongly as he was drawn to her by her ladyhood and the sense she gave him of refinement, he had no feeling that she

had authority over him. So neglected in his childhood, so absolutely trusted by the cottagers, who had never found in him
the slightest occasion for the exercise of authority, he had not
an idea of owing obedience to any but the One.

Mr. Sclater was conscientious in his treatment of him.
The very day following that of their arrival, he set to work
with him. He had been a tutor, was a good scholar and a sen-
sible teacher, and he soon discovered how to make the most
of Gibbie's facility in writing.

What Gibbie made of Mr. Sclater's prayers, either in
congregational or family devotion, I am at some loss to imagine. Beside his memories of the direct outpouring of Janet,
they must have seemed to him like the utterances of some
curiously constructed automaton.

Full of the holy simplicities of the cottage, Gibbie had
a good many things to meet which disappointed and perplexed him. He never came quite to understand the Sclaters.

32   Donal in the City

Donal had not accompanied Mr. Sclater and his ward,
as the minister generally styled him, to the city but continued
at the Mains until another herdboy should be found to take
his place. His last night he spent with his parents on Glashgar
and the next morning set out to join the coach. His mother's
parting words to him were, "Now, remember, you're not a
straw dried on its root, but a growing stalk that must look to
its grain."

It was a cold afternoon, the air half mist, half twilight,
when Donal arrived at the coach office. Mr. Sclater stood waiting, welcomed him with dignity rather than kindness, hired
a porter whom he told where to take the chest, said Sir Gilbert

would doubtless call on him the next day, and left him with the porter.

Once in his lodgings, he approached the fire and sat down to warm himself. A few moments and he was startled by a slight noise, as of suppressed laughter. He jumped up. One of the curtains of his bed was strangely agitated. Out leaped Gibbie from behind it and threw his arms about him.

"Eh, creature! You gave me such a fright!" said Donal. "But, losh! They have made a gentleman of you already!" he added, holding him at arm's length and regarding him with wonder and admiration.

A notable change had indeed passed upon Gibbie. Mrs. Sclater had had his hair cut; his shirt was of the whitest of linen, his necktie of the richest of black silk, his clothes were of the newest cut and best possible fit, and his boots perfect. The result was altogether even to her satisfaction. In one thing only was she foiled: she could not get him to wear gloves. He had put on a pair but found them so miserably uncomfortable that, in merry wrath, he pulled them off on the way home and threw them over the Pearl Bridge. Prudently fearful of overstraining her influence, she yielded for the present and let him go without.

Mr. Sclater also had hitherto exercised prudence in his demands upon Gibbie—not that he desired anything less than unlimited authority with him but, knowing it would be hard to enforce, he sought to establish it by a gradual tightening of the rein. Gibbie had never yet refused to do anything he required of him, yet somehow Mr. Sclater could never feel that the lad was exactly obeying him. He thought it over but could not understand it and did not like it, for he was fond of authority. Gibbie in fact did whatever was required of him from his own delight in meeting the wish expressed, not from any sense of duty or of obligation to obedience. The minister had no perception of what the boy was, and had a foreboding suspicion that the time would come when they would differ.

The boys had then a jolly time of it. They made their tea, for which everything was present, and ate as boys know how: Donal enjoying the rarity of the white bread of the city;

Gibbie, who had not tasted oatmeal since he came, devouring "mother's cakes." When they had done, Gibbie, who had learned much since he came, looked about the room till he found a bell rope and pulled it; whereupon the oddest-looking old woman, not a hair altered from what Gibbie remembered her, entered and, with friendly chatter, proceeded to remove the tray.

When the good woman at length left them, they uncorded Donal's chest, took out everything, put the provisions in a cupboard, arranged the few books, and then sat down by the fire for "a read" together.

The hours slipped away; it was night. And still they sat and read. It must have been after ten o'clock when they heard footsteps coming through the adjoining room. The door opened swiftly; in walked Mr. Sclater and closed it behind him. His look was angry. Gibbie had absented himself without permission, had stayed away for hours, had not returned even when the hour of worship arrived; and these were sins against the respectability of his house which no minister could pass by.

When first he entered, Gibbie rose with his usual smile of greeting, and got him a chair. But he waved aside the attention with indignant indifference and went on with his foolish reproof. Gibbie looked the minister straight in the face. His smile of welcome, which had suddenly mingled itself with bewilderment, gradually faded into one of concern, then of pity, and by degrees died away altogether, leaving in its place a look of question.

The boys remained absolutely silent. But before he had begun to draw to a close, across the blinding mists of his fog-breeding wrath, the minister began to be aware of the eyes of the dumb boy fixed upon him. They jarred him; he began to feel awkward, he hesitated, then ceased. For the moment Gibbie, unconsciously, had conquered; without knowing it he was the superior of the two, and Mr. Sclater had begun to learn that he could never exercise authority over him.

"Donal Grant," he said, "you had better go to bed at once and get fit for your work tomorrow. I will go with you to call upon the principal. Get your cap, Sir Gilbert, and come. Mrs. Sclater was already very uneasy about you when I left her."

Gibbie took from his pocket the little ivory tablets Mrs. Sclater had given him, wrote the following words, and handed them to the minister:

"Dear sir, I am going to slepe this night with Donal. The bed is bigg enuf for 2. Good night sir."

For a moment the minister's wrath seethed again, but he thought better of it.

"Then be sure you are at home by lesson time," he said. "Donal can come with you. Good night. Mind you don't keep each other awake."

Donal said, "Good night, sir," and Gibbie gave him a serious and respectful nod. He left the room, and the boys turned and looked at each other. Donal's countenance expressed an indignant sense of wrong, but Gibbie's revealed a more profound concern. He stood motionless, intent on the receding steps of the minister. The moment the sound of them ceased, he darted soundless after him to follow him home. Donal started to his feet and went as well. On and on went Mr. Sclater, and on and on went Gibbie, careful constantly not to be seen by him; and on and on went Donal careful to be seen of neither. At last the minister went up the steps of a handsome house, took a key from his pocket, and opened the door.

Gibbie turned and was quickly away and Donal was after him like a hound. But Gibbie turned a corner and was gone from his sight. Donal turned too, but Gibbie was already out of sight. Concluding that Gibbie had turned another corner ahead of him, he ran on and on, in the vanishing hope of catching sight of him; but he was soon satisfied he had lost him, and himself as well, for he had not the smallest idea how to return, even as far as the minister's house. It rendered the matter considerably worse that, having never heard the name of the street where he lodged but once—when the minister gave direction to the porter—he had utterly forgotten it.

Presently he found himself on the shore of the river.

He was saying to himself whatever was he to do all night long, when round a corner a little way off came a woman. It was no use asking counsel of her, however, or anyone, he thought, so long as he did not know even the name of the street he wanted. The woman drew near. She was rather tall, erect in the back but bowed in the shoulders, with fierce black eyes which were all that he could see of her face, for she had a little tartan shawl over her head. But those eyes were enough. They were just passing each other under a lamp when she looked hard at him and stopped.

"Man," she said, "I have set eye upon your face before!"

"If that be the case," answered Donal, "you've set your eye upon it again."

"Where do you come from?" she asked.

"That's what I would like to ask myself," he replied. "But, woman," he went on, "I fancy I have set an eye upon your eye before—but I can't well say your face. Where do you come from?"

"Know you a place they call Daurside?" she rejoined.

"Daurside's a long place," answered Donal; "and this must be about the tail end of it, I'm thinkin'."

"You're not far wrong there," she returned. "You have a quick tongue in your head for a lad from Daurside."

"I never heard tongues were cut any shorter there," said Donal; "but I didn't mean any offense."

"There's none taken," answered the woman. "Know ye a place they call the Mains of Glashruach?"

As she spoke she let go her shawl and it opened from her face like two curtains.

"Lord! it's the witch-wife!" cried Donal, retreating a pace in his astonishment.

The woman burst into a great laugh—a hard, unmusical, but not unmirthful laugh.

"Ay!" she said. "Was that how the folk would have it about me?"

"It wasn't much wonder, after you waded through water yards deep, and then went down the flood on a raft."

181

"Well, it was the maddest thing!" she returned, with another laugh which stopped abruptly. "I wouldn't do the like of that again to save my life. But the Almighty carried me through. And how's wee Sir Gibbie?—but we're just at the door of my small room—come in . . . I don't know your name. Come quiet up the stairs and tell me about it."

"Well, I would like to rest for a bit, for I have lost myself, and I am tired," answered Donal. "I just left the Mains yesterday."

"Come in and welcome; and when you're rested, and I'm rid of my basket, I'll send you on your way home."

Donal was too tired and too glad to be once more in the company of a human being to pursue further explanation at present. He followed her, as quietly as he could, up the dark stair. When she struck a light, he saw a little garret room—better than decently furnished, it seemed to the youth from the hills, though his mother would have thought it far from tidy. The moment the woman got a candle lighted, she seated herself and began to relate her adventures in quest of Gibbie. Someday she would tell him, she said, the whole story of her voyage on the raft, which would make him laugh. Then she told him a great deal about Gibbie and his father.

"And now," remarked Donal, "he'll be thinkin' about it all over again as he runs about the town this very minute lookin' for me!"

"Don't trouble yourself about him," said the woman. "He knows the town as well as any of the rats knows the drains. But where do you put up?" she added, "It's time decent folks were going to their beds."

Donal explained that he knew neither the name of the street nor of the people where he was lodging.

"Tell me something about the house or the folk or what they're like, and it may be that I'll know them," she said.

But scarcely had he begun his description of the house when she cried, "Hoot, man! It's at Lucky Murkinson's you are, in the Widdiehill. Come with me, and I'll take you home in a jiffy."

So saying, she rose, took the candle, showed him down the stair, and he followed.

It was past midnight and the moon was down, but the streetlamps were not yet extinguished and they walked along without anything to interrupt their conversation.

Before they reached the Widdiehill, Donal, with the open heart of the poet, was full of friendliness to her and rejoiced in the mischance that had led him to make her acquaintance.

"You know, of course," he happened to say, "that Gibbie's with Master Sclater?"

"Well enough," she answered. "I have seen him too; but he's grown into a grand gentleman now, and I wouldn't like to be affronted laying claim to the acquaintance—welcome as he once was to my house!"

"You little know Gibbie," he said, "if you think that way of him! Go to the minister's door and ask for him! He'll be down the stair like a shot.—But, indeed, maybe he's come back and is in my room now! Will you come up the stair and see?"

"No, I won't do that," said Mistress Croale.

She pointed out the door to him but herself stood on the other side of the way till she saw it opened by Mistress Murkinson in her nightcap and heard her make jubilee over his return.

Gibbie had come home and gone out again to look for him, she said.

"Well," remarked Donal, "there would be small good in my going to look for him. It would be but the sheep going to look for the shepherd."

"You're right there," said his landlady. "A lost child should sit down and sit still."

"Well, you go to your bed, mem," returned Donal. "Let me see how your door works, and I'll let him in when he comes."

Gibbie came within an hour and all was well. They made their communication, of which Donal's was far the more interesting, had their laugh over the affair, and went to bed.

33   The Sinner

The minister's anger went on smoldering all night, and in the morning he rose with his temper very feverish. During breakfast he was gloomy but would confess to no inward annoyance. What added to his unrest was that although he felt insulted, he did not know what precisely the nature of the insult was.

Gibbie made his appearance at ten o'clock, and went straight to the study, where at the hour the minister was always waiting him. He entered with a smile. The minister said, "Good morning," but gruffly, and without raising his eyes. Gibbie seated himself in his usual place, arranged his book and slate and was ready to commence when the minister, having now summoned resolution, lifted his head, fixed his eyes on him and said sternly, "Sir Gilbert, what was your meaning in following me after refusing to accompany me?"

Gibbie's face flushed. He had no idea he'd been seen. But he took his slate, found his pencil, wrote, and handed the slate to the minister. There stood these words: "I thout you was drunk."

His eyes flaming, his cheeks white with passion, Mr. Sclater started to his feet, and with the flat of the slate came down a great blow on the top of Gibbie's head. Happily, the latter was the harder of the two, and the former broke, flying mostly out of the frame. It took Gibbie terribly by surprise. Half-stunned, he started to his feet, and for one moment the wild beast which was in him, as it is in everybody, rushed to the front of its cage. It would have gone ill then with the minister had not as sudden a change followed; the flame of Gibbie's wrath went out, and a smile of compassion overspread his countenance. Bur Mr. Sclater saw no compassionate brother before him, for when Gibbie rose he drew back to better his position. When he stepped back, he stumbled and fell.

Gibbie darted forward and began to help him up like a child.

Having regained his legs, the minister stood for a moment, confused and half-blinded. The first thing he saw was a drop of blood stealing down Gibbie's forehead. He was shocked at what he had done. In truth he had been frightfully provoked, but it was not for a clergyman so to avenge an insult, and as mere chastisement it was brutal. What would Mrs. Sclater say to it? The rascal was sure to make his complaint to her!

And there too was Gibbie's friend, the herdlad, in the drawing room with her!

"Go wash your face," he said, "and come back again directly."

Gibbie put his hand to his face and, feeling something wet, looked, and burst into a merry laugh.

"I am sorry I have hurt you," said the minister, not a little relieved at the sound; "but how dare you write such a— such an insolence? A clergyman never gets drunk."

Gibbie picked up the frame which the minister had dropped in his fall. A piece of the slate was still sticking in one side, and he wrote upon it: "I will kno better the next time. I thout it was alwais whiskey that made people like that. I beg your pardon, sir."

He handed him the fragment, ran to his own room, returned presently looking all right. When Mr. Sclater would have attended to his wound, he would not let him even look at it, laughing at the idea. Still further relieved to find there was nothing to attract observation to the injury, and yet more ashamed of himself, the minister made haste to the refuge of their work.

From that time, after luncheon, which followed immediately upon lessons, Gibbie went and came as he pleased. Mrs. Sclater begged he would never be out after ten o'clock without having let them know that he meant to stay out all night with his friend. Not once did he neglect this request, and they soon came to have perfect confidence not only in any individual promise he might make, but in his general punc-

GEORGE MACDONALD

tuality. Mrs. Sclater never came to know anything of his wounded head.

Mr. Sclater had not been long teaching Gibbie before he began to desire to make a scholar of him. Partly from being compelled to spend some labor at it, the boy was gradually developing an unusual facility in written expression. All he cared about was to say what he meant, and avoid saying something else; to know when he had not said what he meant, and to set the words right.

His guardian lost no time in having his organs of speech examined by a surgeon in high repute, a professor of the university; but Dr. Skinner's opinion put an end to question and hope together. Gibbie was not in the least disappointed. He had got on very well as yet without speech. It was not like sight or hearing. The only voice he could not hear was his own, and that was just the one he had neither occasion nor desire to hear. As to his friends, those who had known him the longest minded his dumbness the least. But the moment the defect was understood to be irreparable, Mrs. Sclater very wisely proceeded to learn finger speech; and as she learned it, she taught it to Gibbie.

As to his manners, which had been and continued to be her chief care, she never could get them to take on the case-hardening needful for what she counted the final polish. They always retained a certain simplicity which she called child-ishness. It came in fact of childlikeness, but the lady was not child enough to distinguish the difference. In after years, however, Gibbie's manner was almost universally felt to be charming.

One night on their way home from an evening party, the minister and his wife had a small difference, probably about something of as little real consequence to them as the knowledge of it is to us; but by the time they reached home, they had gotten to the very summit of politeness with each other. Gibbie was in the drawing room, as it happened, waiting their return. At the first sound of their voices, he knew before a syllable reached him that something was wrong. When they entered, they were too much engrossed in differ-

186

ence to heed his presence and went on disputing—with the utmost external propriety but with a sense of injury in every tone. A discreet, socially wise boy would have left the room, but how could Gibbie abandon his friends? He ran to the side table. With a vague presentiment of what was coming, Mrs. Sclater, feeling rather than seeing him move across the room like a shadow, sat in dread expectation. And presently her fear arrived, in the shape of a large New Testament and a face of keen discomfort. He held out the book to her, pointing with a finger to the words: "Have salt in yourselves, and have peace one with another." What Gibbie made of salt, I do not know; but the rest of the sentence he understood.

The lady's cheeks had been red before, but now they were redder. She rose, cast an angry look at the dumb prophet, a look which seemed to say, "How dare you suggest such a thing?" and left the room.

"What have you got there?" asked the minister, turning sharply upon him. Gibbie showed him the passage.

"What have you got to do with it?" he retorted, throwing the book on the table. "Go to bed."

———

Mistress Croale grew more and more desirous of looking upon the object of her recent windfall and summoned resolution at last. She went to the market a little better dressed than usual and when business there was over and she had shut up her little box of a shop, she walked to Daur Street to the minister's house.

They were in the middle of their soup when the maid informed her master that a woman was at the door wanting to see Sir Gilbert.

Gibbie looked up, put down his spoon, and was rising to go when the minister, laying a hand on his arm, pressed him gently back to his chair, and Gibbie yielded, waiting.

"What sort of a woman?" he asked the girl.

"A decent-looking, working-like body," she answered. "I couldn't see her very well, it's so foggy tonight around the door."

"Tell her we're at dinner; she may call again in an hour or tomorrow morning.—I wonder who she is," he added, turning, he thought, to Gibbie.

But Gibbie was gone. He had passed behind his chair, and all Mr. Sclater saw of him was his back as he followed the girl from the room. In his eagerness he left the door open, and they saw him dart to the visitor, shake hands with her in evident delight, and begin pulling her toward the room.

Now Mistress Croale, though nowise inclined to quail before the minister, would not willingly have intruded herself upon him, especially while he sat at dinner with his rather formidable lady. But she fancied that Gibbie was taking her where they might have a quiet talk together, and remained thus mistaken until she stood on the threshold. Looking up, she started, stopped, made a bow to the minister and another to the minister's lady, and stood doubtful, if not a little abashed.

"Oh . . . it's you, Mistress Croale," said Mr. Sclater, rising, "—I will speak to you in the hall."

Mrs. Croale's face flushed and she drew back a step. But Gibbie still held her and, with a look to Mr. Sclater that should have sent straight to his heart the fact that she was dear to his soul, kept drawing her into the room; he wanted her to take his chair at the table. How friendly the warm air felt! How consoling the crimson walls with the soft flicker of the great fire upon them! How delicious the odor of the cockie-leekie! She could give up whiskey a good deal more easily, she thought, if she had the comforts of a minister to fall back upon! And this was the same minister who had once told her that her soul was as precious to him as that of any other in his parish—and then driven her from respectable Jink Lane to the disreputable Daurfoot! It all passed through her mind in a flash, while yet Gibbie pulled and she resisted.

"Gilbert, come here," called Mrs. Sclater.

He went to her side.

"Really, Gilbert, you must not," she said, rather loud for a whisper. "If you are to be a gentleman, and an inmate of my house, you must behave like other people. I cannot have a woman like that sitting at my table. Do you know what sort of a person she is?"

Gibbie's face shone up. He raised his hands. He was already able to talk a little.

"Is she a sinner?" he asked on his fingers.

Mrs. Sclater nodded.

Gibbie wheeled round and sprang back to the hall, whither the minister had ejected Mistress Croale and was now talking to her with an air of confidential condescension, willing to wipe out any feeling of injury she might perhaps be inclined to cherish at not being made more welcome. To the minister's consternation, Gibbie threw his arms round her neck and gave her a great hug.

"Sir Gilbert!" he exclaimed, the more angry that he knew Gibbie was in the right, "leave Mistress Croale alone, and go back to your dinner immediately ... Jane, open the door."

Jane opened the door, Gibbie let her go, and Mrs. Croale went. But on the threshold she turned to the minister: "Well, sir," she said, with a certain sad injury not unmingled with dignity, "you have stepped over my doorstep many times, and with sorer words in your mouth than I used to pay you back. And I never told you to go. So first you turn me out of my own house and now you turn me out of yours; and what's left for you but to turn me out of the house of the Lord? And, indeed, sir, you need never wonder if the likes of me doesn't care about coming to hear the preached gospel—we would fain see a practiced one!"

"You shall have a plate of soup, and welcome, Mistress Croale!" said the minister, "—Jane, take Mistress Croale to the kitchen with you, and—"

"The devil's tail in your soup!" cried Mistress Croale, drawing herself up suddenly. "When did I turn into a beggar? Was it your soup or your grace I sought for, sir? The Lord judge between me and you! There's first that will be last, and last that will be first. But the one's not me, and the other's not you, sir."

With this she turned and walked down the steps, holding her head high.

"Really, Sir Gilbert," said the minister, going back into the dining room—but no Gibbie was there! Nobody but his wife, sitting in solitary discomposure at the head of the dinner table. The same instant, he heard a clatter of feet down the steps and turned quickly into the hall again, where Jane was in the act of shutting the door.

"Sir Gilbert's run out after the woman, sir!" she said.

"Hoot!" grunted the minister, greatly displeased, and went back to his wife.

"Take Sir Gilbert's plate away," said Mrs. Sclater to the servant.

"That's his New Testament again!" she went on, when the girl had left the room.

"My dear! my dear! take care," said her husband. He had not much notion of obedience to God, but he had some idea of respect to religion.

"Really, Mr. Sclater," his wife continued, "I had no idea what I was undertaking. But you gave me no choice. The creature is incorrigible. But of course he must prefer the society of women like that. They are the sort he was accustomed to when he received his first impressions, and how could it be otherwise? You knew how he had been brought up, and what you had to expect!"

"Brought up!" cried the minister. "You should have seen him about the streets!"

Nothing further was said until the second course was on the table. Then the lady spoke again.

"You really must teach him the absurdity of attempting to fit every point of his behavior to—to—words which were of course quite suitable to the time when they were spoken, but which it is impossible to take literally nowadays. Why! You saw him throw his arms around the horrid creature's neck!—Well, he had just asked me if she was a sinner. I made no doubt she was. With the word, off goes my gentleman to embrace her!"

Here they laughed together.

Dinner over, they went to a missionary meeting, where the one stood and made a speech and the other sat and listened, while Gibbie was having tea with Mistress Croale.

From that day Gibbie's mind was much exercised as to what he could do for Mistress Croale, and now first he began to wish he had his money. As fast as he learned the finger alphabet, he had taught it to Donal and, as already they had a good many symbols in use between them—so many indeed that Donal would often instead of speaking make use of signs—they had now the means of communication almost as free as if they had had between them two tongues instead of one. It was easy therefore for Gibbie to impart to Donal his anxiety concerning her, and his strong desire to help her. And doing so, he lamented in a gentle way his present inability. This communication Donal judged it wise to impart in his turn to Mistress Croale.

"You see, mem," he said in conclusion, "he's some way or another gotten it into his head that you're just a bit over free with the bottle. I don't know. You'll be the best judge of that yourself!"

Mistress Croale was silent for a whole minute. From the moment when Gibbie forsook his dinner to go with her, the woman's heart had begun to grow to the boy, and her old memories fed the new crop of affection.

"Well," she replied at length, "—I may not be so ill as he thinks me, for he had his poor father before his eyes; but the child's mostly in the right, and we must look to it and see what can be done. For eh! I would be loath to disappoint the bonnie lad! My bonnie wee Sir Gibbie—I can't help calling him wee Sir Gibbie. All the town called him that, although he'll be a big man someday. And as for his title, I was always one to give honor where honor is due, and never once, as well as I knew him, did I call his honest father anything but Sir George, even though he was just a hard-working cobbler, and on Saturdays was pleased to have a wash in my bedroom and put on a clean shirt of my dead husband's—rest his soul!— and spend the evening in my place."

34   The Girls

It had come to be the custom that Gibbie should go to Donal's every Friday afternoon about four o'clock and remain with him till the same time on Saturday, which was a holiday with both. One Friday, just after he was gone, the temptation seized Mrs. Sclater to follow him and pay the lads an unexpected visit to see what they were about.

It was a bright, cold afternoon; and in fur tippet and muff, amidst the snow that lay everywhere, she set out. As she was passing a certain baker's shop through a neighboring street approaching the Widdiehill, something made her stop and look in through the glass. There she saw Gibbie seated on the counter, legs dangling, eating a penny loaf. A very pretty girl, with whose company Gibbie was evidently much pleased, stood behind the counter. At the moment she was laughing merrily and talking gaily to Gibbie. Clearly they were on the best of terms and the boy's bright countenance, laughter and eager motions were making full response to the girl's words.

Mrs. Sclater, gazing through the glass, found a large justification for displeasure. She opened the door sharply and stepped in. Gibbie jumped from his seat on the counter and, with a smile of playful roguery, offered it to her. A vivid blush overspread Mysie's fair countenance.

"I thought you had gone to see Donal," said Mrs. Sclater in the tone of one deceived, and took no notice of the girl.

Gibbie gave her to understand that Donal would arrive presently, and they were then going to the pier that Donal might learn what the sea was like in a nor'-easter.

"But why did you make your appointment here?" asked the lady.

"Because Mysie and I are old friends," answered the boy on his fingers.

Then first Mrs. Sclater turned to the girl. Having gotten over her first indignation, she spoke gently and with a frankness natural to her.

"Sir Gilbert tells me you are old friends," she said.

Thereupon Mysie told her the story of the earring, which had introduced their present conversation, and added several other little recollections, in one of which she was drawn into a description, half pathetic, half humorous, of the forlorn appearance of wee Gibbie as he ran about in his truncated trousers. Mrs. Sclater was more annoyed, however, than interested, for in view of the young baronet's future she would have had all such things forgotten.

Hardly anybody was ever in less danger of falling in love than Gibbies. And the thing would not have been worth recording but for the new direction it caused Mrs. Sclater's thoughts; measures, she judged, must be taken.

Recalling what her husband had told her of the odd meeting between the boy and a young lady at Miss Kimble's school, some relation, she wondered whether she might turn the acquaintance to account. There was no reason why she should not ask Miss Kimble to come and spend the evening, and bring two or three of the elder girls with her. A little familiarity with the looks, manners, and dress of refined girls of his own age would be the best antidote to his taste for low society, from that of baker's daughters downward.

Mr. Galbraith had not taken Miss Kimble into his confidence with respect to his reasons for so hurriedly placing his daughter under her care. Hence, when Mrs. Sclater's invitation arrived, the schoolmistress was aware of no reason why Miss Galbraith should not be one of the girls to go with her, especially as there was her cousin, Sir Gilbert, whom she herself would like to meet again in the hope of removing the bad impression which she feared she must have made upon him.

One day, then, at luncheon, Mrs. Sclater told Gibbie that some ladies were coming to tea, and they were going to have supper instead of dinner. He must put on his best clothes, she said. He did as she desired, was duly inspected, approved on the whole, and finished off by a few deft fingers at his necktie and a gentle push or two against his hair thatch, and was seated in the drawing room with Mrs. Sclater when the ladies arrived. Ginevra and he shook hands, she with the sweetest of rose flushes, he with the radiance of delighted surprise. But a moment after, when Mrs. Sclater and her guests had seated themselves, Gibbie, their only gentleman, for Mr. Sclater had not yet made his appearance, vanished from the room. Tea was not brought until some time after when Mr. Sclater came home, and then Mrs. Sclater sent Jane to find Sir Gilbert; but she returned to say he was not in the house. The lady's heart sank; her project had miscarried!

The case was, however, very much otherwise. The moment Gibbie ended his greetings, he had darted off to tell Donal; it was not his custom to enjoy anything shareable alone.

The news that Ginevra was at that moment seated in Mrs. Sclater's house raised such a commotion in Donal's atmosphere that his heart beat like the trample of a trotting horse. He never thought of inquiring whether Gibbie had been commissioned by Mrs. Sclater to invite him, or reflected that his studies were not half over for the night. Gibbie simply told him by two signs that he must put on his Sunday clothes.

Donal's preparations took a long time, and before they reached the house, tea was over and gone. They had had some music; and Mrs. Sclater was now talking kindly to two of the schoolgirls who, seated erect on the sofa, were looking upon her elegance with awe and envy. Ginevra was looking at the pictures of an annual. Mr. Sclater was making Miss Kimble agreeable to herself.

The door opened. Donal entered and walked across the room to Ginevra. Mrs. Sclater rose; Mr. Sclater threw himself back and stared—the latter astounded at the presumption of the youths, the former uneasy at the possible results of their ignorance. To the astonishment of the company, Ginevra rose, respect and modesty in every feature, as the youth, clownish rather than awkward, approached her. Almost timidly she held out her hand to him. He took it in his horny palm, shook it hither and thither sideways until Ginevra took charge of it herself again. Gibbie danced about behind him, all but standing on one leg but for Mrs. Sclater's sake restraining himself. Ginevra sat down and Donal, feeling very clumsy, looked about for a chair; then first espying Mrs. Sclater, he went up to her with the same clamping stride, but without embarrassment, and spoke, holding out his hand.

"How are you tonight, mem! I didn't see your pretty face when I came in. A grand house, like this—and I'm sure, mem, it couldn't be too grand for yourself, but it's perplexin' to plain folk like me that's used to more room, and less in it."

Donal was thinking of the meadow on the Lorrie bank.

"You will soon get accustomed to our town ways, Mr. Grant. I am glad to see you have friends here," she added.

"Only one, mem. Gibbie and me—"

"Excuse me, Mr. Grant, but would you oblige me—of course with me it is of no consequence, but just for habit's sake—would you oblige me by calling Gilbert by his own name, Sir Gilbert, please. I wish him to get used to it."

"As you will, mem. Well, as I was saying, Sir Gibbie—Sir Gilbert, that is, mem—an' myself, we have known Miss Galbraith for a long time, being of the laird's own folk, as I may say."

"Will you take a seat beside her, then," said Mrs. Sclater and, rising, placed a chair for him near Ginevra, wondering how any Scotch laird, the father of such a little lady as she, could have allowed her such an acquaintance.

To most of the company Donal must have looked very queer. Gibbie, indeed, was the only one who saw the real Donal. To the school ladies, mistress and pupils, he was simply a clodhopper and from their report became a treasure of poverty-stricken amusement to the school. Often did Ginevra's cheek burn with indignation at the small insolences of her fellow pupils.

"I thank you, mem," said Donal, as he took the chair;

and fell into some rather long, and to some unintelligible, Scotch storytelling.

Gibbie, behind Donal's chair, was delighted, but the rest of the company, understanding his words yet not comprehending a single sentence he uttered, began to wonder whether he was out of his mind and were perplexed to see Ginevra listening with such respect.

Ginevra said little in reply. She had not much to say. In her world the streams were still, not vocal. But Donal meant to hold a little communication with her which none of them, except indeed Gibbie—he did not mind Gibbie—should understand.

"Well, well, Donal!" broke in the pompous voice of Mr. Sclater, who, unknown to the poet, had been standing behind him almost the whole time, "you have given the ladies quite enough of your romancing. That sort of thing may do very well around the fire in the farm kitchen, but it's not the sort of thing for a drawing room. Besides, the ladies don't understand your word of mouth; they don't understand such broad Scotch. Come with me, and I'll show you something."

He thought Donal was boring his guests, and at the same time was preventing Gibbie from having the pleasure in their society for which they had been invited.

Donal rose, replying, "Do you think so, sir? Didn't you understand me, mem?" he added, turning to Ginevra.

"Every word, Donal," she answered.

Donal followed his host, contented.

Gibbie took Donal's place and began to teach Ginevra the finger alphabet. The other girls found him far more amusing than Donal. And he had such a romantic history! And was a baronet!

In a few minutes Ginevra knew the letters, and presently she and Gibbie were having a little continuous talk together, a thing they had never had before. It was so slow, however, as to be rather tiring. It was mainly about Donal. But Mrs. Sclater opened the piano and made a diversion. She played something brilliant and then sang an Italian song. Then she asked Miss Kimble to play something, who declined but said that Miss Galbraith should sing—"That little Scotch song you sing now and then, my dear," she added.

Ginevra rose timidly but without hesitation and, going to the piano, sang a simple old Scottish air for which had been written five verses. Before she ended, the minister, the late herdboy and the baronet were grouped crescent-wise behind the music stool.

Three of them knew that the verses were Donal's. If the poet went home feeling more like a fellow in a blue coat and fustian trousers or a winged genius of the tomb, I leave my reader to judge. Anyhow, he felt he had had enough for one evening and was able to encounter his work again. Perhaps also, when supper was announced, he reflected that his reception had hardly been such as to justify him in partaking of their food, and that his mother's hospitality to Mr. Sclater had not been in expectation of return. As they went down the stair, he came last and alone behind the two whispering schoolgirls; and when they passed on into the dining room, he left the house and ran home to the furniture shop and his books.

35 Growing

In obedience to the suggestion of his wife, Mr. Sclater did what he could to show Sir Gilbert how mistaken he was in imagining he could fit his actions to the words of our Lord.

But in talking thus to Gibbie, the minister but rippled the air. He was too familiar with truth. The unseen Lord and His reported words were to Gibbie realities. He had never *resolved* to keep the words of the Lord; he just kept them. The effect of it all upon Gibbie was to send him to his room to his prayers, more eager than ever to keep the commandments of Him who had said, "If ye love me...." Comforted then and strengthened, he came down to go to Donal.

It will be plain from what I have told that Donal's imagination was full of Ginevra, and his was not an economy whose imagination could enjoy itself without calling the heart to share. Gibbie and he seldom talked about Ginevra. She was generally understood between them.

Mrs. Sclater showed herself sincere, after her kind, to Donal as well as to Gibbie. She told Gibbie that he must talk to Donal about his dress and his speech. That he was a lad of no common gifts was plain, she said, but were he ever so "talented" he could do little in the world, certainly would never raise himself, so long as he dressed and spoke ridiculously. The wisest and best of men would be utterly disregarded, she said, if he did not look and speak like other people. Gibbie thought with himself this could hardly hold, for there was John the Baptist; he answered her, however, that Donal could speak very good English if he chose. As to his dress, Donal was poor, Gibbie said, and could not give up wearing any clothes so long as there was any wear in them. "If you had seen me once!" he added, with a merry laugh to finish for his fingers.

Mrs. Sclater spoke to her husband, who said to Gibbie that if he chose to provide Donal with suitable garments, he would advance him the money.

Gibbie would thereupon have dragged Donal at once to the tailor; but Donal was obstinate. "No, no," he said; "I'll wear the clothes out. You can tell Mrs. Sclater that by the time I have anything to say to the world, it won't be my clothes that will make folks listen; and if she considers the ones that I have now too much a disgrace for her, she must just not invite me, and I'll not come; for I can't presently help them."

"What will you do when you are a minister?" asked Gibbie on his fingers.

"Me a minister?" echoed Donal. "Me a minister!" he repeated. "Losh, man! If I can save my own soul, it will be all I'm fit for. No, no; if I can be a schoolmaster and help children to be good, as my mother taught me, and have some time to read, and a few shillings to buy books, I'll be a happy man!"

"But wouldn't you like to have a wife, Donal, and children, like your father and mother?" spelled Gibbie.

"No, no; no wife for me, Gibbie!" answered the philosopher. "Who would have a poor schoolmaster or a shepherd?—except it was maybe some lass like my sister Nicie that wouldn't know Euclid from her stockings or Burns from a milldam."

When they met on Friday evening, they would rove the streets, Gibbie taking Donal to the places he knew so well in his childhood and enjoying it the more that he could now tell him so much better what he remembered. The only place he did not take him to was Jink Lane to the house that had been Mistress Croale's. He did take him to the court in the Widdiehill and showed him the Auld Hoose o' Galbraith and the place under the stair where his father had worked. The shed was now gone; the neighbors had by degrees carried it away for firewood. The house was occupied still as then by a number of poor people, and the door was never locked, day or night, anymore than when Gibbie used to bring his father home. He took Donal to the garret where they had slept—one could hardly say lived—and where his father had died. The door stood open and the place was just as they had left it.

"If I was you, Sir Gilbert," said Donal, who now and then remembered Mrs. Sclater's request to use Gibbie's title, "I would have Mr. Sclater keep a sharp lookout for the first chance of buyin' back this house. It would be a great pity if it should get much worse before you get it. Eh! Such tales as this house could tell!"

"How am I to do that, Donal? Mr. Sclater would not mind me. The money's not mine yet, you know," said Gibbie.

"The money is yours, Gibbie," answered Donal; "it's yours just as the kingdom of heaven is yours. It's only that you can't just lay your hands upon it yet. The sooner you let Mr. Sclater know that you know what you're about, the better. And, believe me, when he comes to understand that you want that house, he'll not be a day going to somebody or another about it."

Donal was right, for within a month the house was

bought and certain necessary repairs commenced.

Mrs. Sclater continued to invite young ladies to the house for Gibbie's sake, and when she gave a party, she took care there should be young people at it; but Gibbie, although kind and polite to all, did not much enjoy these gatherings. The little pocket money Mr. Sclater allowed him was chiefly spent at the shop of a certain secondhand bookseller, nearly opposite Donal's room. These volumes were considered by Gibbie to be Donal's, and by Donal, Gibbie's. Every Saturday, as before, Gibbie went to see his father and mother. Janet kept fresh and lively, although age told on her, she said, more rapidly since Gibbie went away.

Six weeks of every summer between Donal's sessions, while the minister and his wife took their holiday, Gibbie spent with Robert and Janet. It was a blessed time for them all. He led then just the life of the former days with Robert and Oscar and the sheep, and Janet and her cow and the New Testament—only he had a good many more things to think about now, and more ways of thinking about them. With his own hands he built a little porch to the cottage door, with close sides and a second door to keep the wind out. Donal and he had carried up the timber and the mortar. But although he tried hard to make Janet say what more he could do for her, he could not bring her to reveal any desire that belonged to this world—except, indeed, for two or three trifles for her husband's warmth and convenience.

They almost always called him Sir Gibbie, and he never objected or seemed either annoyed or amused at it. He took it just as the name that was his, the same way as his hair or his hands were his; he had been called wee Sir Gibbie for so long.

The minister kept Gibbie hard at work, and by the time Donal's last winter came, Gibbie was ready for college also. Mr. Sclater consented to Gibbie's lodging with Donal. He would have insisted on them taking rooms in some part of the town more suitable to the young baronet's position, but by this time Gibbie seldom found difficulty in having his way with his guardian.

One day early in the session, as the youths were approaching the gate of Miss Kimble's school, a thin, careworn man in shabby clothes came out and walked along, eventually meeting them. It was the laird. They lifted their caps, but in return he only stared or, rather, tried to stare, for his eyes seemed able to fix themselves on nothing. He was now at length a thoroughly ruined man and had come to the city to end his days in a cottage he had purchased for his daughter. Mr. Sclater, who was unwearily on the watch over the material interests of his ward, had already, through his lawyer and without permitting his name to appear, purchased the whole of the Glashruach property. For the present, however, he kept Sir Gilbert in ignorance of the fact.

36   Fergus Duff

In every way the Laird had sunk to the bottom of manhood. It was very sad to Ginevra to see him thus shrunk and withered. Nothing interested him; he never looked at the paper, never cared to hear a word of news. It was a comfort that now in his misery she was able, if not to forget those painful thoughts about him, at least to dismiss them in the hope that as already such a change had passed upon him, further and better change might follow.

She was still the same small brown bird as of old. She had the sweetest, rarest smile—not frequent and flashing like Gibbie's, but stealing up from below, like the shadowy reflection of a greater light. Her atmosphere was an embodied stillness; she made a quiet wherever she entered. She was not beautiful, but she was lovely; and her presence at once made a place such as one would desire to be in. The most pleasant of her thoughts were of necessity those with which the two youths were associated. How dreary but for them would the retrospect of her life have been! Several times every winter they had met at the minister's, and every summer she had again and again seen Gibbie with Mrs. Sclater; once or twice she had had a walk with them, and every time Gibbie had something of Donal's to give her.

Twice Gibbie had gone to see her at the school, but the second time she asked him not to come again as Miss Kimble did not like it. He gave a big stare of wonder; but followed the stare with a swift smile, for he saw she was troubled; he asked no questions, waiting for the understanding of all things. But now, when or where was she ever to see them? Gibbie was no longer at the minister's and she dared not ask Donal to call; her father would be indignant. And for her father's sake she would not ask Gibbie; it might give him pain. Also, the thought that he would of a certainty behave so differently to him now that he was well-dressed and mannered like a gentleman was almost unendurable to her.

Mr. and Mrs. Sclater had called upon Ginevra and her father the moment they were settled in the cottage; but Mr. Galbraith would see nobody. When the gate bell rang, he always looked out and, if a visitor appeared, withdrew to his bedroom.

One brilliant Saturday morning, the second in the session, the ground was hard with an early frost; Mrs. Sclater rang the said bell. Mr. Galbraith, peeping from the window, saw a lady's bonnet. She walked in, followed by Gibbie, and asked Ginevra to go with them for a walk. She went and asked her father.

"Why do you ask me?" returned her father. "My wishes are nothing to anyone now; to you they never were anything."

"I will stay at home if you wish, Papa—with pleasure," she replied, as cheerfully as she could after such a reproach.

"By no means. If you do I shall go and dine at the Red Hart," he answered.

It made her miserable for a while, of course, but she had gotten so used to his way of breaking a gift as he handed it that she answered only with a sigh. In haste she put on her little brown-ribboned bonnet, took the moth-eaten muff that had been her mother's, and joined Mrs. Sclater and Gibbie, beaming with troubled pleasure. Life in her was strong, and their society soon enabled her to forget not her father's sadness but his treatment of her.

At the end of the street, they found Donal waiting them—without greatcoat or muffler, the picture of such health as suffices to its own warmth. Away they walked together westward, then turned southward. Mrs. Sclater and Gibbie led, and Ginevra followed with Donal. And they had not walked far before something of the delight of old times on Glashruach began to revive in the bosom of the sober girl. In vain she reminded herself that her father sat miserable at home, but the sun and the bright air like wine in her veins were too much for her. Donal had soon made her cheerful, and now and then she answered his talk with even a little flash of merriment.

They crossed the bridge, hung high over the Dour, by which on that black morning Gibbie had fled. And there, for the first time, with his three friends about him, he told on his fingers the dire deed of the night and heard from Mrs. Sclater that the murderers had been hanged. Ginevra grew white and faint as she read his fingers and gestures, but it was more at the thought of what the child had come through than from the horror of the narrative. They then turned eastward to the sea and came to the top of the rock border of the coast, with its cliffs rent into gullies—eerie places to look down into, ending in caverns into which the waves rushed with bellow and boom. Although so nigh the city, this was always a solitary place; yet rounding a rock they came upon a young man, who hurried a book into his pocket and would have gone by the other side; but, perceiving himself recognized, he came to meet them, and saluted Mrs. Sclater, who presented him to Ginevra as Rev. Mr. Duff.

"I have not had the pleasure of seeing you since you were quite a little girl, Miss Galbraith," said Fergus.

Ginevra said coldly she did not remember him. The

youths greeted him in careless student fashion. They had met now and then about the college; and little, meaningless talk followed.

He was to preach the next day—and for several Sundays following—at a certain large church in the city, at the time without a minister. And when they came upon him he was studying his sermon—not the truths of the Book but his manuscript, studying it in the sense in which actors use the word, learning it by heart.

Fergus never forgot that he was a clergyman, always carrying himself according to his idea of the calling; therefore when the interchange of commonplaces flagged, he began to look for some remark to make sufficiently tinged with his profession to be suitable.

"I was watching these waves when you found me; they seem to be such a picture of the vanity of human endeavor! But just as little as those waves would mind me if I told them they were wasting their labor on these rocks will men mind me when I tell them tomorrow of the emptiness of their ambitions."

"Hoots, Fergus!" said Donal. "Why should you, in that case, go on preaching, setting them such a poor example?"

Fergus gave him a high-lidded glance, vouchsafing no replying. He just stared. What did his father's herdboy mean by talking such to him? Although now about to take his degree of Master of Arts, Donal was still to Fergus the cleaner-out of his father's stalls, an upstart whose former position was his real one—toward him at least, who knew him. And did the fellow challenge him to a discussion? Or did he presume on the familiarity of their boyhood and wish to sport his acquaintance with the popular preacher? On either supposition, this fellow was impertinent!

A good deal of discussion followed, most of it to Fergus's discomfort.

"I hope, ladies, your wits are not quite swept away in this flood of Highland logic," he said at length.

"You have a poor opinion of the stability of our brains, Mr. Duff," said Mrs. Sclater.

"I was only judging by myself," he replied, a little put out. "I can't say I understood our friends here. But this is Saturday, and tomorrow is my workday, you know, ladies," he said. "If you would oblige me with your address, Miss Galbraith, I should do myself the honor of calling on Mr. Galbraith."

Ginevra told him where they lived, but added she was afraid he must not expect to see her father, for he had been out of health lately and would see nobody.

"At all events I shall give myself the chance," he rejoined and, bidding the ladies good-bye and nodding to the youths, turned and walked away.

On Monday Fergus went to pay his visit to Mr. Galbraith. As Ginevra had said, her father did not appear; but Fergus was far from disappointed. He had taken it into his head that Miss Galbraith sided with him when that ill-bred fellow made his ungrateful attack upon him, and was much pleased to have a talk with her. Ginevra thought it would not be right to cherish against him the memory of the one sin of his youth in her eyes, but she could not like him. She was heartily tired of him before he went. When he was gone, she found as she sat with her father that she could not recall a word he had said. As to what had made the fellow stay so long, she was therefore positively unable to give her father an answer; the consequence of which was that the next time he called, Mr. Galbraith, much to her relief, stood the brunt of his approach and received him.

The ice thus broken, his ingratiating manners and the full-blown respect he showed Mr. Galbraith so won upon him that when he took his leave, he gave him a cordial invitation to repeat his visit. He did so, in the evening this time and, remembering a predilection of the laird's, begged for a game of backgammon. The result of his policy was that for many weeks that followed, every Monday evening at least, he spent with the laird. Ginevra was grateful to him for his attention to her father and his efforts to draw him out of his gloom, so she came gradually to let a little light of favor shine upon him. And if the heart of Fergus Duff was drawn to her, that is not to be counted to him a fault—neither that, his heart thus drawn, he should wish to marry her. He could easily have gotten a rich wife, but he was more greedy of distinction than money; and to marry the daughter of a man to whom he had been accustomed in childhood to look up to as the greatest in the known world was in his eyes like a patent of nobility and would be a ratification of his fitness to mingle with the choice of the land.

37   The Quarry

It was a cold night in March, cloudy and blowing. Donal and Gibbie were at the North Church to hear Fergus preach in the pulpit that had now become his own. The people had been gathering since long before the hour, and the youths could find only standing room near the door.

There was, however, no mistaking either Ginevra's bonnet or the long neck of her father. They sat a good way in front, about the middle of the great church. At the sight of them, Gibbie's face brightened and Donal's turned pale as death. For only the last week he heard of the frequent visits of the young preacher to the cottage and the favor in which he was held by both father and daughter. Donal's state of mind since had not been, with all his philosophy to rectify and support it, an enviable one. That he could not for a moment regard himself as a fit husband for the lady-lass, or dream of revealing himself or her to the insult which his offer as a son-in-law would bring on them both from the laird, was not a reflection to render the thought of such a bag of wind as Fergus Duff marrying her one whit the less horrible.

Had the laird been in the same social position as before, Donal would have had no fear of his accepting Fergus; but misfortune alters many relations. Fergus's father was a man of considerable property, Fergus himself almost a man of influence and already in possession of a comfortable income. It was possible to imagine that the impoverished Thomas Galbraith, Esq., late of Glashruach, might contrive to swallow what annoyance there could not but in any case be in wedding his daughter to the son of John Duff, formerly his own tenant of the Mains.

The young men were among the first out and, going round to another door by which they judged Ginevra and her father must issue, there stood waiting. Fergus soon was standing beside them but seemed not to see them, and they were nowise inclined to attract his attention. At last out came Ginevra—like a daisy among the mown grass!—with her father. She saw Donal, glanced from him to Gibbie, cast down her sweet eyes, and made no sign. Fergus had already advanced and addressed the laird.

"Ah, Mr. Duff!" said Mr. Galbraith. "Excuse me, but would you oblige me by giving your arm to my daughter? I see a friend waiting to speak to me. I shall overtake you in a moment."

Fergus murmured his pleasure, and Ginevra and he moved away together. The youths for a moment watched the father. He dawdled—evidently wanting to speak to no one. They then followed the two, walking some yards behind them. Every other moment Fergus would bend his head toward Ginevra; once or twice they saw the little bonnet turn upward in response or question. When the youths reached the street where the cottage stood, they turned the corner after them and walked quickly up to them where they stood at the gate waiting for it to be opened.

"Such a grand night!" said Donal, after the usual greetings. "Sir Gibbie and me's been having a walk in the moonlight. The moon's so bright you'd think she had light enough to keep the clouds off her, wouldn't you, mem? But no! they'll be upon her, I'm afraid, soon enough. See the clouds there among the moon? ... Well, good night, mem. Good night, Fergus."

Therewith Donal walked on, doubtless for the moment

a little relieved. But before they had walked far, he broke down altogether. "Gibbie," he said, "the rascal's going to marry the lady-lass! And it drives me mad to think it. If I could but have a chance to speak to her—once—just once! Lord! what'll come of all the gowans upon the Mains, and the heather upon Glashgar!"

Gibbie's face had grown white in the moonglow and his lips trembled. He put his arm through Donal's and clung to him, and in silence they went home. When they reached Donal's room, Donal entered and shut the door behind him, leaving Gibbie outside. He stood for a moment like one dazed, then suddenly coming to himself, turned, left the house, and ran straight to Daur Street.

When the minister's door was opened to him, he went to the dining room, knowing Mr. and Mrs. Sclater would then be at supper. Happily for his intent, the minister was at the moment having his tumbler of toddy after the labors of the day. His wife, therefore, when she saw Gibbie, rose and, meeting him, took him with her to her own little sitting room where they had a long talk. The result appeared the next night in a note from Mrs. Sclater to Gibbie, asking him and Donal to spend the evening of Tuesday with her.

The next night Donal, trembling, accompanied Gibbie. The hospitable crimson room, with its round table set out for a Scottish tea and its fire blazing hugely, received them. And there sat Ginevra by the fire with her pretty feet on a footstool before it! (In those days ladies wore open shoes, and showed dainty stockings.) Her face looked rosy from the firelight. She received them, as always with the same simple sincerity that had been hers on the bank of the Lorrie burn. But Gibbie read some trouble in her eyes, for his soul was all touch and, like a delicate spiritual seismograph, responded at once to the least tremble of a neighboring soul.

When tea was over, Gibbie went to the window and peeped out. Returning presently he spelled with fingers and signed with hands to Ginevra that it was a glorious night; would she not come for a walk? Ginevra looked to Mrs. Sclater.

"Gibbie wants me to go for a walk," she said.

"Certainly, my dear—if you are well enough to go with him," replied her friend.

"I am always well," answered Ginevra.

"I can't go with you," said Mrs. Sclater, "for I expect my husband any moment; but what occasion is there, with two such knights to protect you?"

Perceiving Gibbie's design, Donal cast him a grateful glance while Ginevra rose hastily and ran to put on her outer garments. Plainly to Donal, she was pleased to go.

When they stood on the pavement, there was the moon, the very cream of light, ladying it in a blue heaven. The steps of the youths rang on the pavement, and Donal's voice seemed to him too loud. He spoke low, and Ginevra answered him softly. They walked close together and Gibbie flitted to and fro, now on this side, now on that, now in front of them, now behind.

"How did you like the sermon last evening, mem?" asked Donal.

"Papa thought it a grand sermon," answered Ginevra.

"And yourself?" persisted Donal.

"Papa tells me I am no judge," she replied.

"That's as much as to say you didn't like it as well as he did!" returned Donal, in a tone expressing some relief.

"Mr. Duff is very good to my father, Donal," she rejoined, "and I don't like to say anything against his sermon; but all the time I could not help thinking whether your mother would like this and that. For, you know, any good there is in me I have got from her and from Gibbie—and from you, Donal."

The youth's heart beat with a pleasure that rose to physical pain.

Donal remaining silent, Ginevra presently returned him his own question.

"How did you like the sermon, Donal?"

"Do you want me to say, mem?" he asked.

"I do, Donal," she answered.

"Well, I would just say, in general, I can't think much

of a sermon that might make someone think more of a preacher than Him that he comes to preach about. I mean that I don't see how anybody was to love God or his neighbor a jot more for hearing that sermon on Sunday night."

"That's just what I was feeling," she replied. "I am sorry for Mr. Duff if he has taken to preaching where he does not understand."

They had left the city behind them and were walking on a wide-open road, with a great sky above it. On its borders were small, fenced fields and a house here and there with a garden. But this night the earth was nothing; what was in them and over them was all. Donal felt that with this wonder by his side, to be doomed to go on walking to all eternity would be a blissful fate were the landscape turned to a brick-field and the sky to persistent grey.

"Would you take my arm, mem?" he said at length, summoning courage. "I just find myself like a horse with a rein broken, going through the air this way."

Before he had finished the sentence, Ginevra had accepted the offer. It was the first time. His arm trembled. He thought it was her hand.

"You're not cold, are you, mem?" he said.

"Not in the least," she answered.

A moment more and Donal broke out singing:

My thoughts are like fireflies, pulsing in moonlight;
    My heart is a silver cup, full of red wine;
My soul a pale gleaming horizon, whence soon light
    Will flood the gold earth with a torrent divine.

"What was that, Donal?" cried Ginevra.

"Oh, nothing," answered Donal. "It was only my heart laughing."

"Say the words," said Ginevra.

"I can't—I don't know them now," replied Donal.

"Oh, Donal! Are those lovely words gone—altogether—forever? Shall I not hear them again?"

"I'll try to remember them when I go home," he said.

"I can't think of them now. I can think of nothing but one thing."

"And what is that, Donal?"

"Yourself," answered Donal.

Ginevra's hand lifted just a half of its weight from Donal's arm, like a bird that had thought of flying, then settled again.

"It is very pleasant to be together once more as in the old time, Donal—though there are no daisies and green fields.—But what place is that?"

Instinctively, almost unconsciously, she wanted to turn the conversation. The place she pointed to was an opening immediately on the roadside, through a high bank—narrow and dark, with one side half-lighted by the moon. She had often passed it, walking with her schoolfellows, but had never thought of asking what it was. In the shining dusk it looked strange and a little dreadful.

"It's the quarry, mem," answered Donal; "don't you know that? That's where most of the whole town came from. It's an eerie kind of place to look at in this light. I'm surprised you never saw it."

"I have seen the opening there but never took much notice of it before," said Ginevra.

"Come and I'll let you see it," said Donal. "You wouldn't be afraid to come and see what the moon makes of it, would you, mem?"

"No, Donal. I would not be frightened to go anywhere with you. But—"

"Eh, mem! it makes me right proud to hear you say that. Come, then."

So saying, he turned aside and led her into the narrow passage, cut through granite. Gibbie, thinking they had gone to have but a peep and return, stood in the road looking at the clouds and the moon and crooning to himself. By and by, when he found they did not return, he followed them.

When they reached the end of the cutting, Ginevra started at the sight of the vast gulf, the moon showing the one wall a ghastly grey, and from the other throwing a shadow half across the bottom. But a winding road went down into it, and Donal led her on. The side of the quarry was on one hand, and on the other she could see only into the gulf, and she was afraid to take her hand from his arm.

"Oh, Donal!" she said at length, almost in a whisper, "this is like a dream I once had, of going down and down a long, roundabout road, inside the earth."

Presently Donal again began to sing.

"Are you sure there are no holes—full of water—down there?" she faltered.

"Ay, there's one or two," replied Donal, "but we'll keep out of them."

Ginevra shuddered but was determined to show no fear. They stepped at last on the level below, covered with granite chips and stones and great blocks. There shone the moon on the corner of a pool, the rest of which crept away in the blackness under an overhanging mass. She caught his arm with both hands. He told her to look up. Steep granite rock was above them all around—on one side dark, on the other, mottled with the moon and the thousand shadows of its own roughness. Over the gulf hung vaulted the dark blue, cloud-blotted sky, whence the moon seemed to look straight down upon her, asking what they were about.

Suddenly Donal caught her hand. She looked in his face. It was not the moon that could make it so white.

"Ginevra!" he said with trembling voice.

"Yes, Donal," she answered.

"You're not angry with me for calling you by your name? I never did it before."

"I always call you Donal," she answered.

"That's natural. You're a grand lady, and I'm nothing but a herd-laddie."

"You're a great poet, Donal, and that's much more than being a lady or a gentleman."

"Ay, maybe," answered Donal listlessly, "but a poor lad like me dares not lift an eye to a grand lady like you, mem. My time is nearly over at the college, and I see nothing for it but to go home and hire myself out. I'll be better working with my hands than with my head when I have no hope left of seeing your face again. Eh, mem, but you are pretty! But you don't know yourself how pretty you are ... what a subversion you make in my heart and my head."

Still she looked him in the eyes, like one bewildered, unable to withdraw her eyes from his. Her face too had grown white.

"Tell me to hold my tongue, mem, and I'll hold it," he said.

Her lips moved, but no sound came.

"I well know," he went on, "you can never look on me as anything more than a kind of human bird that you would keep in a cage and listen to when he sang. And whether you grant me my prayer or not, you will never see me again. The only difference will be that I'll either hang my head or hold it up for the rest of my days. I would fain know that I wasn't despised."

"What is it, Donal?" said Ginevra, half inaudibly and with effort; she could scarcely speak for a fluttering in her throat.

"I beseech you upon my knees," he went on, as if she had not spoken, "at the favor of your sweet soul, to lay upon me—as upon the lips of the soul that sang you the songs you liked so well to hear when you were but a lassie—one solitary kiss. I swear by the Truth I'll think of it but as you think, and no man or woman or child, not even Gibbie himself, shall know—"

The last word broke the spell upon Ginevra.

"But, Donal," she said, as quietly as when years ago they talked by the Lorrieside, "would it be right?—a secret with you I could not tell to anyone?—not even if afterward—"

Donal's face grew so ghastly with despair that absolute terror seized her; she turned from him and fled, calling, "Gibbie! Gibbie!"

He was not many yards off, approaching the mound as she came from behind it. He ran to meet her. She darted to him like a dove pursued by a hawk, threw herself into his arms, laid her head on his shoulder, and wept. Gibbie held her fast, and with all the ways in his poor power sought to comfort her. She raised her face at length. It was all wet with tears which glistened in the moonlight. Hurriedly Gibbie asked on his fingers:

"Was Donal not good to you?"

"He's beautiful," she sobbed; "but I couldn't, you know, Gibbie, I couldn't . . . I don't care a straw about position and all that—who would with a poet?—But I couldn't, you know, Gibbie. I couldn't let him think I might have married him—in any case; could I now, Gibbie?"

She laid her head again on his shoulder and sobbed. Gibbie did not well understand her. Donal, where he had thrown himself on a heap of granite chips, heard and understood, felt and knew and resolved all in one. The moon shone, and the clouds went flitting about, and still the two, Ginevra and Gibbie, stood motionless—Gibbie with the tears in his eye, and Ginevra weeping as if her heart would break. And behind the granite blocks lay Donal.

Again Ginevra raised her head.

"Gibbie, you must go and look after poor Donal," she said.

Gibbie went, but Donal was nowhere to be seen. To escape the two he loved so well, he had crept away softly into one of the many recesses of the place. Again and again Gibbie made the noise with which he was accustomed to call him, but Donal gave back no answer; and they understood that wherever he was he wanted to be left to himself. They climbed again the winding way out of the gulf and left him the heart of its desolation.

"Take me home, Gibbie," said Ginevra, when they reached the high road.

As they went, not a word more passed between them. Ginevra was as dumb as Gibbie, and Gibbie was sadder than he had ever been in his life—not only for Donal's sake, but because, in his inexperienced heart, he feared that Ginevra would not listen to Donal because she could not, because she had already promised herself to Fergus Duff. With all his love to his kind, he could not think it well that Fergus should be made happy at such a price. He left her at her own door and went home, hoping to find Donal there before him.

He was not there. Hour after hour passed, and he did not appear. At eleven o'clock, Gibbie set out to look for him, but with little hope of finding him. He went all the way back to the quarry. Gibbie went home again, and sat up all night, keeping the kettle boiling, ready to make tea for him the moment he should come in. But even in the morning Donal did not appear.

He might hear of him at the college, he thought, and went at the usual hour. Sure enough, as he entered the quadrangle, there was Donal going in at the door leading to the moral philosophy classroom. For hours, neglecting his own classes, Gibbie watched about the court, but Donal never showed himself. Gibbie concluded he had gone home by Crown Street, and himself returned, almost sure of now finding him in his room—although probably with the door locked. The room was empty and no one had seen him.

Donal's final examination, upon which alone his degree now depended, came on the next day. Gibbie watched at the certain corner and, unseen, saw him pass—with a face pale but strong, eyes that seemed not to have slept. After that he did not see him once till the last day of the session arrived. Then in the public room he saw him go up to receive his degree. As they came from the public room, Gibbie lay in wait for him once more, but again in vain.

When he reached his lodging, he found a note from Donal waiting him in which he bade him good-bye, said he was gone home, and asked him to pack up his things for him.

A sense of loneliness, such as in all his forsaken times he had never felt, overshadowed Gibbie. It troubled him a little that he must now return to Mr. Sclater. But it would not be for long.

Mr. Sclater had thought of making a movement toward gaining an extension of his tutelage beyond the ordinary legal period, on the ground of unfitness in his ward for the management of his property. But Gibbie's character and scholarship had deterred him from the attempt. In the month of May, therefore, when, according to the registry of his birth in the parish book, he would be of age, he would also be his own master so far as other mortals were concerned.

Gibbie was in no haste to return to Daur Street. He packed Donal's things, with all the books they had bought together, and committed the chest to the landlady. He then told her he would rather not give up his room yet, but would like to keep it on for a while, and come and go as he pleased.

He told her he would sleep there that night, and she got him his dinner as usual; after which, putting a Greek book in his pocket, he went out, thinking to go to the end of the pier and sit there awhile.

The next day Gibbie went back to his guardians. At his request Mrs. Sclater asked Ginevra to spend the following evening with them; he wanted to tell her about Donal. She accepted the invitation. But in a village near the foot of Glash-gar, Donal had that morning done what was destined to prevent her from keeping her engagement; he posted a letter to her. He had recalled the verses he sang to her as they walked that evening, and now sent them—complete in a very different tone. Not a word accompanied them.

My thoughts are like fireflies pulsing in moonlight;
    My heart like a silver cup full of red wine;
My soul a pale gleaming horizon, whence soon light
    Will flood the gold earth with a torrent divine.

My thoughts are like worms in a starless gloamin';
    My heart like a sponge that's fillit wi' gall;
My sowl like a bodiless ghaist sent roamin',
    To bide i' the mirk till the great trumpet call.

But peace by upo' ye, as deep as ye're lo'esome!
    Brak na an hoor o' yer fair-dreamy sleep,
To think o' the lad wi' a weicht in his bosom,
    'At ance sent a cry till ye oat o' the deep.

Some sharp rocky heicht, to catch a far mornin'
    Ayont a' the nichts o' this warld, he'll clim',
For nane shall say, Luik! he sank doon at her scornin',
    Wha rase by the han' she hield frank oot to him.

The letter was handed, with one or two more, to Mr. Galbraith at the breakfast table. He did not receive many letters now and could afford time to one that was for his daughter. He laid it with the rest by his side and after breakfast took it to his room and read it. He could no more understand it than Fergus could the Epistle of the Romans. But he had begun to be afraid of his daughter. He laid the letter aside, said nothing and waited, inwardly angry. After a while he began to flatter himself with the hope that perhaps it was but a sort of impertinent valentine, the writer of which was unknown to Ginevra. From the moment of its arrival, however, he kept a stricter watch upon her and that night prevented her from going to Mrs. Sclater's.

38   Of Age

There was no rejoicing upon Gibbie's attainment of his twenty-first year. His guardian, believing he alone had acquainted himself with the date and desiring in his wisdom to avoid giving him a feeling of importance, made no allusion to the fact, as would have been most natural, when they met at breakfast on the morning of the day. But, urged thereto by Donal, Gibbie had learned the date for himself and finding nothing was said, fingered to Mrs. Sclater, "This is my birthday."

"I wish you many happy returns," she answered. "How old are you today?"

"Twenty-one," he answered—by holding up all his fingers twice and then a forefinger.

She looked struck and glanced at her husband who, thereupon in his turn, gave utterance to the usual formula of goodwill and said no more. Seeing he was about to leave the table, Gibbie claimed his attention, spelling on his fingers very slowly (for Mr. Sclater was not adept at following this mode of communication).

"If you please, sir, I want to be put in possession of my property as soon as possible."

"All in good time, Sir Gilbert," answered the minister, with a superior smile, for he clung with hard reluctance to the last vestige of his power.

"But what is good time?" spelled Gibbie with a smile, which nonetheless that it was of genuine friendliness indicated there might be difference of opinion on the point.

"Oh! We shall see," returned the minister coolly. "These are not things to be done in a hurry," he added, as if he had been guardian to twenty wards before. "We'll see in a few days what Mr. Torrie proposes."

"But I want my money at once," insisted Gibbie. "I have been waiting for it, and now it is time; why should I wait still?"

"To learn patience, if for no other reason, Sir Gilbert," answered the minister with a hard laugh, meant to be jocular. "But indeed such affairs cannot be managed in a moment. You will have plenty of time to make a good use of your money, if you should have to wait another year or two."

So saying he pushed back his plate and cup and rose from the table.

"When will you see Mr. Torrie?" asked Gibbie, rising too and working his telegraph with greater rapidity than before.

"By and by," answered Mr. Sclater and walked toward the door. But Gibbie got between him and it.

"Will you go with me to Mr. Torrie today?" he asked.

The minister shook his head. Gibbie withdrew, seeming a little disappointed. Mr. Sclater left the room.

"You don't understand business, Gilbert," said Mrs. Sclater.

Gibbie smiled, got paper and pen and, sitting down at the table, wrote as follows:

"Dear Mr. Sclater: As you have never failed in your part, how can you wish me to fail in mine? I am now the one accountable for this money, which surely has been idle long enough, and if I leave it still unused, I shall be doing wrong, and there are things I have to do with it which ought to be set about immediately. I am sorry to seem impertinent, but if by twelve o'clock you have not gone with me to Mr. Torrie, I will go to Messrs. Hope & Waver, who will tell me what I ought to do next, in order to be put in possession. It makes me unhappy to write like this but I am not a child any longer, and having a man's work to do, I cannot consent to be treated as a child. I will do as I say. I am, dear Mr. Sclater, your affectionate ward, Gilbert Galbraith."

He took the letter to the study and, having given it to Mr. Sclater, withdrew. The minister might have known by this time with what sort of a youth he had to deal! He came down instantly, put the best face on it he could, said that if Sir Gilbert was so eager to take up the burden, he was ready enough to cast it off, and they would go at once to Mr. Torrie.

With the lawyer, Gibbie insisted on understanding everything, and that all should be legally arranged as speedily as possible. Mr. Torrie saw that if he did not make things plain or gave the least cause for doubt, the youth would most likely apply elsewhere for advice. Therefore he took trouble to set the various points, both as to the property and the proceedings necessary, before him in the cleanest manner.

"Thank you," said Gibbie, through Mr. Sclater. "Please remember I am more accountable for this money than you, and am compelled to understand!" Janet's repeated exhortations on the necessity of sending for the serpent to take care of the dove had not been lost upon him.

The lawyer being then quite ready to make him an advance of money, they went with him to the bank where Gibbie wrote his name and received a checkbook. As they left the bank, he asked the minister whether he would allow him to keep his place in his house till the next session and was almost startled at finding how his manner to him was changed. He assured Sir Gilbert, with a deference and respect both painful and amusing, that he hoped he would always regard his house as one home, however many besides he might now choose to have.

So now at last Gibbie was free to set about realizing a long-cherished scheme.

The repairs upon the Auld Hoose o' Galbraith were now nearly finished. In consequence of them, some of the tenants had had to leave, and Gibbie now gave them all notice to quit at their earliest convenience, taking care, however, to see them provided with fresh quarters, for several of the houses in the neighborhood had been bought for him at the same time with the old mansion. As soon as it was empty, he set more men to work, and not a little of the old stateliness began to reappear. He next proceeded to furnish certain of the rooms. By the time he had finished, his usual day for going home had arrived. While Janet lived, the cottage on Glashgar was home. Just as he was leaving, the minister told him that Glashruach was his. Mrs. Sclater was present and read in his eyes what induced her instantly to make the remark: "How could that man deprive his daughter of the property he had to take her mother's name to get!"

"He had misfortunes," indicated Gibbie, "and could not help it, I suppose."

"Yes, indeed!" she returned, "—misfortunes so great that they amounted to little less than swindling. I wonder how many he has brought to grief besides himself! If he had Glashruach once more, he would begin it all over again."

"Then I'll give it to Ginevra," said Gibbie.

"And let her father coax her out of it, and do another world of mischief with it!" she rejoined.

Gibbie was silent. Mrs. Sclater was right! To give is not always to bless. He must think of some other way.

He would liked to have seen Ginevra before he left but had no chance. He had gone to the North Church every Sunday for a long time now for the sake of seeing his lost friend. Had he not lost her when she turned from Donal to Fergus? Did she not forsake him too when she forsook his Donal? His heart would rise into his throat at the thought, but only for a moment. Now and then he had from her a sweet smile, but no sign that he might go and see her. Whether he was to see Donal when he reached Daurside, he could not tell; he had heard nothing of him since he went. His mother never wrote letters.

Notwithstanding his new power, it was hardly with his usual elation that he took his seat on the coach. But his reception was the same as ever. At his mother's persuasion, Donal, he found, instead of betaking himself again to bodily labors as he had purposed, had gone in search of some situation as a tutor.

"He'll be the better for it in the end," she said with a smile of the deepest sympathy, "though, being my own, I can't help being sorry for him. But the Lord was in the earthquake, and the fire, and the wind that blew the rocks, though the prophet couldn't see him. Donal will come out of this with more room in his heart and more light in his spirit."

Gibbie took his slate and wrote, "If money could do anything for him, I have plenty now."

"I know your heart, my child," replied Janet; "but no; the poor fellow must wrestle out of the thicket as best he can—sore scratched, no doubt. Eh! It's a fearful and wonderful thing that drawing of heart to heart, and then a great snap and a start back, and there's miles between them! The Lord alone knows the bottom of it."

Gibbie told her that Glashruach was his. Then first the extent of his wealth seemed to strike his old mother.

"Eh! You'll be the laird, will you, then? To think of this house and all being wee Gibbie's! Well, it beats all. The ways of the Lord are to be thought upon! He made David a king, and Gibbie He's made the laird! Blest be His name."

"They tell me the mountain is mine," Gibbie wrote. "Your husband shall be laird of Glashgar if he likes."

"No, no," said Janet, with a loving look. "He's too old for that. What better would Robert be to be laird? We pay no rent as it is, and he has as many sheep to love as he can well know one from the other. I know nothing that he lacks but Gibbie to go with him about the hill. A neighbor's laddie comes and goes, to help him, but, eh, says Robert, he's no Gibbie!—But if Glashruach be your own, my bonnie man, you must go down there this very night, and give a look to the burn; for the last time I was there, I thought it was creeping in underneath the bank fearfully like for what's left of the old house, and the sooner it's looked after the better. Eh, Sir Gibbie, but you should marry the bonnie lady, and take her back to her own house."

Gibbie gave a great sigh to think of the girl that loved the hill and the heather and the burns shut up in the city, and every Sunday going to the great church. To him Glashgar was full of God; the North Church or Mr. Sclater's church— well, he had tried hard, but had not succeeded in discovering temple signs about either.

The next day he sent to the city for an architect; and within a week masons and quarrymen were at work, some on the hill, blasting blue boulders and red granite, others roughly shaping the stones, and others laying the foundation of a huge facing and buttressing wall, which was to slope up from the bed of the Glashburn fifty feet to the foot of the castle, there to culminate in a narrow terrace with a parapet. Others again were clearing away what of the ruins stuck to the old house in order to leave it, as much as might be, in its original form. There was no space left for rebuilding, neither was there any between the two burns for adding afresh. The channel of the second remained dry, the landslip continuing to choke it, while the stream fell into the Glashburn. But Gibbie would not consent that the burn Ginevra had loved should sing no more as she had heard it sing. Her chamber was gone and could not be restored, but another chamber should be built for her, beneath whose window it should again rain; when she was married to Fergus, and her father could not touch it, the place should be hers.

More masons were gathered and foundations blasted in the steep rock that formed the other bank of the burn. The main point in the building was to be a room for Ginevra. He planned it himself—with a windowed turret projecting from the wall, making a recess in the room overhanging the stream. The turret he carried a story higher than the wall, and in the wall placed a stair leading to its top, whence over the roof might be seen great Glashgar and its streams coming down from heaven and singing as they came. Then from the middle of the first stair in the old house—the wall a yard and a half thick having been cut through—a solid stone bridge with a pointed arch was to lead across the burn to a like landing in the new house—a closed passage, with an oriel window on each side, looking up and down the stream, and a steep roof. And while these works were going on below, two masons high on the mountain were adding to the cottage a warm bedroom for Janet and Robert.

The architect was an honest man and kept Gibbie's secret, so that, although Gibbie was constantly about the place, nothing disturbed the general belief that Glashruach had been bought and was being made habitable by a certain magnate of the county adjoining.

39 The Auld Hoose o' Galbraith

One cold afternoon in the end of October, when Mistress Croale was shutting up her shop in the market, Gibbie came walking up the long gallery with the light hill step which he never lost. Startling her with a hand on her shoulder, he made signs that she must come with him. She made haste to lock her door, and they walked side by side to the Widdiehill.

They turned into the close of the Auld Hoose o' Galbraith, and Gibbie led her up the dark stair. At the top, on a wide hall-like landing, he opened a door. She drew back with amazement. But his smile reassured her and she stepped in.

It was a grand room, rich and somber in color, old-fashioned in its somewhat stately furniture. A glorious fire was blazing and candles were burning. The table was covered with a white cloth and laid for two. Gibbie shut the door, placed a chair for Mistress Croale by the fire, seated himself, took out his tablet, wrote, "Will you be my housekeeper? I will give you 100 pounds a year," and handed it to her.

"Lord, Sir Gibbie!" she cried, jumping to her feet, "have you lost your wits? How would an old wife like me look in such a place—and in such duds as this? It would make Satan laugh, and that he does but seldom."

Gibbie rose and, taking her by the hand, led her to the door of an adjoining room. It was a bedroom as grand as the room they had left, and if Mistress Croale was surprised before, she was astonished now. A fire was burning here too, candles were alight on the dressing table, a hot bath stood ready, and on the bed lay a dress of rich black satin, with linen and everything to collars, cuffs, mittens, cap and shoes. All these things Gibbie had bought himself, using the knowledge he had gathered in shopping with Mrs. Sclater and the advice of her dressmaker, whom he had taken into his confidence and who had entered heartily into his plan. He made signs to Mistress Croale that everything there was at her service, and left her.

Like one in a dream she yielded to the rush of events, not too much bewildered to dress with care, and neither too old nor too wicked nor too ugly to find pleasure in it. She might have been a born lady just restored to the habits of her youth, to judge by her delight over the ivory brushes and tortoise-shell comb and great mirror. In an hour or so she made her appearance—I can hardly say reappeared, but wiping the tears from her eyes like a too-blessed child. Gibbie was so satisfied with her appearance that, come of age as he was and vagrant no more, he first danced around her several times with a candle in his hand—much to the danger but nowise to the detriment of her finery—then set it down and executed his old lavolta of delight, which, as always, he finished by standing on one leg.

They then sat down to a nice nondescript meal, also of Gibbie's own providing.

When it was ended, he went to a bureau and brought thence a paper plainly written to this effect: "I agree to do whatever Sir Gilbert Galbraith may require of me, so long as it shall not be against my conscience; and consent that, if I taste whiskey once, he shall send me away immediately, without further reason given."

He handed it to Mistress Croale. She read and instantly looked about for pen and ink; she dreaded seeming for a moment to hesitate. He brought them to her, she signed, and they shook hands.

He then conducted her all over the house—first to the rooms prepared for his study and bedroom, and next to the room in the garret which he had left just as it was when his father died in it. Then, on the floor between, he showed her a number of bedrooms, all newly repaired and freshly painted, including double windows, the inside ones filled with frosted glass. These rooms, he gave her to understand, he wished her to furnish. Going back to the sitting room, he proceeded to explain his plans, telling her he had furnished the house that he might not any longer be himself a stranger as to have no place to take a stranger to. Then he got a Bible which was in the room and showed her those words in the book of Exodus, ". . . also, thou shalt not oppress a stranger; for ye know the heart of a stranger, seeing ye were strangers in the land of Egypt." While she thought again of her wanderings through the country and nights in the open air, he made her understand that whomsoever he should at any time bring home, she was to treat as his guest. She might get a servant to wait upon herself, he said, but she herself must help him to wait upon his guests.

She expressed hearty acquiescence but would not hear of a servant; the more work, the better for her, she said. She would tomorrow arrange for giving up her shop and disposing of her stock and the furniture in her garret. Next he insisted that she should never utter a word as to the use he intended making of his house; if the thing came out, it would ruin his plans. And thereupon he took her to the ground floor and showed her a door in communication with a poor little house behind, by which he intended to introduce and dismiss his guests, that they should not know where they had spent the night. Then he made her read to him the hundred and seventh Psalm, after which he left her, saying he would come to the house as soon as the session began, which would be in a week; until then he should be at Mr. Sclater's.

Left alone in the great house—like one with whom the most beneficent of fairies had been busy—the first thing Mistress Croale did was to go and have a good look at herself from head to foot. She was satisfied with everything she saw there except her complexion, and that she resolved should improve. She was almost painfully happy. Out there was the Widdiehill, dark and dismal and cold, through which she had come, sad and shivering and haunted with miserable thoughts, into warmth and splendor and luxury and bliss! Wee Sir Gibbie had made a lady of her! If only poor Sir George were alive to see it!

40 The Laird and the Preacher

Since he came to town, Gibbie had seen Ginevra but once—that was in the North Church. She looked so sad and white that his heart was very heavy for her. Could it be that she repented? She must have turned down Donal to please her father! If she would marry Donal, Gibbie would give her Glashruach. She should have Glashruach all the same whatever she did, only it might influence her father. He paced up and down before the cottage once for a whole night, but no good came of that. He paced before it from dusk to bedtime again and again in the hope of speaking to Ginevra, but he never saw even her shadow on the white blind. He went up to the door once, but in the dread of displeasing her lost his courage and paced the street the whole morning instead, but saw no one come out.

Fergus had gradually become essential to the small remaining happiness of which the laird was capable. He had gained his favor chiefly through the respect and kindly attention he showed him. The young preacher knew little of the laird's career, and looked upon him as an unfortunate man, toward whom loyalty now required even a greater show of respect than while he owned his father's farm.

Fergus at length summoned courage to ask him if he might pay his addresses to Miss Galbraith. The old man started, cast on him a withering look, murmured "The heiress of Glashruach!" then remembered, threw himself back in his chair, and closed his eyes. The father reflected that if he accepted him, he might leave the miserable cottage and go to the manse; it would be of consequence to have a clergyman for a son-in-law. Slowly he raised himself in his chair.

"You have my permission, Mr. Duff."

The young preacher hastened to find Ginevra but only to meet a refusal, gentle and sorrowful. He pleaded for permission to repeat his request after an interval, but she distinctly refused. Disappointed and annoyed he was, but he sought and fancied he found reasons for her decision which were not unfavorable to himself, and continued to visit her father as before, saying to him he had not quite succeeded in drawing from her a favorable answer but hoped to prevail. He nowise acted the despairing lover, but made grander sermons than ever and, as he came to feel at home in his pulpit, delivered them with growing force. But delay wrought desire in the laird; and at length one evening, having by cross-questioning satisfied himself that Fergus made no progress, he rose and, going to his desk, handed him Donal's verses. Fergus read them and remarked he had read better, but the first stanza had a slight flavor of Shelley.

"What I want to know is," said Mr. Galbraith,

"whether they do not suggest a reason for your want of success with Ginny. Do you know the writing?"

"I cannot say I do. But I think it is very likely that of Donal Grant; he sets up for the Burns of Daurside."

"Insolent scoundrel!" cried the laird.

"But, my dear sir," said Fergus, "if I am to understand these lines—if you will excuse me for venturing to say so—what I read in them is that whoever the writer may be, the lady, whoever she may be, had refused him."

"You cannot believe that the wretch had the impudence to make my daughter—the heiress of—at least—What! make my daughter an offer! She would at once have acquainted me with the fact, that he might receive suitable chastisement. Let me look at the stuff again."

"It is quite possible," said Fergus, "it may be only a poem some friend has copied for her from a newspaper."

While he spoke, the laird was reading the lines and persuading himself he understood them. With sudden resolve, the paper held torchlike in front of him, he strode into the next room where Ginevra sat.

"Do you tell me," he said fiercely, "that you have so far forgotten all dignity and propriety as to give a dirty cowboy the encouragement to make you an offer of marriage? The very notion sets my blood boiling."

Ginevra had turned white; but looking him straight in the face, she answered, "If that is a letter for me, you know I have not read it."

"There! See for yourself."

She took the verses from his hand and read them. Even with her father standing there watching her like an inquisitor, she could not help the tears coming into her eyes as she read.

"There is no such thing here, Papa," she said. "They are only verses bidding me good-bye."

"And what right has any such fellow to bid my daughter goodbye? Explain that to me, if you please."

"Why should I make both him and you uncomfortable, Papa—when there was not going to be anything more of it?"

"Why, then, do you go hankering after him still, and refusing Mr. Duff? It is true he is not exactly a gentleman by birth, but he is such by education, by manners, by position, by influence."

"Papa, I have already told Mr. Duff, as plainly as I could without being rude, that I would never let him talk to me so. What lady would refuse Donal Grant and listen to him!"

"You are a bold, insolent hussy!" cried her father in a rage, and left the room to rejoin Fergus.

They both sat silent for a while—then the preacher spoke.

"Other communications may have reached her from the same quarter," he said.

"That is impossible," rejoined the laird.

"I don't know that," insisted Fergus. "There is a foolish—a half-silly companion of his about town. They call him Sir Gibbie Galbraith."

"Ginny knows no such person."

"Indeed she does, I have seen them together."

"Oh! You mean the lad the minister adopted! The urchin he took off the streets!—Sir Gibbie Galbraith!" he repeated sneeringly, but as one reflecting, "—I do vaguely recall a slanderous rumor in which a certain female connection of the family was hinted at.—Yes! That's where the nickname comes from. And you think she keeps up a communication with the clown through him?"

"I don't say that, sir. I merely think it possible she may see this Gibbie occasionally; and I know he worships the cowboy."

For a while thereafter Ginevra tried hard to convince her father that his notion of her conduct, or Gibbie's or Donal's was mistaken. He would listen to nothing she said, continually insisting that the only amends for her past was to marry according to his wishes; to give up poetry and cowboys and dumb rascals, and settle down as a respectable matron. Then Ginevra became absolutely silent. He stormed at her for her sullenness, but she persisted in her silence, sorely distressed to find how dead her heart seemed to be growing under his treatment of her.

41 Differences

Gibbie found everything at the Auld Hoose in complete order for his reception. Mistress Croale had been very diligent and promised well for a housekeeper—looked well, too, in her black satin and lace. She had a good meal ready for him with every adjunct in proper style.

Everything went comfortably. Gibbie was so well in mathematics, thanks to Mr. Sclater, that he did all requisite for honorable studentship; but having no desire to distinguish himself, he had plenty of time for more important duty. Now that he was by himself, as if old habit had returned in the shape of new passion, he roamed the streets every night. His custom was this: after dinner, which he had when he came from college about half past four, he lay down and slept till half past six; then he had tea and after that studied till ten o'clock, where he took his Greek Testament. At eleven he went out for an hour longer—during which time Mistress Croale was in readiness to receive any guest he might bring home.

Some nights he would not meet a single wanderer; occasionally he would meet two or three in the same night. When he found one, he would stand regarding him until he spoke. If the man was drunk he would leave him; such were not those for whom he could now do most. If he was sober he made him signs of invitation. If he would not go with him, he left him but kept him in view and tried him again. If still he would not, he gave him a piece of bread and left him. If the stranger called to him, he stopped and by circuitous ways brought him to the little house at the back. It was purposely quite dark. If the man was too apprehensive to enter, he left him; if he followed, he led him to Mistress Croale. If anything suggested the possibility of helping further, a possibility turning entirely on the person's self, the attempt was set on foot; but in general, after a good breakfast, Gibbie led him through a dark passage into the darkened house, and dismissed him from the door by which he had entered. He never gave money and never sought such guests except in the winter. Indeed, he was never in the city in the summer. It was a tolerable beginning, and during the time not a word reached him indicating knowledge of his proceedings, although within a week or two a rumor was rife in the lower parts of the city of a mysterious being who went about doing this and that for poor folk.

Mr. and Mrs. Sclater could not fail to be much annoyed when they found he was occupying the Auld Hoose with "that horrible woman" for a housekeeper; they knew, however, that expostulation with one possessed by such a headstrong sense of duty was utterly useless.

Fergus had now established himself in the manse of the North Church, and thither he invited Mr. and Miss Galbraith to dine with him on a certain evening. Her father's absolute desire compelled Ginevra's assent; she could not, while with him, rebel absolutely. Fergus did his best to make the evening a pleasant one and had special satisfaction in showing the laird that he could provide both a good dinner and a good bottle of port. Two of his congregation, a young lawyer and his wife, were the only other guests. The laird found the lawyer an agreeable companion, chiefly from his readiness to listen to his old law stories, and Fergus laid himself out to please the two ladies. Secure of the admiration of one, he hoped it might help to draw the favor of the other.

It grew late. The dinner had been at a fashionable hour; they had stayed an unfashionable time. It was nearly twelve o'clock when guests and host left the house in company. The lawyer and his wife went one way, and Fergus went the other with the laird and Ginevra.

Hearing the pitiful wailing of the child and the cough

of a woman as they went along a street bridge, they peeped over the parapet and saw upon the stair leading to the lower street a woman with a child asleep in her lap, trying to eat a piece of bread and coughing as if in the last stage of consumption. On the next step below sat a man hushing in his bosom the baby whose cry they had heard. They stood for a moment, the minister pondering whether his profession required of him action, and Ginevra's gaze fixed on the head and shoulders of the foreshortened figure of the man, who vainly as patiently sought to soothe the child by gently rocking it to and fro. But when he began a strange humming song to it, which brought all Glashgar before her eyes, Ginevra knew beyond a doubt that it was Gibbie.

At the sound the child ceased to wail, and presently the woman with difficulty rose, laying a hand for help on Gibbie's shoulder. Then Gibbie rose also, cradling the infant on his left arm and making signs to the mother to place the child on his right. She did so and, turning, went feebly up the stair. Gibbie followed with the two children, one lying on his arm, the other with his head on Gibbie's shoulder, both wretched and pining with grey cheeks and dark hollows under their eyes. From the top of the stair they went slowly up the street, the poor woman coughing and Gibbie crooning to the baby, who cried no more but now and then moaned. Then Fergus said to the laird:

"Did you see that young man, sir? That is the so-called Sir Gilbert Galbraith we were talking of the other night. They say he has come into a good property, but you may judge for yourself whether he seems fit to manage it!"

Ginevra withdrew her hand from his arm.

"Good God, Ginny!" exclaimed the laird, "you do not mean to tell me you have ever spoken to a young man like that?"

"I know him very well, Papa," replied Ginevra collectedly.

"You are incomprehensible, Ginny! If you know him, why do I not know him? Why have you concealed from me your acquaintance with this—this—person?"

"Because I thought it might be painful to you, Papa," she answered, looking in his face.

"Painful to me! Why should it be painful to me—except indeed that it breaks my heart as often as I see your invincible fondness for low company?"

"Do you desire me to tell you, Papa, why I thought it might be painful to you to make that young man's acquaintance?"

"I do distinctly. I command you."

"Then I will: that young man, Sir Gilbert Galbraith—"

"Nonsense, girl! There is no such Galbraith. It is the merest of scoffs."

Ginevra did not care to argue with him this point. In truth she knew little more about it than he.

"Many years ago," she recommenced, "when I was a child—excuse me, Mr. Duff, but it is quite time I told my father what has been weighing upon my mind for so many years."

"Sir Gilbert!" muttered her father contemptuously.

"One day," again she began, "Mr. Fergus Duff brought a ragged little boy to Glashruach—the most innocent and loving of creatures, who had committed no crime but that of doing good in secret. I saw Mr. Duff box his ears on the bridge; and you, Papa, gave him over to that wretch, Angus MacPholp, to whip him—so at least Angus told me, after he had whipped him till he dropped senseless. I can hardly keep from screaming now when I think of it."

"All this, Ginny, is nothing less than cursed folly. Do you mean to tell me you have all these years been cherishing resentment against your own father for the sake of a little thieving rascal, whom it was a good deed to frighten from the error of his ways? I have no doubt Angus gave him merely what he deserved."

"You must remember, Miss Galbraith, we did not know he was dumb," said Fergus, humbly.

"If you had had any heart," said Ginevra, "you would have seen in his face that he was a perfectly angelic child. He ran to the mountain without a rag to cover his bleeding body, and would have died of cold and hunger had not the Grants, the parents of your father's herdboy, Mr. Duff, taken him to their hearts and been father and mother to him."—Ginevra's mouth was opened at last.—"After that," she went on, "Angus shot him like a wild beast when he was quietly herding Robert Grant's sheep. In return Sir Gilbert saved his life in the flood. And just before the house of Glashruach fell—the part in which my room was—he caught me up, because he could not speak, and carried me out of it; and when I told you that he had saved my life, you ordered him out of the house, and when he was afraid to leave me alone with you, you dashed him against the wall and sent for Angus to whip him again. But I should have liked to see Angus try it then!"

"I do remember an insolent fellow taking advantage of the ruinous state the house was in, to make his way into the study," said the laird.

"And now," Ginevra continued, "Mr. Duff makes question of his wits because he finds him carrying a poor woman's children, going to get them a bed somewhere! If Mr. Duff had run about the streets when he was a child, like Sir Gilbert, he might not perhaps think it so strange he should care about a houseless woman!"

Ginevra burst into tears.

"Abominably disagreeable!" muttered the laird. "Hold your tongue, Ginny, you will wake the street. All you say may or may not be quite true; I do not say you are telling lies, or even exaggerating; but I see nothing in it to prove the lad a fit companion for a young lady. Very much to the contrary. I suppose he told you he was your injured, neglected, ill-used cousin? He may be your cousin; you may have any number of such cousins, if half the low tales concerning your mother's family be true."

Ginevra did not answer him—did not speak another word. When Fergus left them at their own door, she neither shook hands with him nor bade him good night.

"Ginny," said her father the moment he was gone, "if I hear of your once speaking again to that low vagabond— and now I think of it," he cried, interrupting himself with a

234

sudden recollection "—there was a cobbler fellow in the town here they used to call Sir Somebody Galbraith!—that must be his father! Whether the Sir was title or nickname, I neither know nor care. A title without money is as bad as a saintship without grace. But this I tell you, that if I hear of your speaking one word, good or bad, to the fellow again, I will turn you out of the house."

To Ginevra's accumulated misery, she carried with her to her room a feeling of contempt for her father, with which she lay struggling in vain half the night.

42 Ginevra

Although Gibbie had taken no notice of the laird's party, he had recognized each of the three as he came up the stair and in Ginevra's face read an appeal of deliverance. It seemed to say, "You help everybody but me! Why do you not come and help me too? Am I to have no pity because I am neither hungry nor cold?" He did not, however, lie awake thinking what he should do; long before the poor woman and her children were in bed, he had made up his mind.

As soon as he came home the next day and had hastily eaten his dinner, acting upon his vague knowledge of law business lately acquired, he bought a stamped paper, wrote upon it, and put it in his pocket. Then he took a card and wrote on it, "Sir Gilbert Galbraith, Baronet of Glashruach," and put that in his pocket also. Thus provided he walked deliberately along Pearl Street out into the suburb and, turning to the right, rang the bell at the garden gate of the laird's cottage. When the maid came, he gave her his card and followed her into the house. She carried it into the room where, dinner over, the laird and the preacher were sitting with a bottle of the same port between them which had pleased the laird at the manse. Giving time to read the card and no more, Gibbie entered the room; he would not risk a refusal to see him.

It was a small room with a round table. The laird sat sideways to the door; the preacher sat between the table and the fire.

"What the devil does this mean?" cried the laird.

His big tumbling eyes had required more time than Gibbie had allowed. When with this exclamation he lifted them from the card, they fell upon the object of his imprecation standing in the middle of the room between him and the open door. The preacher, snug behind the table, scarcely endeavored to conceal the smile with which he took no notice of Sir Gilbert. The laird rose in the perturbation of mingled anger and unpreparedness.

"Ah!" he said, but it was only a sound, not a word, "to what—may I ask ... have I—I have not the honor of your acquaintance, Mr. . . . Mr.—" Here he looked again at the card he held, fumbled for and opened a double eyeglass, then with deliberation examined the name upon it, thus gaining time and gathering his force for more. "Mr. . . . ah, I see! Galbraith, you say.—To what, Mr., Mr. . . . ."—another look at the card— "Galbraith, do I owe the honor of this unexpected ... and ... and—I must say—unlooked-for visit—and business, I presume, it must be that brings you, seeing I have not the honor of the slightest acquaintance with you?"

He dropped his eyeglass with a clatter against his waistcoat, threw the card into his finger-glass, raised his pale eyes, and stared at Sir Gilbert with all the fixedness they were capable of; he had already drunk a good deal of wine. Gibbie answered by drawing from the breastpocket of his coat the paper he had written and presented it like a petition. Mr. Galbraith sneered and would not have touched it had not his eye caught the stamp, which from old habit at once drew his hand. From similar habit, or perhaps to get it nearer the light, he sat down. Gibbie stood, and Fergus stared at him with insolent composure. The laird read, but not aloud: "I, Gilbert Galbraith, Baronet, hereby promise and undertake to transfer to Miss Galbraith, only daughter of Thomas Galbraith, Esq., on the day when she shall be married to Donal Grant, Master of Arts, the whole of the title deeds of the house and lands of Glashruach, to have and to hold as hers, with absolute power to dispose of the same as she may see fit. Gilbert Galbraith, Old House of Galbraith, Widdiehill, March," etc., etc.

The laird stretched his neck like a turkeycock and gobbled inarticulately, threw the paper to Fergus and, turning on his chair, glowered at Gibbie. Then suddenly starting to his feet, he cried, "What do you mean, you rascal, by daring to insult me in my own house? Damn your insolent foolery!"

"A trick! A most palpable trick! And an exceedingly silly one!" pronounced Fergus, who had now read the paper. "Quite as foolish as unjustifiable! Everybody knows Glashruach is the property of Major Culsalmon!"—Here the laird sought the relief of another oath or two. "Make haste before worse comes of it. You have been made a fool of."

When Fergus began to speak, the laird turned and, while he spoke, stared at him with lackluster yet gleaming eyes. Poor Gibbie stood shaking his head, smiling, and making eager signs with hands and arms; but in the laird's condition of both heart and brain, he might well forget that Gibbie was dumb.

"Why don't you speak, you fool?" he cried. "Get out and don't stand making faces there. Be off with you."

Gibbie pointed to the paper, which lay before Fergus, and placed a hand first on his lips, then on his heart.

The laird swore at him, choking with rage. "Go away, or, by God! I will break your head!"

Fergus at this rose and came round the table to get between them. But the laird caught up a pair of nutcrackers and threw it at Gibbie. It struck him on the forehead and the blood spurted from the wound. He staggered backward. Fergus seized the laird's arm and sought to pacify him.

Her father's loud tones had reached Ginevra in her room. She ran down and that instant entered; Gibbie all but fell into her arms. The moment's support she gave him and the look of loving terror she cast in his face restored him, and he was again firm on his feet, pressing her handkerchief to his forehead. Fergus, leaving the laird, advanced with the intention of getting him safe from the house. Ginevra stepped between them. Her father's rage thereupon broke loose. He seized hold of her with violence and dragged her from the room. Fergus laid hands upon Gibbie more gently, and would have half forced, half persuaded him to go. A cry came from Ginevra; refusing to be sent to her room before Gibbie was in safety, her father struck her.

Gibbie would have darted to help her. Fergus tried to hold him fast but knew nothing of Gibbie's strength, and the next moment he found himself on his back upon the table, amidst the crash of wineglasses and china. Having locked the door, Gibbie sprang to the laird who was trying to drag his daughter, now hardly resisting, up the first steps of the stair. He took him round the waist from behind, swept him to the other room, and there locked him up also. He then returned to Ginevra where she lay motionless on the stair, lifted her in his arms, and carried her out of the house. He did not stop until, having reached the farther end of the street, he turned the corner of it into another equally quiet.

Under a dull, smoky oil lamp Gibbie stopped. He knew by the tightening of her arms that Ginevra was coming to herself.

"Let me down," she said feebly.

He did so but kept his arm round her. She gave a deep sigh, and gazed bewildered. When she saw him, she smiled.

"With you, Gibbie!" she murmured. "—But they will be after us!"

"They shall not touch you," signified Gibbie.

"What was it all about?" she asked.

Gibbie spelled on his fingers. "Because I offered to give you Glashruach if your father would let you marry Donal."

"Gibbie! How could you?" she cried almost in a scream; pushing away his arm, she turned from him and tried to run; but after two steps, she tottered to the lamppost and leaned against it.

"Then come with me and be my sister, Ginevra, and I will take care of you," spelled Gibbie. "I can do nothing to take care of you while I can't get near you."

"Oh, Gibbie! Nobody does like that," returned Ginevra, "—else I should be so glad to!"

"There is no other way then that I know. You won't marry anybody, you see."

"Won't I, Gibbie? What makes you think that?"

"Because of course you would never refuse Donal and marry anybody else; that is not possible."

"Oh! don't tease me, Gibbie."

"Ginevra, you don't mean you would?"

In the dull light, and with the imperfect means of Gibbie for the embodiment of his thoughts, Ginevra misunderstood him.

"Yes, Gibbie," she said, "I would. I thought it was understood between us ever since that day you found me on Glashgar. In my thoughts I have been yours all the time."

She turned her face to the lamppost. But Gibbie made her look.

"You do not mean," he spelled very hurriedly, "that you would marry *me?—Me?* I never dreamed of such a thing!"

"You didn't mean it then!" said Ginevra with a cry— bitter but feeble with despair and ending in a stifled shriek. "What have I been saying then! I thought I belonged to you! I thought you meant to take me all the time!" She burst into an agony of sobbing. "I have been alone all the time and did not know it!"

She sank on the pavement at the foot of the lamppost, weeping sorely and shaken with her sobs. Gibbie was in sad perplexity. Heaven had opened before his gaze; its colors filled his eyes; its sounds filled his ears and heart and brain. But the portress was busy crying and would not open the door. Neither could he get at her to comfort her—her eyes being wanted to cry with, his poor signs were of no use. Gibbie held one of her hands and stroked it. Then he pulled off his coat and laid it softly upon her. She grew a little quieter.

"Take me home, Gibbie," she said in a gentle voice.

Gibbie put his arms around her and helped her to her feet. She looked at him and saw a face glorious with bliss. Never, not even on Glashgar in the skincoat of the beast-boy had she seen him so. And in his eyes was that which triumphed, not over dumbness but over speech. It brought the rose-fire rushing into her wan cheeks; she hid her face on his bosom; and under the dingy, red flame of the lamp in the stony street, they held each other, as blessed as if they had been under an orange tree haunted with fireflies. For they knew each the heart of the other.

How long they stood thus, neither of them knew. The lady would not have spoken if she could, and the youth could not if he would. But the lady shivered; and because she shivered, she would have the youth take his coat. He mocked at cold. He made her put her arms in the sleeves, and buttoned it around her; both laughed to see how wide it was. Then he took her by the hand and led her away, obedient as when first he found her and her heart upon Glashgar. Like two children, holding each other fast, they hurried along, in dread pursuit. He brought her to Daur Street and gave her to Mrs. Sclater's arms. Ginevra told her everything, except that her father had struck her, and Gibbie begged her to keep his wife for him till they could be married. Mrs. Sclater behaved like a mother to them, sent Gibbie away and Ginevra to a hot bath and to bed.

Gibbie went home as if Pearl Street had been the stairs of Glashgar and the Auld Hoose a mansion in the heavens. Love had been gathering and ever storing itself in his heart so many years for this brown dove! Now at last the rock was smitten and its treasure rushed forth. Gibbie's was love simple, unselfish, undemanding—not merely asking for no return but asking for no recognition, requiring not even that its existence should be known. He was a rare one, who did not make the common desire, namely to be loved, for love itself.

Some would count worthless the love of a man who loved everybody. There would be no distinction in being loved by such a man!—and distinction, as a guarantee of their own great worth is what such seek. There are women who desire to be the sole object of a man's affection, and are all their lives devoured by unlawful jealousies. A love that had never gone forth upon human being but themselves would be to them the treasure to sell all that they might buy. And the man who brought such a love might in truth be all-absorbed therein himself. The poorest of creatures may well be absorbed in the poorest of loves. The man who loves most will love best. The man who thoroughly loves God and his neighbor is the only man who will love a woman ideally—who can love her with the love God thought of between them when He made man male and female.

Because Gibbie's love was toward everything human, he was able to love Ginevra as Donal was not yet grown able to love her. His love to Ginevra stood like a growing thicket of aromatic shrubs, until her confession set the fire of heaven to it. He had never imagined, never hoped, never desired she should love him like that. She had refused his friend, the strong, the noble, the beautiful, Donal the poet; and it never could but from her own lips have found way to his belief that she had turned her regard upon wee Sir Gibbie, a nobody, who to himself was a mere burning heart running about in tattered garments. Immeasurably the greater therefore was his delight. The sum of happiness in the city, if gathered that night into one wave, could not have reached halfway to the crest of the mighty billow tossing itself heavenward as it rushed along the ocean of Gibbie's spirit.

43 Preparations

Having reflected that Ginevra was underage and they must be careful, the next morning, the first thing after breakfast, Mr. Sclater resumed with considerable satisfaction his office of guardian. Holding no previous consultation with Gibbie, he walked to the cottage and sought an interview with Mr. Galbraith.

"I have to inform you, Mr. Galbraith," he began, "that Miss Galbraith—"

"Oh!" said the laird, "I beg your pardon; I was not aware it was my daughter you wished to see."

He rose and rang the bell. Mr. Sclater, annoyed at his manner, held his peace.

"Tell your mistress," said the laird to the maid, "that the Rev. Mr. Sclater wishes to see her."

The girl returned with a scared face and the news that her mistress was not in her room. The laird's loose mouth dropped looser.

"Miss Galbraith did us the honor to sleep at our house last night," said Mr. Sclater deliberately.

"The devil!" cried the laird, relieved. "Why!—What!—Are you aware of what you are saying, sir?"

"Perfectly; and of what I saw too. A blow looks bad on a lady's face."

"Good heavens! The little hussy dared to say I struck her?"

"She did not say so; but no one could fail to see someone had. If you do not know who did it, I do."

"Send her home instantly, or I will come and fetch her!" cried the laird.

"Come and dine with us if you want to see her. For the present she remains where she is. You want her to marry Fergus Duff; she prefers my ward, Gilbert Galbraith, and I shall do my best for them."

"She is underage," said the laird.

"That fault will rectify itself as fast in my house as in yours," returned the minister. "If you invite the publicity of a legal action, I will employ counsel and wait the result."

"Mr. Sclater," said the laird at length, "I am shocked, unspeakably shocked, at my daughter's conduct. To leave the shelter of her father's roof in the middle of the night and—"

"About seven o'clock in the evening," interjected Mr. Sclater.

"—and take refuge with strangers!" continued the laird.

"By no means strangers, Mr. Galbraith!" said the minister. "You drive your daughter from your house and are shocked to find she has taken refuge with friends!"

"She is an unnatural child. She knows well enough what I think of her, and what reason she has given me so to think."

"When a man happens to be alone in any opinion," remarked the minister, "even if the opinion should be of his own daughter, the probabilities are he is wrong. Everyone but yourself has the deepest regard for Miss Galbraith."

"She has always cultivated strangely objectional friendships," said the laird.

"For my own part," said the minister, as if heedless of the laird's last remark, "I do not know a lady I should prefer for a wife to my ward."

The minister's plain speaking was not without effect upon the laird. It made him uncomfortable. He sat silent a while. Then, gathering all the pomp and stiffness at his command, he announced, "Oblige me by informing my daughter," he said, "that I request her, for the sake of avoiding scandal, to return to her father's house until she is of age."

"And in the meantime you undertake—"

"I undertake nothing!" shouted the laird in his feeble yet harsh voice.

"Then I refuse to carry your message. I will be no bearer of that from which, as soon as delivered, I should dissuade."

"Allow me to ask, are you a minister of the gospel and stir up a child against her own father?"

"I am not here to bandy words with you, Mr. Galbraith. It is nothing to me what you think of me. If you will engage not to urge your choice upon Miss Galbraith, I think it probable she will at once return to you. If not—"

"I will not force her inclinations," said the laird. "She knows my wish, and she ought to know the duty of a daughter."

"I will tell her what you say," answered the minister, and took his departure.

When Gibbie heard, he was not at all satisfied with Mr. Sclater's interference to such result. He wished to marry Ginevra at once in order to take her from under the tyranny of her father. But he was readily convinced it would be better, now things were understood, that she should go back to him and try once more to gain him. The same day she did go back.

Ginevra soon found that her father had not yielded the idea of having his own way with her, but her spirits and courage were now so good that she was able not only to endure with less suffering but to carry herself quite differently.

At the end of the month Gibbie went home to Glashgar as usual, telling Ginevra he must be present to superintend what was going on at Glashruach to get the house ready for her. But he said nothing of what he was building there. By the beginning of the winter, they had gotten the buttress wall finished, also the shell of the new house roofed in. Since the first day the weather had permitted, the masons were at work again. The bridge was built, the wall of the old house broken through, the turret carried aloft. All the hollow where the little burn had carried away pinewood and shrubbery, gravel drive and lawn, had been planted mostly with fir trees; and a weir of strong masonry, a little way below the house, kept the water back, so that it rose and spread and formed a still pool just under the house. If Ginevra pleased, Gibbie meant to raise the weir and have quite a little lake in the hollow. A new approach had been contrived and was nearly finished before Gibbie returned to college.

44   The Wedding

In the meantime, Fergus by degrees lost heart and hope so far as concerned Ginevra and at length told the laird that, much as he valued his society and was indebted for his kindness, he must deny himself the pleasure of visiting anymore at the cottage. The laird blustered against his daughter and expostulated with the preacher. But Fergus had at last learned his lesson and was no longer to be blinded. Besides, there had lately come to his church a certain shopkeeper, retired rich, with one daughter; and as his hope of the dignity of being married to Ginevra faded, he had come to feel the enticement of Miss Lapraik's money and good looks. Within three months, he married Miss Lapraik, and lived respectably ever after. He took to writing hymns, became popular afresh through his poetry, and exercised a double influence for the ultimate humiliation of Christianity.

As soon as Gibbie returned, Ginevra let him know things were going badly with her father. They met, consulted, and agreed that the best thing was to be married at once. They made their preparations, confident that, if asked, he would refuse his permission, and proceeded, for his sake, as if they had had it.

One morning as he sat at breakfast, Mr. Galbraith received from Mr. Torrie, whom he knew as the agent in the purchase of Glashruach and whom he supposed to have bought it for Major Culsalmon, a letter, more than respectful, stating that matters had come to light regarding the property which rendered his presence on the spot indispensable for their solution, especially as there might be papers of consequence in some drawer or cabinet of those he had left locked behind him. The present owner, therefore, through Mr. Torrie, begged most respectfully that Mr. Galbraith would sacrifice two days of his valuable time and visit Glashruach. The result, he did not doubt, would be to the advantage of both parties. If Mr. Galbraith would kindly signify to Mr. Torrie his assent, a carriage with postilions, in order that he might make the journey in all possible comfort, should be at his house the next morning at ten o'clock, if that hour would be convenient.

For weeks the laird had been an unmitigated bore to himself, and the invitation laid hold upon him by the most projecting handle of his being, namely, his self-importance. He wrote at once to signify his gracious assent; and in the evening told his daughter he was going to Glashruach on business and had arranged for Miss Kimble to come and stay with her till his return.

At nine o'clock the schoolmistress came to breakfast, and at ten a traveling carriage with four horses drew up at the door looking nearly as big as the cottage. With monstrous stateliness and a fur coat on his arm, the laird descended to his garden gate and got into the carriage, which instantly dashed away for the western road, restoring Mr. Galbraith to the full consciousness of his inherent grandeur. If he was not exactly laird of Glashruach again, he was something quite as important. His carriage was just out of the street when a second, also with four horses, drew up at the garden gate, to the astonishment of Miss Kimble. Out of it stepped Mr. and Mrs. Sclater, then a young gentleman whom she thought very graceful until she discovered it was that low-lived Sir Gilbert, and Mr. Torrie the lawyer! They came trooping into the little drawing room, shook hands with them both, and sat down, Sir Gilbert beside Ginevra—but nobody spoke.

What could it mean! A morning call? It was too early. And four horses to a morning call! A pastoral visitation? Four horses and a lawyer to a pastoral visitation! A business call? It must after all be a pastoral visitation, for there was the minister commencing a religious service!—during which, however, it suddenly revealed itself to the horrified spinster that she was part and parcel of a clandestine wedding! An anxious father had placed her in charge of his daughter, and this was how she was fulfilling her trust! There was Ginevra being married in a brown dress! And to that horrid lad, who called himself a baronet and hobnobbed with a low market woman!

But alas! Just as she was recovering her presence of mind, Mr. Sclater pronounced them husband and wife! She gave a shriek, at which the company, bride and bridegroom included, broke into "a loud smile." The ceremony over, Ginevra glided from the room and returned almost immediately in her little brown bonnet. Sir Gilbert caught up his hat and Ginevra held out her hand to Miss Kimble. Then at length the abashed and aggrieved lady found words of her own.

"Ginevra!" she cried, and burst into tears.

Ginevra kissed her and said: "Never mind, dear Miss Kimble. You could not help it. The whole thing was arranged. We are going after my father, and we have the best of horses."

Mr. Torrie laughed outright.

"A new kind of runaway marriage!" he cried. "The happy couple pursuing the obstinate parent with four horses! Ha! ha! ha!"

"But after the ceremony!" said Mr. Sclater.

Here a servant ran down the steps with a carpetbag and opened the gate for her mistress. Lady Galbraith got into the carriage; Sir Gilbert followed. There was kissing and tears at the door. Mrs. Sclater drew back; the postilions spurred their horses; off went the second carriage faster than the first. And the minister's party walked quietly away, leaving Miss Kimble to declaim to the maid of all work, who cried so that she did not hear a word.

Between the second stage and the third, Gibbie and Ginevra came in sight of their father's carriage. Having arranged that the two carriages should not change horses at the same places, they easily passed unseen by him. He was thinking of nothing so little as their proximity as he sat in state before the door of a village inn.

Just as Mr. Galbraith was beginning to hope the major had contrived a new approach to the place, the carriage took an unexpected turn. He found presently they were climbing, by a zigzag road, the height over the Lorrie burn; but the place was no longer his, and to avoid a sense of humiliation, he avoided taking interest in the change.

A young woman—it was Donal's eldest sister, but he knew nothing of her—opened the door to him and showed him up the stair to his own study. There a great fire was burning; but, beyond that, everything, even to the trifles on his writing table, was just as when last he left the house. His chair stood in its usual position by the fire, and wine and biscuits were on a little table near.

"Very considerate!" he said to himself. "I trust the major does not mean to keep me waiting, though. Deuced hard to have to leave a place like this!"

Weary with his journey, he fell into a doze, dreamed of his dead wife, woke suddenly and heard the door of the room open. There was Major Culsalmon entering with outstretched hand! and there was a lady—his wife, doubtless! But how young the major was! He had imagined him a man in middle age at least!—Bless his soul! Was he never to get rid of this impostor fellow! It was not the major! It was the rascal calling himself Sir Gilbert Galbraith!—the half-witted wretch his fool of a daughter insisted on marrying! And—bless his soul again! There was the minx, Ginny! Looking as if the place was her own! The silly tears in her eyes too! It was all too absurd! He had just been dreaming of his dead wife, and clearly that was it! He was not awake yet!

He tried hard to wake, but the dream mastered him.

"Ginny!" he said as the two stood for a moment regarding him a little doubtfully, but with smiles of welcome, "what is the meaning of this? I did not know Major Culsalmon had invited you! And what is this person doing here?"

"Papa," replied Ginevra, with a curious smile, half merry, half tearful, "this person is my husband, Sir Gilbert Galbraith of Glashruach; and you are at home in your own study again."

"Will you never have done masquerading, Ginny?" he returned. "Inform Major Culsalmon that I request to see him immediately."

He turned toward the fire and took up a newspaper. They thought it better to leave him. As he sat, the truth by degrees grew plain to him. But not one other word on the matter did the man utter to the day of his death. When dinner was announced, he walked straight from the dining room door to his former place at the foot of the table. But Robina Grant was equal to the occasion. She caught up the dish before him and set it at the side. There Gibbie seated himself; and, after a moment's hesitation, Ginevra placed herself opposite her husband.

The next day Gibbie provided him with something to do. He had the chest of papers found in the Auld Hoose o' Galbraith carried into Mr. Galbraith's study, and the man found both employment and interest for weeks in deciphering and arranging them. Among many others concerning the property, its tenures and boundaries, appeared some papers which, associated and compared, threw considerable doubt on the way in which portions of it had changed hands. The laird was keen of scent as any nose-hound after dishonesty in other people. In the course of a fortnight he found himself so much at home in his old quarters, and so much interested in those papers and his books, that when Sir Gilbert informed him Ginevra and he were going back to the city, he pronounced it decidedly the better plan, seeing he was there himself to look after affairs.

For the rest of the winter, therefore, Mr. Galbraith played the grand seigneur as before among the tenants of Glashruach.

45 The Burn

The moment they were settled in the Auld Hoose, Gibbie resumed the habits of the former winter. What a change it was to Ginevra—from imprisonment to ministration!

Every winter for many years, Sir Gilbert and Lady

Galbraith occupied the Auld Hoose; which by degrees came at length to be known as the refuge of all that were in honest distress. The next year they built a house in a sheltered spot on Glashgar, and thither from the city they brought many invalids to spend the summer months under the care of Janet and her daughter Robina, whereby not a few were restored. The first summer, Nicie returned to Glashruach to wait on Lady Galbraith, was more her friend than her servant, and when she married, was settled on the estate.

For some time Ginevra was fully occupied in getting her house in order and furnishing the new part of it. When that was done, Sir Gilbert gave an entertainment to his tenants. The laird preferred a trip to the city, "on business," to the humiliation of being present as other than the greatest; though perhaps he would have minded it less had he ever himself given a dinner to his tenants.

Jean Mavor was beside herself with joy to see her broonie now lord of the land and to be seated beside him in respect and friendship. But her brother said it was "clean ridic'lous"; and not to the last would he consent to regard the new laird as other than half-witted, insisting that everything was done by his wife, and that the talk on his fingers was a mere pretense.

When the main part of the dinner was over, Sir Gilbert and his lady stood at the head of the table and, he speaking by signs and she interpreting, made a little speech together. In the course of it, Sir Gibbie took the occasion to apologize for having once disturbed the peace of the countryside by acting the supposed part of a broonie. In relating his adventures of the time, he accompanied his wife's text with such graphic illustration of gesture that his audience laughed at the merry tale till the tears ran down their cheeks. Then with a few allusions to his strange childhood, he thanked the God who led him through thorny ways into the very arms of Robert and Janet Grant, from whom—and not from the fortune he had since inherited—came all his peace.

"He desires me to tell you," said Lady Galbraith, "that he was a stranger, and you folk of Daurside took him in. And if ever he can do a kindness to you or yours, he will. He desires me also to say that you ought not to be left ignorant that you have a poet of your own, born and bred among you— Donal Grant, the son of Robert and Janet, the friend of Sir Gilbert's heart, and one of the noblest of men. And he begs you to allow me to read you a poem he had from him this very morning—probably just written. It is called 'The Laverock.' I will read it as well as I can. If any of you do not like poetry, he says—I mean Sir Gilbert says—you can go to the kitchen and light your pipes, and he will send your wine there to you."

She ceased. Not one stirred, and she read the verses.

After the reading of the poem, Sir Gilbert and Lady Galbraith withdrew and went toward the new part of the house, where they had their rooms. On the bridge, over which Ginevra scarcely ever passed without stopping to look both up and down the channel in the rock, she lingered as usual, gazing from its windows. Below, the burn opened out on the great valley of the Daur; above was the landslip, and beyond it the stream rushing down the mountain. Gibbie pointed up to it. She gazed a while, and gave a great sigh.

"Let us see it from my room, Gibbie," said Ginevra.

They went up, and from the turret window looked down upon the water. They gazed until, like the live germ of the gathered twilight, it was scarce to be distinguished but by abstract motion.

"It's my ain burnie," said Ginevra, "an' it's ain auld sang, I'll warran' it hasna forgotten a note o' 't! Eh, Gibbie, ye gie me a' thing!"

"Gien I was burnie, wadna I rin!" sang Gibbie, and Ginevra heard the words, though Gibbie could utter only the air he had found for them so long ago. She threw herself into his arms and, hiding her face on his shoulder, clung silent to her silent husband. Over her lovely bowed head, he gazed into the cool spring night, sparkling with stars and shadowy with mountains. His eyes climbed the stairs of Glashgar to the lonely peak dwelling among the lights of God; and if upon their way up the rocks they met no visible sentinels of heaven, he needed neither; ascending stairs nor descending angels, for a better than the angels was with them.

You can read of the later travels and adventures of Donal in the sequel, *The Shepherd's Castle*. And if you enjoyed *The Baronet's Song*, don't miss the other MacDonalds in this series: *The Fisherman's Lady* and *The Marquis' Secret*.